THREE WORRIES

THREE WORRIES

MADELAINE LAWRENCE

Betsey,
So great to see you!
Hugs always
Madelaine

Charleston, SC
www.PalmettoPublishing.com

Three Worries

First Edition

Paperback ISBN: 979-8-8229-1560-2

eBook ISBN: 979-8-8229-1561-9

This is a work of fiction inspired by some real-life experiences; however, the names, characters, places, and incidents are entirely based on the author's imagination and are fictionalized.

Also by Madelaine Lawrence

Fiction

A Pocketful of $20s

Why Kill a Parapsychologist?

A Hypnotic Suggestion

Nonfiction

The death view revolution:
A guide to transpersonal experiences surrounding death.

In a World of Their Own: Experiencing Unconsciousness

For my Beta readers, Kathy, Bette,
Margaret, and Barbara, whose reviews
have been exceptionally valuable.

CHAPTER 1

As Lynn poured over next week's nursing staff schedule, she heard a light knock on her office door. She could tell by his outline through the frosted glass door that it was Peter, Dr. Peter Fry, to be exact.

"Come in," Lynn responded, her heart beating quickly.

"Good morning, sweetie. How's my favorite ER nursing director today?" asked Peter.

Smiling, Lynn glanced up with just a light twinkle in her eye and a mischievous smile. "Well, good morning, Dr. Fry."

"What's wrong with this picture?" Peter stepped into her office, setting two cups of coffee on the edge of her overflowing desk. "I call you sweetie, and you call me Dr. Fry. Is there something I should know?"

"Good morning, Peter," she corrected herself, eyeing the coffee. "And to answer your question, everything is fine. Or I will be when I get next week's emergency department or ED schedule done." Lynn said with emphasis. Since most hospitals have several rooms that make up their emergency center, they have changed the name to emergency department rather than the emergency room.

But Peter wasn't listening. He was too busy shutting the door and leaning over to kiss Lynn's lips.

"My morning is always better when you drop in," said Lynn.

Lynn thought a lot about what was so appealing about Peter. She knew she was happier when they were together, but she couldn't quite put her finger on her attraction. Maybe it was how his blue eyes looked at her with affection and attention. Perhaps it was the energy that exuded from his tall, lean body. Or better yet, he was a good man.

"I know the coffee gets me in the room," laughed Peter.

"Well, there is that," said Lynn. "However, I'm always happy to see you, even without coffee."

"Unfortunately, I cannot stay and chat this morning. I have an OR case. This poor fellow fell off his ladder while putting Christmas lights on his roof. He fractured his tibia in two places. He should be fine, but I'm not sure the lights are still viable," said Peter. "Are you free for dinner at my place tonight? Virginia is dropping Hanna off this afternoon. Hanna's already asking for you!"

"I'm free. I can make it around 6:30. Does that work for you?"

"Yep! Can't wait for some together time," said Peter, and then he was gone.

Lynn had wondered if she would bump into Virginia, Peter's ex-wife. They hadn't met yet. As she thought about meeting Virginia, she started twisting her thick, brown hair on the side of her face. That was always her tell when she played cards or was nervous.

All she knew about Peter's ex-wife was that she was into art and interior decorating. Peter says their relationship was amicable now with shared custody of eight-year-old Hanna but is that for real? Lynn and Hanna already had a great relationship going. Virginia was still the unknown.

A text from her friend Wanda, the nursing director in obstetrics, caught Lynn's attention.

Got time for lunch, or has Dr. Pete reserved that time?

Lynn texted back.

I'm all yours! See you at 1:00.

Wanda sent a thumbs-up emoji back. Lynn finished her staff schedule and was on her way to check the supply room on the unit. As she walked by the glass ED door, she heard a car pull up, and saw a woman tumble from the car onto the sidewalk.

"Beatrice, help! Bring a stretcher!" Lynn yelled to Beatrice, the ED's nurse manager. She ran outside quickly, catching a glimpse of the car and its license plate. She noticed it was a dark blue SUV, maybe a Chevy Suburban. *Was that a fish and the number 85 on the license plate?* She asked herself.

"How's she doing?" asked Beatrice, who had quickly exchanged her management paperwork for a stretcher.

"Not good, I'm afraid. She has a thready pulse and is barely breathing. She's pretty banged up, too. Check out the black eye and cheek bruises. Even her hair is bloody. She's so young." Two additional staff arrived with an oxygen tank. They expertly lifted the young woman onto the stretcher, attached the oxygen, and rushed her to the trauma room in the ED.

"What's going on?" Dr. Tom McNamara asked, joining the group of nurses as they ran by. As the ED doctor, Tom saw many emergency patients but rarely was one dumped out on the sidewalk.

"Someone just tossed this woman out of a car and drove away at warp speed," said Lynn. "She is not looking good, badly bruised, with a rapid pulse and respirations. She's maybe late teens, early twenties."

In the trauma room, Dr. Tom took charge of the resuscitation. "Start an IV of Lactated Ringer's. What are her vitals?"

"BP is 85/60; her pulse is thready about 88. Breathing is shallow," said Beatrice.

Almost immediately, Beatrice and her team had the woman hooked up, with her vital signs and ECG rhythm brightly lit on the wall monitors. The oxygen mask covered her face but not all the bruises.

As it was expected of someone in a director position, Lynn stepped back to observe and only intervene if necessary. Some days it was hard for her to do that, and this was one of those times that she missed being in the middle of the activity.

"No breath sounds from the chest on her right, very bruised," said Beatrice. "X-ray is on its way."

Lynn examined the young woman's clothes for identification. All her pockets were empty. She also texted Detective Stan Gregowski, the ED's liaison police officer, letting him know about a criminal case in the ED.

"V-Tach," Beatrice shouted. A wide, regular, rapid menacing rhythm escalated across the cardiac monitor.

Lynn held her breath and prayed they could save this young woman.

"120 joules," demanded Dr. Tom. He grabbed for the cardiac paddles. "Clear," he shouted. Everyone in the room took their hands off the woman and stepped away from the stretcher as the young woman's body jumped slightly.

Lynn watched the monitor. The cardiac rhythm did not change.

"150 mgs of amiodarone IV 30 mg/min," ordered Dr. Tom.

Lynn saw a flat line across the screen.

"200 joules," Dr. Tom ordered. "Clear."

Lynn took a deep breath and sighed as the flat line continued on the monitor.

"1.0 mg of epinephrine, IV," Dr. Tom ordered.

The flat line continued after another attempt to shock the young woman's heart.

"Call it," said Dr. Tom reluctantly.

"Time of death, 11:02 am," Beatrice said.

Lynn said a silent prayer.

"I'm sorry we couldn't save her," Dr. Tom said to Lynn as they left the trauma room. His head and shoulder slumped down.

"You did your best, Tom. You always do," Lynn said. "Unfortunately, she was dropped here too late. What could have happened to this young woman?"

"Given the bruises, maybe a trafficked victim. What a scourge that is," Dr. Tom said angrily.

Lynn noticed Detective Stan Gregowski waiting for her down the hall. She knew he would start a criminal investigation right away.

"Beatrice, Stan's waiting to see me," Lynn said. "You and your team did the most anyone could have done. Let's debrief later."

Stan smiled as Lynn approached him. It was a friend's smile and then some. The last time they had lunch together, Lynn talked about how excited she was to spend more time with Dr. Pete to avoid Stan mistaking their friendship for a possible romance.

"Good to see you, Stan. I'm assuming you want information about this poor woman who just died," said Lynn.

She told Stan she saw the woman being pushed from the car and what she saw of the car and license plate, including a fish.

"That's more info than I usually get," Stan said. "But then you are particularly good at your job."

When Stan smiles at me, Lynn thought, *his face lights up. His brown eyes have a different softness, and his 6'2" frame feels comforting, not intimidating like some of the other police detectives.*

"Thank you, but I'm not so sure about this report. Could I have seen a fish?' Lynn asked.

"Yes, and that is very helpful. Some fishing groups and fishermen like the fish design on their license plates. That narrows the search a lot. You weren't just seeing things."

"That's good. Here's a maybe. I think I saw a flash of red on the back window, but I'm not sure. Everything happened so fast."

"We'll check on it," replied Stan. "I'm going to also block off part of your entrance as a crime scene. We'll be quick. Come show me where the woman was dropped."

While walking to the ED entrance with Lynn, Stan called his captain to report the crime and to get the forensic team sent over. Bright yellow barricade tape saying **POLICE LINE DO NOT CROSS** in black letters soon stood out in front of the ED.

Another view of the dark side of humanity, thought Lynn, as she looked down on the sidewalk, still picturing the young woman lying there, bruised and barely alive. *If only we could have saved her*, she thought.

CHAPTER 2

After a debriefing with the staff, Lynn left the unit to meet up with Wanda in the hospital cafeteria, usually a happy-sounding place with lively chatter. Today, Lynn didn't pick up on happy sounds.

"Great day for lunch here with chicken pot pie on the menu. I'll bet a different chef makes this," said Wanda as Lynn joined her table. For whatever reason, unlike most of the cafeteria food, the chicken pot pie surpassed edible and landed firmly in 'delicious.' The lines were always longer on the days that pot pie was on the menu, and today was no exception.

Inhaling the scents of freshly baked dough and roast chicken with anticipation, Lynn sat down next to Wanda. As usual, her friend was perfectly coiffed, her scrubs ironed, and her makeup impeccable. But the dark circles beneath her eyes told the truth – Wanda had had another sleepless night, most likely because of that worthless husband of hers, always putting her down.

Lynn wanted to tell her to give the man the boot, worrying she might end up like the young woman that had just died in the ED. She wanted to tell Wanda again that she was beautiful and special, smart, and if Roger couldn't appreciate that, he didn't deserve a woman like her.

"How are things going for you?" Lynn asked.

"We're quiet. One patient came up from your department this morning, and that's it. She's got a way to go before delivering, but she is doing OK. How's everything with you? You look like you have something on your mind," said Wanda.

"It started like a typical day. A man came in with chest pain, a woman with an overdose that we caught early but then we just lost a young woman. Someone dumped her out of a car onto the entrance and just drove off. You should have seen her all beat up and barely breathing. We couldn't save her."

"That's awful. Are you OK?" Wanda asked.

"No, but I will be. This poor woman looked to be in her early 20s. I don't even want to think about how awful her last years must have been," Lynn replied.

"Knowing you and your team, she got the best care possible. As you know, very few patients die in OB, but the few that do leave a lasting memory. I feel for you," Wanda said.

"I did see the car and got a partial license plate. I hope they catch these guys," said Lynn. She had lost her appetite again, even for the pot pie.

"Are they going to ask you to testify in court if they catch the driver of the car?" A worried look had come over Wanda's face.

"Maybe, I guess. I've done it before, although these could be bad guys. It wouldn't surprise me if this poor girl was being trafficked. We'll know more when the medical examiner does the autopsy. It's always something, isn't it?" said Lynn. Lynn thought this could be more than just something; it could be dangerous to testify.

"Hopefully, they won't need you. How about happier events? How's everything with you and Dr. Pete going?

"Peter and I are getting to the point where I might be meeting up with his ex-wife, Virginia, soon. No experience there," Lynn replied.

"Ugh!!! No great news there, either. I do know a little about Virginia from a confrontation with her. Dr. Pete was helping a pregnant woman up on my floor who had fallen and dislocated her shoulder. He had left Virginia a message, telling her he would be late for some event. She called the unit, screaming at me for keeping him here and not letting her talk to him immediately," said Wanda.

"What did you do?" asked Lynn. Now she wondered if Peter was being realistic about no more screaming scenes with Virginia.

"I told her I'd give Dr. Pete her message and hung up," said Wanda. "But about an hour later, she appeared on the unit dressed like a movie star. She was angry. If she could generate smoke, it would have come out of ears."

Lynn chuckled at that image.

"I invited her to take a seat in the waiting room and said that I'd tell Dr. Pete she was there. She insisted on seeing him immediately. You know me; I don't respond well to demands. I told her I had hospital security on speed dial. Her choice was to wait in the waiting room or get escorted out of the hospital," Wanda said.

"Good for you! Poor Peter! Then what happened?" asked Lynn.

"Dr. Pete went to talk with her – I told him to use my office – then she left. He's a good guy. We all felt for him. However, being married to a doctor isn't easy," said Wanda, "As we all know. "

"Let's hope she's not in my life too much," said Lynn.

Lynn's further reply was interrupted by her phone announcing a text from Peter.

Got another case. Won't make it home at 5:00 to meet up with Virginia and Hanna. I hate asking, but is it possible for you to meet them?

"So much for wishful thinking about Virginia," Lynn told Wanda, showing her the text.

She texted Peter back, saying she would be there a little before five, and included a heart emoji.

"How's your stock of protective gear?" asked Wanda.

Laughing, Lynn and Wanda left their table and bussed their plates to the moving conveyer, which fortunately wasn't jammed by a fork this afternoon.

"Thanks for being such a good friend, Wanda," Lynn said. They hugged and went on to meet what was in store for them the rest of the day.

CHAPTER 3

The doorbell rang. "Come in," said Dorothy Price. Lynn's brother George and wife Angie entered Lynn's mother's neat, spacious three-bedroom apartment in her assisted living quarters. The front door opened into the living room, which housed a casual silver upholstered three-seater couch, a love seat, and a comfortable blue leather recliner. Today, Dorothy was sitting upright in the recliner.

"Hi, Mom," said George. "Good to see you. Why are you still in your pajamas? You are usually right at the door with your lovely smile. Your hair isn't even combed."

"So good of you to come over and bring Chinese food for dinner," Dorothy replied, ignoring the pajama question.

"But of course. I have the best mother ever," he said, bending his 6'1" frame to give Dorothy a kiss on the cheek.

"Do you mind setting the table and putting out the dishes? I'm feeling more tired than usual tonight," Dorothy said.

"OK, Mom. 'Fess up. What's going on? You always have the table set and ready for us. Are you even too tired to get dressed?" asked George.

"I'm fine, just a little tired," said Dorothy.

George noticed his mother was breathing harder than usual, even sitting down.

"Where are those gizmos you use to check your blood pressure and oxygen?" asked George.

"That's not necessary," replied Dorothy.

Angie came over to sit next to Dorothy, holding her hand.

"Dorothy, you would be doing me a big favor by letting me take your vital signs. You know how George gets when he's worried. The last time he was worried about little Bernie, he went out and bought us all a two-week stay in Hawaii during the times the kids were still in school."

"I remember that, but I'm fine," said Dorothy.

"You could end up with round-the-clock people living in. You don't know what George will do. He is used to fixing problems in a big way from being the CEO of his pharmaceutical company," said Angie.

"Hey, I'm not that bad," said George. "Maybe just two shifts of caretakers."

"OK, OK," said Dorothy. "The blood pressure machine and the pulse oximeter are in the top drawer of that wooden cabinet."

Angie put the pulse oximeter on Dorothy's finger and took her blood pressure on the opposite arm. "Your oxygen level is 90%, and blood pressure is 176 over 89. Your pulse is 88. That's not great," said Angie.

"That is different than it has been running," admitted Dorothy, now getting concerned, too.

"I'm calling your doctor," said George. George rang Dr. Becky Moreno's office, reporting Dorothy's vital signs. The receptionist said she would give Dr. Becky the message.

"I'm calling Lynn," George said to Dorothy.

"Please don't do that. She'll worry. Lynn's so busy these days," said Dorothy.

"Mom, you know she will beat me with a stick if I don't call her. You know how she gets," said George, smiling.

"All right, George. I know she won't beat you with a stick, but you are right; she will get upset if you don't call her," said Dorothy reluctantly.

George dialed Lynn's phone.

"Hi, George. How's it going?" said Lynn answering the phone.

"I'm with Mom. I told her you would beat me with a stick if I didn't call you about her BP," said George.

"Hey, the stick beating is an idea," said Lynn, teasing her brother. "What's her BP doing?"

George gave Lynn a report on Dorothy, also adding that he had called Dr. Becky's office.

"So glad you and Angie caught this. Mom has a pad where she keeps track of her vital signs. Dr. Becky will want to know what the results have been. Check if her feet are swollen," Lynn said. "I'll hang on."

Lynn could hear George asking Angie to check Dorothy's feet.

"Angie's checking," said George. "How's the ED? How's Dr. Pete? When are you two getting married?"

"George, stop teasing your sister," said Dorothy.

Lynn laughed. "No plans yet," said Lynn. "Have you talked with him, your good college buddy, lately? I'm going to Peter's to meet with Virginia and Hanna. Any advice?"

"Just let Hanna in the house. Leave Virginia outside. That's the safest move," said George.

"Oh, come on! Virginia can't be that bad," said Lynn.

"You know Virginia is an interior decorator with an excellent reputation with the elite of the general Wilmington area with reaches to the people in Chapel Hill and other swanky North Carolina places. She's used to being admired on a pedestal. Virginia was like that even in college. Being married to Peter didn't change her; instead, she got worse. When Peter couldn't meet all her demands to attend parties, she was nasty with a vengeance. Be careful," said George.

"Thanks for the heads up from you, too. Unfortunately, my friend Wanda had something similar to say," said Lynn.

"OK, Angie's reporting mom has plus 1+ pitting edema. I have no idea what that means," said George.

"It just means there is a slight swelling of her feet but with a barely detectable impression. "Mention that to Dr. Becky," said Lynn. "Call me about what she says."

"OK. I'll call you when I hear from Dr. Becky. You be careful around Virginia. She's got a temper," said George.

"We'll both be in touch—hug Mom for me. Thanks to Angie. Love you, Bro," said Lynn.

"Love you back, Sis," replied George.

After alerting Dr. Tom about Dorothy potentially appearing in the ED, Lynn was ready to leave work. She wanted to get to Peter's house 15 minutes before Virginia arrived. She did one more tour of the ED to ensure all was good and to check on Mrs. Bustillo, who had attempted suicide this morning. As Lynn entered Mrs. Bustillo's room, she saw a young man with long straggly hair, dressed in jeans and an oversized sweater, approaching her bed. He had no visitor badge.

"Hi, can I help you?" Lynn asked. The man turned quickly and rushed out the door, nearly knocking Lynn over. Lynn pushed the emergency button for the staff to come to the room.

"What happened? Are you OK?" asked Beatrice.

"Some guy was here trying to get into Mrs. Bustillo's room without a visitor badge. Notify security about a man in his 20s with an oversized navy sweater and jeans, probably running to leave the hospital. I might be able to identify him," Lynn said.

"What's happening? I was sound asleep until I heard this commotion," said Mrs. Bustillo. "Is everything OK?"

"It is now," Lynn said. "There was a strange man in your room, but he's gone, and security is chasing him down. We are going to put a security guard on your door in case he comes back. We will have Dr. Tom check on you to make sure you are OK. How do you feel?"

"I feel fine. I'm ready to go home," Mrs. Bustillo replied.

Lynn left a message for Stan to call her in the morning so she could report another potential assault. God, what a day, Lynn thought to herself as she got into her car to go to Peter's house.

CHAPTER 4

Lynn loved driving up to Peter's house with its circular driveway and large columned front porch. The cushioned chairs on the porch always looked so inviting, a perfect setting for a glass of wine in the evening. The house had a keypad entrance system to which Lynn knew the code. She wondered if Peter had changed the entrance code after his divorce.

She texted Peter.

Here at the house. Virginia has not arrived yet. Do you want me to start dinner?

Peter replied.

Bless you. You are the best! I was going to make spaghetti and meatballs. Go ahead and start them if you want. I should be home around 6:30.

Lynn started cleaning up leftover breakfast dishes when the doorbell rang. She peeked out the window and saw that Virginia and Hanna had arrived. "Hi," said Lynn, opening the door. "You must be Virginia. And you must be Hanna."

"You know I am Hanna already," said Hanna, hugging Lynn.

"Yes, I do, and I am happy to see you," said Lynn. Hanna doted right by Lynn to her toy room.

Lynn turned toward Virginia and said, "Would you like to come in and have a cup of tea or coffee?" Lynn remembered George's advice but decided to try a friendly approach.

"So, where is Peter? He was supposed to meet me here and not send his girlfriend of the moment to greet me," replied Virginia, hands on hips. "You are at least more attractive and better dressed than some I've met."

Now I see where Hanna learned to put her hands on her hips, thought Lynn.

"I guess that's a no to the tea question. I'll pass your message on to Peter," said Lynn, shutting the door before Virginia could enter.

I'll be damned if I'm going to get into an argument with her, Lynn thought.

"Hanna, is everything good in the playroom?" Lynn asked, receiving "yep" for an answer.

Aware of the noise on the door keypad, Lynn looked to see Virginia trying to unlock the door. *It looks like Peter did change that code,* thought Lynn. *That's nervy of her to try to get in. She'll either ring the doorbell or go away*. The doorbell rang.

"Damn," said Lynn.

"Yes, can I help you with something?" asked Lynn.

"I just want to apologize," said Virginia. "You were nice, and I was taking out my frustration with Peter on you. Sorry about that."

"Apology accepted. The offer for tea or coffee still stands," replied Lynn, but she was not sure she should have repeated the invitation.

"Thanks! I'd like that," Virginia said as she walked in.

"Coffee would be good. I take it with a dab of cream and one packet of stevia," said Virginia. She sat on the cushioned light blue Italian designer couch in front of the glass coffee table. Lynn watched as Virginia organized the scattered books and the red and white silk orchid floral arrangement that donned the coffee table. She also fussed with her hair and smoothed out the bottom of her chartreuse Jason Wu dress Lynn recognized from the Bloomingdales catalog. Lynn had to admit she was an attractive woman.

"I'm sure Peter appreciated you coming here to meet Hanna and me. He always needs a helper," said Virginia.

"I'm happy to help," said Lynn. "Your daughter is delightful."

Lynn delivered the coffee in Peter's denim-colored mugs, ensuring Virginia saw the stevia packet on the side. Lynn sat on the ivory barrel chair opposite Virginia.

"Thanks! I enjoy being with Hanna so much and miss her when she's here," said Virginia.

"I can imagine that is hard," replied Lynn.

"Do you have children?" Virginia asked.

"No. Maybe someday," said Lynn.

"I wouldn't advise having a child with Peter. He was never around. I felt like I had to do all the caretaking of Hanna when she was a baby. I knew nothing about taking care of a baby," said Virginia.

I want to avoid listening to Peter bashing. This is tricky, thought Lynn.

"Have you seen a counselor since the divorce?" asked Lynn. "That might help with the frustration you had or have with Peter."

Virginia's eyes opened wide. Her lips tightened. "I'm guessing you don't want to hear how difficult a time I had with Peter when we were married," Virginia said.

"What went on with you and Peter is really between you two. Honestly, you are right. I don't want to be your sounding board about your marriage," Lynn said.

"Don't you want to be warned about how horrible a relationship with Peter can be?" asked Virginia.

Lynn sighed. *Let this end soon,* she thought.

"Peter and I are making our own history. No relationship is perfect. Peter and I will probably have issues different from those you had with him because you and I are different people. Being a nurse and helping with my brother's children taught me how to care for babies, for example. I work with Peter at the hospital. That makes a difference, too."

"So, you think you will be better than I was at making a relationship or even a marriage with Peter work?" asked Virginia. "You think it was all my fault the marriage ended?"

Lynn noticed Virginia's clenched jaw, reddened skin, clenched fist, and a look that made her think Virginia was ready to pounce.

Wow! thought Lynn. *Maybe I should have listened to George about not letting Virginia in the house. What do I say to that?*

"I don't know what happened between you and Peter. It's also not my business. I don't see us competing for the best relationship. I had hoped you and I could have at least a friendly relationship. Being friendly might make those situations more comfortable and better for all of us, including Hanna, but I guess that's not happening," said Lynn.

"Are you suggesting I am not concerned about Hanna's wellbeing?" asked Virginia.

Oh, God, thought Lynn. *Where's the button that moves her off this path?*

At the sound of her name, Hanna came into the room. She turned to Lynn and asked, "Are we going to make brownies tonight?"

"Sure," said Lynn, after which Hanna smiled and returned to the playroom.

Virginia's shoulders slumped down, and tears were in her eyes.

"Hard times, huh?' suggested Lynn.

"I lost my husband, and now I'm losing my daughter. The losses don't stop happening," said Virginia.

"You need to consider me an occasional babysitter who will take good care of your daughter. I'm not in competition with you. You will always be her mother, which is incredibly special," said Lynn. "Is there something you would enjoy doing tonight? I always like a mani-pedi when I have some free time or dinner with friends."

Virginia looked up at Lynn and smiled. "You are kind, and I'm being bitchy," Virginia said.

"I know this is a tough time for you. I don't want to make it tougher," Lynn said.

"I have friends I can talk with, but we talk about how awful men are. The conversations are not helping me move on or feel better," said Virginia.

Lynn got up from her chair and went to the desk drawer, where she kept folders and cards. She handed Virginia a business card. "This is one of the counselors I recommend to people, so I have a stack of her cards. Let her know I suggested you to her," Lynn said. Lynn stayed standing, hoping Virginia would get up off the couch and head toward the door.

Virginia had gotten up from her chair and took the card with the counselor's name. She went to the playroom to say goodbye to Hanna. When she came back into the living room, she hugged Lynn.

"Thanks for the coffee," Virginia said.

"You take care," Lynn replied as Virginia left the house.

Lynn collapsed on the couch and let out a deep breath. *That was a tough one*, she thought. *I hope future encounters with Virginia will be more comfortable or avoided. My life is busy enough without confrontations like this one.*

Lynn's moment of respite was short-lived. Hanna had entered the living room with her hands on her hips. The word 'munchkin' always came to mind when Lynn engaged with Hanna, with her curly brown hair, big brown eyes, endless energy, and mischievous smile.

"You know you promised we would make brownies," Hanna said.

"And we always keep our promises, right?" said Lynn, walking to the kitchen with Hanna.

"Right," said Hanna. "Especially when it comes to making brownies."

CHAPTER 5

"Hanna, the stove timer for the brownies is ringing," said Lynn.

"Are they ready?" asked Hanna. "Can we check with the toothpick?"

"Let's do the toothpick test," said Lynn placing the hot brownies on the hot plate on Hanna's table. "Be careful not to touch the sides of the pan," warned Lynn.

Hanna reached out her arm and carefully stuck the toothpick into the cooked brownies. "There's nothing on the toothpick, Ms. Lynn. Doesn't that mean they are ready?" asked Hanna.

"It sure does. We'll leave the brownies here to cool. They will make a great dessert for after dinner," said Lynn, emphasizing the after-dinner.

"OK, I'll just watch them but won't eat any until after dinner. When is Daddy coming home?" Hanna asked.

"He said, at 6:30, that's in about 10 minutes. Do you want to help me set the table?" asked Lynn.

"I don't think so," said Hanna. "I have some homework to finish."

Soon, Lynn heard the keypad on the door being activated. Peter was home.

"Hello, Sweetie, how's everything?" Peter said, handing Lynn a bouquet of mixed flowers, including six red roses.

"Everything is good, and thank you for the lovely flowers," she said before kissing Peter. "What's the occasion?" she asked.

Hanna came running into the kitchen. "Hi, Daddy," said Hanna, hugging Peter.

"Hi, Sweetheart," Peter said, reaching out to give Hanna a hug.

Hanna's expression changed suddenly from happiness to upset.

"Daddy, what did you do to Ms. Lynn? You brought her flowers. Did you make her mad?" Hanna asked accusingly.

Why would Hanna think Peter did something? Thought Lynn. *It's not like we were arguing. He just brought flowers.* "Hanna, your dad didn't do anything to me. Men bring flowers to women they care about all the time," said Lynn.

"My daddy brought flowers for my mommy when she was mad at him," said Hanna. "She got a lot of flowers."

Lynn stifled a smile. "But I'm not mad at your dad," said Lynn. "In fact, I just kissed him. Everything is OK here."

"OK, mushy stuff. I have homework to do," said Hanna.

"Did you think I'd be mad at you for some reason?" Lynn asked Peter after Hanna left.

"Yes, I thought you might be. I asked you to leave work early and meet up with Virginia for the first time without me even being here," said Peter. "I'm sorry about that."

"Virginia and I had a little talk. It was tense at times, but I think it worked out, maybe better because you weren't here. What I told her I'm saying to you now. She and I are different people. The issues you and I will have will differ from those you and Virginia had," Lynn said, smiling at Peter.

"I'm so happy to have you in my life," Peter said, pulling Lynn to him. "It feels like a miracle. I'm used to expecting anger and disappointment to always show up."

"Remember, too; we've had some years of negotiating patient issues in the ED, some a lot more difficult than Virginia. We seem to have done OK with that," Lynn said.

"That is true. So, what did you and Virginia say to each other," asked Peter. "Did she tell you how horrible I was to live with?"

"Yep, but I stopped her. I told her any issues she has with you need to be discussed with you, not me. She's in pain, Peter. I could see that. I did give her Marissa's card if she decides to see a counselor. I doubt Virginia and I will ever be friends, but I'm hoping for friendly," said Lynn. "Most of all, I'm motivated by how much I care for you. If I can work out a decent relationship with Virginia, it's better for all of us," Lynn suggested.

"You know how much I care about you, too," said Peter. He held Lynn close in his arms.

"More mushy stuff," said Hanna appearing suddenly. "I'm hungry. Is it time for supper yet?"

"We need to get you squeaky shoes, so we know when you are nearby.," said Peter, laughing.

"The meatballs, sauce, and salad are ready. I just need to cook the spaghetti," said Lynn.

"Let me do that," said Peter. "I'll also pour some wine. Merlot for you?"

"Sounds good," replied Lynn.

"Lynn and I made brownies, too," said Hanna. "Lynn says they come out even better when I help."

"She's a pretty smart woman," said Peter, smiling. "We are lucky she is part of our lives."

CHAPTER 6

It was quiet in the house now, with Hanna asleep after dinner. Lynn felt a moment of bliss as she and Peter cuddled in front of the dancing flames in the fireplace. The smell of wood and the sound of crackles as it burned added to the cozy mood.

"I have some worrisome and interesting news," said Lynn. "Mom has been complaining about feeling tired. George and Angie went and checked on her. Her BP was up, and her pulse ox was slightly lower than usual. George ended up calling Dr. Becky, who wanted to see Mom at the hospital. I'm waiting to see what happened."

"I'm sorry about your mom, but glad she's seeing Dr. Becky. I'm here for you, you know, whatever you need," said Peter.

"Thank you. That means a lot. I have some other news, too. My idea about giving a sort of workshop for five people who want to know the ins and outs of giving out $20s and helping their recipients as needed is approved. The administration said I can use the B6 conference room.

"Can I sign up?" Peter asked.

"I'm happy to give you private lessons," Lynn said, snuggling closer to Peter.

"There's more news that I could use your help with. I got a call from Stephanie Rogers from the Wilmington Tribune. She wants to write a story about the $20 gifts at Christmas. I'm not sure that's a good idea," Lynn said.

Lynn's phone buzzed.

Angie and I brought Mom to the doctor. Dr. Becky's admitting her to the hospital. Not critical but worrisome.

Lynn texted back.

I'm on my way to the hospital. See you there.

"George?" Peter asked.

"When Dr. Becky examined Mom, she admitted her to the hospital," Lynn explained to Peter.

"You go see your mom. Text or call me when you find out what's going on. If it's urgent, I'll get someone to stay with Hanna and will be there, too," said Peter.

"OK," said Lynn. Her voice was shaking, eyes close to tears. "I can't lose my mother," she said.

"Knowing George, he's making sure your mom is getting the best of care. You and I both know that Dr. Becky is our top cardiologist. Are you OK to drive?"

"I'm all right," Lynn said. "I just want my mom to be all right, too."

"She'll dance at our wedding. You go to her," said Peter.

Lynn grabbed her coat and left. *Did Peter say dance at our wedding?* she remembered. *Does he want to get married? I don't know if I'm ready to get married.*

Peter's house was only 15 minutes from the hospital. Lynn rushed up to the cardiac floor.

At least she's not in the ICU, Lynn thought.

"Hi, Mom," Lynn said, entering Dorothy's room. George had gotten her a private room, Lynn noticed. Dorothy was hooked up to a cardiac monitor and getting oxygen. An intravenous infusion was going into her left arm with medication to reduce her blood pressure from the notation on the IV bag. "How are you feeling?'

"I'm fine, just a little more tired than usual," Dorothy said. "This is just too much fuss about me."

Lynn went over and hugged George and Angie. "Thank you," she whispered to them.

"Mom had an echocardiogram done already," said Angie. "Dr. Becky said she would be back to tell us the results. Her blood pressure increased when we were at Dr. Becky's office."

"Mom's got a little white coat syndrome. It's not unusual for her BP to go up in any doctor's office," Lynn explained.

"Hi, Lynn," said Dr. Becky as she entered Dorothy's room. "Good to see you." She turned to Dorothy.

"Miss Dorothy, is it OK to talk about your condition in front of these folks? I don't have your office chart to know whom you designated as people with whom I can share information," asked Dr. Becky.

"It depends," said Dorothy.

"Mother!" exclaimed George and Lynn.

"OK, include them," said Dorothy.

Dr. Becky laughed. "Here's the story. Your left ventricle's ejection fraction is hovering around 38. That's a little lower than the 42 it was the last time I saw you. As we discussed during your last visit, a normal ejection fraction is between 50 to 70 percent, which indicates the percentage of blood the left ventricle pumps out when it contracts. Your heart is pumping out less blood than normal when it contracts. Once an ejection fraction is under 40, you drift into a different and unfortunate lower category of heart function that can lead to heart failure," explained Dr. Becky.

"Is that why I was feeling tired?" asked Dorothy. "Can this be fixed?"

"Yes, and yes," to answer your questions. I'm hoping that the antihypertension medicine in the IV will bring that ejection fraction number up a little and lower your BP. If it does, we will happily send you home with a prescription for a slightly higher dose of BP medication. If it doesn't change, we will talk about other options, and I'll run some more tests. How does that sound?" asked Dr. Becky.

"Seems reasonable," said Dorothy. "What about medicine for these three worrywarts? Shouldn't they go home now that I'm here getting excellent care?"

"I know this crew. They are tough, but they care a lot about you. We can bring in a recliner, so one of them can stay overnight comfortably," said Dr. Becky.

"I'll stay," said Lynn. "George, you, and Angie go home to your kids. I'm good with staying here."

"That's solved. Good. I'm going for some tea later. Want to join me?" Dr. Becky asked Lynn.

"Absolutely! Text me when you are ready," replied Lynn.

Lynn watched Dorothy as she drifted off to sleep. Her blood pressure was receding nicely to a normal range. She texted Peter.

Mom's sleeping. BP is OK now. Meeting Dr. Becky soon for tea. Staying over in Mom's room.

Peter texted back.

Glad to hear. Keep me posted. I'm here if you need me. Love you!

Love you? Wow! thought Lynn. The word love had never come up before, and he mentioned their wedding. She decided that it was a conversation for another day or maybe to be avoided altogether.

CHAPTER 7

"Sorry about canceling our tea date last night," said Dr. Becky at the hospital cafeteria the next morning. Lynn always admired how Becky could look the consummate professional in her lab coat covering her clothes but simultaneously exuding warmth and friendliness.

"Your schedule is crazy. Happy to be meeting for breakfast. I was glad to leave the recliner in Mom's room, where I slept last night. Is the patient you needed to see OK?" said Lynn.

"Yes, he did fine. He now has a pacemaker that should keep his heart at a steady rate so he doesn't pass out."

"How are you always so well dressed, relaxed, and just lovely all the time? I know how many hours you spend with patients. I'd be bedraggled,' Lynn commented.

Dr. Becky laughed. "Just good living, I guess, and a wonderful husband. How are you doing?" asked Dr. Becky.

"Yesterday was a horror show. We lost a young woman yesterday morning that someone tossed out of a car onto our sidewalk. I just can't get over someone doing that," Lynn responded.

"There are always some cases that live with you for a long time. It's like PTSD - you keep going over in your head what else you could have done until, finally, you realize not much more would have helped the situation. Too bad this isn't dinner. You could have something stronger than coffee," Becky said.

"That was just the beginning. Then I had to meet and greet Peter's ex-wife at his house. It ended up OK, but it was God awful for a while."

"I heard she's a tough cookie but never had the pleasure. You are lucky to be still standing, from what I heard."

"We established some ground rules, I hope. Between losing that young woman, meeting up alone with Virginia, and then mom not doing as well as usual, I'm beat. At least I didn't have to drive to work today, but I only slept off and on the recliner," said Lynn.

"I can be the bearer of good news this morning. Your Mom can go home tomorrow. I already told her. Pulse ox is up to 95% oxygen, the ejection fraction is 50, and BP is 132/78. I called in a prescription for a stronger dose of her BP meds. I still want to watch her for another day, but she is stable now," said Dr. Becky. "Don't forget you still owe me dinner so I can hear more about you and Dr. Pete. The rumor mill has you eloping this weekend. You know I'm happy for both of you. He's a good guy, and you are nothing short of terrific and beautiful!" said Dr. Becky.

"We just need to work for the staff here harder – too much extra time for gossip. I can assure you that Peter and I are not eloping this weekend. Next, they will be saying I am pregnant," replied Lynn.

"That's already there – twins, in fact. See you later," said Dr. Becky as she got up from the table.

Lynn shook her head in disbelief.

"Thanks for all you do, Becky," Lynn said, giving her colleague and friend a hug.

She walked quickly back to her mother's room, relieved she was doing better.

"Good news, Mom. Dr. Becky said you can go home tomorrow. I'm going to go down to the ED to finish one report, and then I'll come back up to visit," Lynn said.

"Don't rush, Dear. I know you are busy. I'm sorry to be a bother," replied Dorothy.

Lynn went over and kissed her mother on the cheek. "Love you, Mom," she said.

"What are you doing here?" asked Beatrice when Lynn came on to the unit. "I know your mom came in last night, and you slept in her room on a recliner, no less. Go home and get some real sleep. We can manage. It's quiet here this morning – one man with chest pain who is going to the cardiac unit, a woman in labor came and went to delivery, and we are still watching a ten-year-old with an asthma attack. She's doing fine."

"OK, I have one report to finish, and I'll call it a day! Thanks," said Lynn.

Lynn was about to text Peter when he walked into her office carrying two cups of coffee.

"This morning, I'm not sure what's making me happier – seeing you or the cup of coffee. I guess both," Lynn said.

Peter handed Lynn her cup and plunked himself down in the chair before her desk.

"Mom's going home tomorrow," Lynn said. "I was just going to text you."

"Dr. Becky, the fixer. She's amazing. I'm happy for you and your mom," said Peter.

"How's your day?" Lynn asked.

"Good. Mrs. Appleton came over to take care of Hanna. I get to see you. There have been no nasty, screaming phone calls from Virginia. Patients are doing well. Your Mom's going home. All is surprisingly good in the kingdom," said Peter. "What are your plans today?"

Lynn laughed. *Peter always seemed to put a funny plug into whatever he was discussing. She loved his sincerity, too. There was a lot she liked about him*, she thought.

"I'm going to finish up a report and then head home for some real sleep. I'm getting slides ready for my first session with my $20s group. A new adventure begins," said Lynn.

"Maybe I'm putting too much on my plate. There seems to be a lot going on lately."

"I'm sure your mom being sick was worrisome. I know you love working with people who want to give away $20 to people who could use a boost. Are you still undecided about being interviewed by the reporter?"

"I don't know what to do. What do you think?" asked Lynn.

"I always look at situations with a will it help or will it hurt glasses. Can this interview be helpful or harmful?"

"I'm a little worried about the privacy issues. Stephanie mentioned interviewing the members of my group and the recipients. I don't think either one of them wants or would be helped by their names and stories in the press. The publicity would be good just getting information out about doing more to help people in the community," replied Lynn.

"Would Stephanie be amenable to just talking with you?" asked Peter.

"I don't know, but I can find out. Good suggestion. Thank you, Dr. Fry. Much appreciated."

"Glad to help. Know that I'm always here for you. I can see life with you is going to be an amazing journey," Peter said, getting up from the chair. He came over and kissed Lynn on her cheek and left, humming a song, maybe, *You Make Loving Fun*, Lynn thought.

Did he say life with me? Peter's up to something, thought Lynn. She was happy and anxious at the same time.

Lynn did one more check on her computer. She reread the email saying the Board meeting scheduled for tomorrow was canceled and then on to her mother's room to let her know she was going home for a nap and a change of clothes.

CHAPTER 8

On her way home for some real sleep, Lynn's head was full of thoughts about Peter. Was he thinking seriously about getting engaged or married? Was she ready for that? What about her career, the times she spent with friends and her family? Would that all change?

As she walked into her home, she almost tripped on the mail that fell from the letter slot on the front door.

Oh, an envelope from the University of North Carolina in Chapel Hill, Lynn noticed. "I'm in," she shouted out loud. It was an acceptance letter into the online part-time Doctor of Nursing Practice program.

Lynn texted Peter, George, and Angie.

Wahoo! I got into the nurse practitioner program at UNC!!! Ready for a nap and some wonderful dreams now!

Sleep came easily to Lynn, but one dream was disturbing. She was in a canoe paddling across the choppy waters of a lake. There were two clusters of lights on the shore across the lake. The boat would turn toward one cluster, then turn toward the other one, going back and forth. Finally, Lynn woke up feeling tired.

A text came through from George.

Congrats from Angie and me! We, of course, anticipate free checkups when you graduate – maybe for all my employees, too.

Lynn laughed. The last count from George was that he had about 200 employees, she remembered. *I haven't finished school and already have a full-time job*, she thought.

Showered and dressed, she filled a small bag with overnight necessities and headed back to the hospital for another night in the recliner. Sleep came easily.

"Good morning, dear," Dorothy said. "You slept through Dr. Becky's visit this morning. I'm discharged. Just waiting for the nurse to come back."

"I can't believe I slept that hard," Lynn said. "I'm going to wash up and get dressed, and then on our way to take you home, Mom."

Dorothy headed straight for her living room recliner after she and Lynn entered her apartment. She let out a sigh of both relief and relaxation as she raised the foot slightly and covered herself with her blue and yellow Afghan.

"Would you like a cup of tea?" Lynn asked. She was relieved to have her mother feeling OK and looking comfortable in her favorite chair.

"I can get my own tea," Dorothy protested.

"I know you can, Mom, but I would like to see you rest a bit, and I am happy to bring you tea,"

"I'm fine. There is way too much fussing over me," said Dorothy.

"You know we love you, and we are happy to fuss over you." Lynn found her mother's favorite turquoise Shabby Rose porcelain teacup and saucer. It was an aesthetic lift just looking at the lovely turquoise background with the white, yellow, and pink floral design.

The tea brought a nice smile to Dorothy's lips, too.

"Mom, there are a few things I need to go over with you. I ordered an alert pendant for you. Someone from the Medical Alert company will be coming to drop it off and show you how to work it. Neither George, Angie, nor I want any argument from you about wearing it. If you fall or get too dizzy to walk, it's the fastest and easiest way to get help. We already instructed them to put George and me on the list of people to call."

"But," Dorothy started to say.

"No, buts," said Lynn. "Just know, George, and I will feel much better knowing you can call for help right away if you need to. Also, know we will check to see if you are wearing it, too."

"All right, all right. I'll call the desk to let them know someone from Medical Alert is coming. If it stops you two from worrying, I'll wear it," said Dorothy.

Lynn's phone was buzzing with a phone call from the office of Dr. Don Brown.

"Hi, Jawana, what's up?"

"The medical board meeting is going to start in 30 minutes. Dr. Brown asked me to find out when you will be here, so maybe you can chat ahead of time," said Jawana.

"That's a surprise. I got an email yesterday that said that the meeting was canceled. When did it get re-scheduled?" asked Lynn.

"It was never canceled. I don't know who sent you that notice, but it wasn't me or anyone from this office. Can you make it to this meeting?" Jawana asked.

"I just brought my mother home from the hospital. I need to find someone to stay with her. I'll call you back," said Lynn.

"I can stay by myself," argued Dorothy. "I don't need a sitter. I feel fine."

"Mom, please don't argue. When you have the alert necklace on, I'll feel fine with you here by yourself," Lynn responded, dialing Angie simultaneously.

"Angie, I'm in a pickle. Can you come over and stay with Mom until the Medical Alert fellow gets here? Earlier, someone emailed me saying a board meeting was canceled, but it was either a hoax or a joke. I don't know what's happening, but I must get to that board meeting."

"I'll be right there," answered Angie.

"You are a lifesaver."

"Is Angie coming over?" asked Dorothy.

"Yes."

"Then you can go. She will be here in 10 minutes. I can stay alone for 10 minutes. I have my tea in this beautiful cup," Dorothy said. "I promise I won't get up out of this chair."

"Here is how I see this scene," Lynn said. "I could leave you now, but I would be worried all the time I'm driving back to the hospital. That worry could make me sick or cause me to be in an accident. I would rather not be worrying. Your safety and mine are more important than being on time for this board meeting. They will understand about someone sending me that cancellation message."

"Well then, make yourself some tea. I know you like the pink teacup with the blue, yellow, and pink flowers," said Dorothy.

"Love you, Mom," said Lynn.

"Love you more," said Dorothy.

Lynn left when Angie arrived and made it to the board meeting just as it started. Dr. Brown asked her to meet with him in his office for a few minutes when the meeting was over.

CHAPTER 9

Lynn was seated in the waiting area outside Dr. Donald Brown's office. This is like getting called to the principal's office, Lynn thought. It could be good or bad news. Even the lettering on the door to his office that said Dr. Donald Brown, CEO, was intimidating.

"Come in, Lynn," Dr. Brown's booming voice said. "Have a seat. Heard your mother was admitted a few days ago. How is she doing?"

"Dr. Becky did her magic, and my mom has been discharged and is home resting comfortably in her recliner except for complaining about my brother and sister-in-law fussing over her," Lynn answered. Dr. Brown laughed and shook his head in agreement. A broad smile appeared.

"I know your mom through the philanthropic work she does. She's raised a lot of money for the hospital, for which we are very grateful. I know her to be quite independent. Any time you need something for her, just call this office, and it will be done."

"Thanks, that's much appreciated." Lynn wanted to add what a great job the staff always do anyway but figured she would accept Dr. Brown's offer to help as proffered.

"I'm sure you are wondering why I asked you to meet with me. As you heard at the meeting, we are reorganizing some of the areas of the hospital. The plan is to put the ED with expanded walk-in clinics under the same umbrella. As you know better than most people, several ED patient visits are not true emergencies but require some treatment. We would like to better triage patients to the walk-in clinic and the ED.

"I can totally understand the need for that," replied Lynn.

"I'm glad you said that because we would like you to be the director of this new configuration. Not only would you be the emergency department director but also the director of the walk-in clinics, including obstetrics. You have done an amazingly good job with the ED. We need someone who can help us set up procedures and policies for which patients are best triaged in each of these areas. We feel you are our best candidate," Dr. Brown finished.

"Thank you for that. Seems like a great opportunity and challenge," Lynn replied.

"So far, so good," Dr. Brown said. "There's a little more to be added. We want to become a Level 1 Trauma Center. We can do much as a Level II Center, but we are at least two hours from a Level 1 Center. That two-hour transportation distance has cost the lives of some patients."

"Over the next few years, we will add resources to accomplish that goal. So, whoever takes over as the new ED/Walk-in clinic director will be integral to this transition. Jim Walker, who now supervises the walk-in clinic, would be your associate director unless you have someone else you would prefer."

"I see," said Lynn. *Wow*! She was thinking.

"Obviously, this position comes with a considerable raise and more vacation weeks than you have now. You will probably need them, too. It's a big job."

"As I understand the plan, as the non-urgent patients currently being seen in the ED shift to the walk-in clinics, which leaves more space, so to say, for more trauma patients to be seen in the ED. Is that right?" asked Lynn.

"You hit the nail on the head. It also means no one in the ED will lose their job. Take some time and think over this but we need to know by January 3. For us here, you are a known outstanding candidate. We are hoping; actually, I'm praying every night that you will accept this offer!"

Dr. Brown had gotten up from behind his desk. He came over to shake Lynn's hand and walk her to the door.

"Thanks for thinking of me. It's an outstanding opportunity. I will get back to you as soon as possible."

Lynn was deep in thought, entering the ED. *Could she possibly do that job and everything else that's on her plate already?*

"Hi, Beatrice! How's it going today?" asked Lynn when back in the ED.

"Not too bad. There's a man with chest pain in Room one, but the docs are sure it's just angina. A woman in labor came in, but she is already on the maternity floor. Earlier, we had a man fall off a ladder, putting up Christmas lights on the edge of his roof. He's in surgery. I think he's Dr. Pete's case, so maybe you heard about him already," said Beatrice, the ED's nurse manager.

"I noticed something about you lately, if you don't mind me saying so," said Beatrice.

"Go ahead and tell me," replied Lynn. "I'm not afraid."

"These days, both you and Dr. Pete are much happier people. I want you to know the staff, and I am happy for you," said Beatrice. "You are both good people and make a great couple."

"Thanks for that. Much appreciated. Anything else your radar picked up?" asked Lynn.

"After you spend time doing schedules and ordering supplies, you come out to spend time in the trenches. I think you miss taking care of patients," said Beatrice.

"You got me pegged. I like it when we are swamped, and I can help. Although, I do like keeping things organized," admitted Lynn.

"Maybe we can brainstorm how to get you more involved out here. The staff does like it when you get involved with the patients," Beatrice said.

On her ride home from work, Lynn's head was spinning. Her emotions fluctuated between loving the idea of managing this new configuration of the ED and the walk-in clinic and being part of building a Level I Trauma Center and wondering if it was the right career move for her. What about her growing relationship with Peter? What about being a nurse practitioner and getting back into patient care instead of administration?

She decided not to mention Dr. Brown's offer and her acceptance into the nurse practitioner program until she and Peter were together. She wanted to see his reaction live. Everything seemed to be on hyperdrive this week. Her life was turning, but what direction did she want it to go in? she questioned.

CHAPTER 10

When Lynn got to work the next day, she relaxed. *It's impressive that running an Emergency Department is less stressful than managing my personal life,* she thought. Before her paperwork, she did her rounds on the unit and sat down with the night nurse, John Hollander.

"Hi, John. Do you have time to give me the night report?"

"Sure, of course. At 8:00 pm, two patients came in with injuries from a minor car accident. One person had a fractured wrist, and another had a bruised chest, but no fractures or lung issues showed up on the x-rays. Another woman, around 2:00 am, came in unconscious from an overdose of Lexapro and alcohol. When we gave her Narcan, she woke up right away. Dr. Franklin wanted to keep her here overnight to ensure she was OK. She's sleeping in room 6, hooked to a monitor.

"Sounds like she's doing well," Lynn commented. "But there seems to be something else."

"When she woke up, she was saying strange things, like in the movies, seeing dead people. We are watching her to see if she needs a psych referral," John said. "Would you go talk with her?"

"Sure," Lynn said. "Always happy to talk with patients."

Mrs. Bustillo was sitting up in bed, looking through a newspaper. Her hair was combed, make-up highlighted the curves of her face, and a warm smile appeared when Lynn walked into her room. Lynn had checked her chart and knew she was 56 years old.

"Hi, Mrs. Bustillo. I'm Lynn Price, the ED director. How are you feeling this morning?"

"I feel great except embarrassed by what I did. I should never have taken all those pills and drank that wine. I was so depressed. The depression seems to be gone, though. I don't understand why I feel better," Mrs. Bustillo answered.

"Wow! That sounds like a big change," said Lynn. "The nurses think you had some kind of different experience while you were unconscious. Do you want to talk about it?"

"I am afraid you will think I'm off my rocker if I tell you what happened. Going through a tunnel and meeting up with dead people doesn't sound normal to me," answered Mrs. Bustillo.

"It sounds like maybe you had a near-death experience," said Lynn. "That's nothing to be embarrassed or worried about. Usually, it is a good thing."

Mrs. Bustillo jumped a little, and her mouth opened in surprise. "Is that what happened to me?"

"Maybe," said Lynn. "Tell me what you remember that happened?"

"I remember feeling so depressed and down on myself. My family life is not great. One son got in trouble with the law and moved away with his family. My daughter barely talks to me. I was drinking red wine and taking a lot of anti-depression pills. Then I passed out. I vaguely remember my daughter crying and holding my hand as they put me into the ambulance. Then it was like I was out of my body. It was strange, looking down at myself from on high. I could see the EMT guys putting a needle in my arm and running an IV in. But I felt fine – not worried about where I was. Better than fine – like being a loving cocoon. I remember a tunnel, too. Some people were at the end of the tunnel with a river behind them. A woman I didn't recognize said I had to return; it wasn't my time to cross the river. I needed to live out the rest of my life. I had something more to finish. Swish! I was back in my body here in the hospital. Is this a sign of craziness after taking pills?"

"What you described is a near-death experience. Patients tell us these stories a lot. I guarantee the experience is not due to craziness. No experiences are the same, but they have similar pieces: feeling embraced by a loving feeling, being out of the body, and seeing a tunnel. The good news is that patients do get a new lease on life with more positive energy. Is that what you are experiencing?" said Lynn.

"Yes, absolutely. I don't feel at all depressed, and I want to do stuff – what I'm not sure about yet."

"There is a national association about near-death experiences with local groups, some in NC, for people to discuss and learn about these events and some aftereffects. One of them, for example, involves people becoming more altruistic and less materialistic. We had one patient on his drive home a chilly morning, make his wife stop so he could give a scantily dressed man his coat," Lynn explained.

"I'll have Beatrice bring you one of their handouts. This often happens enough that we keep information on hand. Any questions for me?" Lynn asked.

"Just thank you for stopping in and telling me all this. Always good to know that I am not ready for the looney bin," said Mrs. Bustillo.

"We are here for you," Lynn said, squeezing Mrs. Bustillo's hand.

John was finishing his night report as Lynn approached the nurses' station.

"You thought she might have had an NDE, right?" Lynn asked.

"Yes, Ma'am," John said. "You are the best at identifying and explaining them to our patients. You have helped avoid a lot of unnecessary sedation that I was afraid going to happen to Mrs. Bustillo."

"Well, thanks, but maybe next time we get a patient like this, you come with me and listen to my spiel. We will add that to your professional bag of tricks!" Lynn said.

"You got a deal," John said, extending his hand to shake with Lynn.

In her office, Lynn looked for her email that said the board meeting had been canceled. That message was gone. She checked her deleted files, but it wasn't there either. "What is going on?" Lynn whispered.

I didn't imagine that email, Lynn thought. *But who could have deleted it? I wonder if security or the IT people can find the ghost of that email.*

"Hi, Jim. This is Lynn from the ED. I think maybe someone broke into my computer's system. I got a fake notice, but now it is gone. Can I get someone to check my computer and find that deleted email?"

"I'm going to send Mike Morales, from IT, up to check it. There might be a ghost, so to speak, of the email left on your computer. If it's there, he'll find it," Jim Rogers answered with confidence.

CHAPTER 11

There was a familiar knock on Lynn's door. "Enter, please, especially if it is you, Peter, with coffee!

"I am so happy to enter. Is that what you say to all those who knock?" said Peter.

"No, just those whose image looks like yours through the opaque glass door. I can tell from this desk who has entrance to my hideout!"

Peter laughed as he sat in the chair in front of Lynn's desk, handing her a coffee. The sit-down was short-lived when another knock struck the office door.

"Come in, Mike," Lynn said, recognizing the male form with longish dark hair through the door glass. Lynn got up from her computer. "Yesterday, I received an email saying my meeting with the hospital board was canceled. It was a fake notice. It's gone now. Do you think you can find it?"

"I'll give my best shot. It might take about half an hour. If you have someplace to be, I can text you when I'm done," Mike said.

"You got time for a little chat?" Lynn turned to Peter.

"Always a pleasure to chat with you, Ms. Price. My next case isn't for two more hours," Peter replied.

"Let's go to one of the empty conference rooms. This is highly classified information," Lynn said.

"I'm intrigued. Beauty and mystery. It doesn't get much better than that," said Peter.

Conference Room 4 had a round wooden table with six cushioned chairs. There was something comforting about the mauve walls dotted with calm seascape paintings.

"Should I be worried about what you are going to tell me? What's with the mysterious email? You didn't mention that," said Peter.

"Let me start from there. The day before yesterday, I got an email saying the board meeting scheduled for noon yesterday was canceled. I went and brought Mom home. At my mother's, I got a call from Dr. Brown's office saying he wanted to speak to me before the meeting. I told Jawana I got the message that it was canceled, but she said no, it wasn't, and that she hadn't sent that message."

"I got Angie to come and stay with mom, and I rushed to the meeting, just making it on time. Dr. Brown wanted me to stay to talk after. This is the confidential part. The short version is that the board wants to combine the ED and the walk-in clinic under one roof with me as the Director."

"That's great! Congratulations."

"That's just the beginning. The board also wants to work toward being a Level I trauma center,"

"Oh, I see. Work the non-emergency patients into the walk-in clinic, saving room for the newly expected trauma patients for the ED," replied Peter. "That's a very big job."

"Yep, and there's more. Yesterday I got an acceptance letter into the Ph.D. nurse practitioner program at Chapel Hill. It's part-time and mostly online," Lynn added.

"Can I assume you are not sure about what to do?" asked Peter.

Lynn looked intensely at Peter. Whatever he was feeling wasn't showing on his face. It was more that he was just listening to her problem.

"For sure! I could manage the part-time school with my current job and still have time to spend with you and Hanna, and my family. Running two departments along with the development of a Level I trauma center could be a huge time and energy draw! I'm also not sure if staying in administration rather than being more involved with patient care is my best choice. So, confusion reigns in my head," said Lynn.

"Wow! That's a lot, but the way to an answer is rather simple. Where's your passion? What does your heart tell you? As you go through your days, what and who makes you smile and happy? Of course, I'm hoping I'm on that list. Knowing I will be seeing you makes everything else better for me. I hope that's true for you," said Peter, now holding her hand.

"You know I love being an orthopedic surgeon," Peter continued. "I like the technical part of the OR and seeing patients improve so that they can walk better and have less pain every day. It's rewarding. But at the end of the day, my heart craves companionship and love. It's a circular thing for me. Right now, having you and Hanna in my life makes me happy. That happiness makes me better at work, especially during tough cases. What I have learned, though, is that companionship and love require time, too. They require me to say no, sometimes to some cases."

"I get what you are saying," said Lynn. "Put the time and energy into what's important and heartfelt."

"That's my perspective," said Peter, "but you might see it differently."

"Great food for thought," Lynn said. "You are such a great guy." Lynn gave Peter a hug. They walked to the elevators holding hands. He blew her a kiss before the doors closed, and he ascended to the OR floor.

CHAPTER 12

Lynn walked back to her office, thinking about what Peter had said when a text message from officer Stan brought her back to the current reality.

"I have some information on the young woman who was dumped on your doorstep. What a world we live in," Stan texted. "Do you have time for lunch?"

"Sure, Sea Grill at 1:30?" Lynn responded.

Stan sent a thumbs-up emoji.

"Beatrice, I'm meeting with Stan about our Jane Doe. I should be back in about an hour," Lynn said.

"Take your time. We are doing good so far. I'll text you if it gets busy!" Beatrice replied.

Stan was waiting at a table when Lynn approached the restaurant. She liked Stan a lot but not in a romantic way. She often wondered what led to missing romantic feelings with other people. One of life's mysteries, she surmised. Stan waved her over to his table as she entered.

"I'll have a crab cake with some sweet potato fries and a glass of unsweetened tea," Lynn said to the waitress.

"Make that two," Stan responded.

"I'm excited to hear what you learned about our Jane Doe. I wish we could have saved her," Lynn said.

"We learned that wasn't likely to happen," Stan replied. "Her blood work showed toxic levels of Rohypnol plus alcohol. She also had severe damage to her brain, particularly in the back of her head, the occipital area, I was told. She could have been struggling with someone and fallen backward onto a coffee table or some other hard piece of furniture. She had twisted arm bruises, signs of sexual assault, and was severely underweight. Pretty likely she was being trafficked."

"Oh, that poor woman. Do we know who she is?" asked Lynn.

"We ran her DNA and found a match to a woman from Miami. She went missing when she was 17 and was 22 when she died. Her name is Sharon Vega. So far, we have not located any family. It seems like she was on her own at 17, easy prey for the perpetrators," Stan said angrily. "Traffickers are such animals."

"I hate to think of her living that life for five years. What a horror that must have been," Lynn said, almost in tears. "Unfortunately, she's not the only trafficked person we've seen in the ED."

"We do have some good news, thanks to you. We found the car that they used. It was stolen, but we found fingerprints on the sun visor that didn't belong to the car owner.

Criminals always forget to wipe off the visor, which is great for us. The driver who dumped Sharon has a rap sheet for drug possession and distribution and sexual assault. His name is Reginald Smith. He has been arrested for killing Sharon. We are looking for others who are involved in this trafficking ring."

"All right, that is good news," Lynn said. "My staff will be happy with that news."

"There's more news that's not so good. Maybe we will need you to testify about seeing the car and license plate. That could be dangerous, but you are the one who can put that car at that scene."

"Oh, I see," Lynn said. "Do I need to go into some kind of protection?"

"Not right now. So far, your name is only used as contacting us about Ms. Sharon getting dumped at the entrance of the ED. Nothing reports you saying anything about the car or the license plate. We have the perpetrator's fingerprints on a stolen car. We also have the video from the security camera that shows the car slowing down and driving away but not the plates. Unfortunately, you and some of your staff are on part of the video. I'd like to have you come down to the station so you can see the video. It doesn't seem to show you looking at the license plate – you look like you are just focused on Ms. Sharon.

"From what you are saying, if you have enough evidence to convict this suspect, you won't need me. Is that right?"

"That's the plan! I'm guessing, but not certain; we won't need you to testify. It's just a maybe. Be sure to tell any staff who knows you saw the plate and the car not to say anything to anyone. We don't want your name getting out as a potential witness," Stan said.

"I got it. I don't know if I said anything to anyone except maybe Wanda, my friend in OB. I'll give that some thought," Lynn answered.

"You call me anytime if you have questions or get worried. I'm here for you, always," Stan said.

"Thanks, that's much appreciated," Lynn said, giving Stan a hug as they walked to their separate cars.

Unbeknownst to Stan or Lynn, their hug was recorded.

Two men who are there for me. I wonder if I look like I need help or just attract good guys these days. Lynn thought back to the days of some other boyfriends who were not so caring. *Glad those days are over,* she whispered to herself.

Back in her office, Lynn finished up her paperwork and checked the patients in the ED. She called Stephanie to arrange their meeting at her house on Saturday.

CHAPTER 13

"Good morning, Stephanie," Lynn said while opening the door to the reporter. "Pleased to meet you."

"Hi," said Stephanie. "Likewise."

"Come in and have a seat." Stephanie reached out to shake Lynn's hand, which was quite firm. She was reminded of a research article she had read that described people with a firm handshake as being more extroverted, open to experiences, and less neurotic. This would be an opportunity for her to check out those results.

"Coffee is ready. Would you like some?" asked Lynn.

"That sounds great. I can put the fixings in myself," replied Stephanie as she headed to the kitchen with Lynn.

She's assertive, thought Lynn, *and maybe wealthy*, recognizing the $400 silver ball bracelet from Tiffany's. *Pretty in a classic but kind of distant ways, like all business*, Lynn thought. For Lynn, warmth shining through a person made them more attractive. At least at this early stage, Stephanie did not show warmth.

Once settled on the couch, Stephanie put her recorder on the coffee table and started the interview. Lynn was happy that she didn't try rearranging the candle and bowl of seashells on the coffee table as Virginia had done at Peter's.

"So, tell me how your mom started handing out $20s at Christmastime," Stephanie asked.

"My mother used to give to a lot of charities, especially buying bikes for kids at Christmas. She was happy to do that, but it lacked some satisfaction for her. There were rumors that some parents sold some donated bikes for cash. I'm sure that was rare, if at all, but for my mom, she wanted something that she was sure was helping someone," explained Lynn.

"One day in the grocery store, there was a man in front of her at the checkout counter who did not have enough money to pay for all his choices. My mom discretely gave the cashier enough money to cover the man's charges and wished him a Merry Christmas. That was when she decided to give out $20s to five people at Christmastime to help out. Now she's not well enough to be out and about a lot."

"So, you have picked up the tradition of doing the $20 giving. How's that going for you?" asked Stephanie.

Lynn recognized Stephanie's lack of interest in her mother's health. Most people, Lynn thought, would have said something like, I hope your mother is doing OK, at least.

"My mother left out some pieces of information that I learned when doing this myself. First, I found it's important to present the $20s in a way that's acceptable to the potential receiver. Giving someone $20s at a restaurant is easy. They expect a tip, and the twenty is just extra. Handing over a twenty over to someone who can't pay for something takes more finesse. I have learned blaming my mother works well," said Lynn, smiling.

Stephanie laughed. "How do you blame your mother?"

"I tell people I'm giving this money out for her because she can't do it anymore. It will make her happy and get me off the hook. They usually laugh. The important thing, though, is to not make people feel less than. I want them to feel visible – acknowledging that I see them as people who could use a bump up, even if it is a small one."

"I can see how that's an important part of this gift-giving. What else is important?" asked Stephanie.

"One thing I didn't realize was that not only did my mother give out the twenties, but she also helped many of these people in other ways. I learned that was part of the process," said Lynn.

"Tell me more about that," said Stephanie.

"Last year, when I handed out my five twenties, I continued to get involved with all the people who were recipients. Two of them were women with families looking to improve their lives. One woman had a physically abusive husband, another was a trafficked victim, and another had a critically ill family member in the hospital. I don't want to give you too many details to protect their identity," said Lynn.

"So, what do you get from doing this besides making your mom happy?" asked Stephanie.

"For me, it's like giving back. I have a good life. I've worked hard, but I've also been lucky to have a wonderful family who supports me in many ways. I'm not wealthy, but like a lot of people, I can afford to give $100 a year to five people who could use some help. Twenty dollars is not a lot of money, but it can make some people's lives just a little better and give them a feeling that someone sees them and cares about them," Lynn replied.

"Now you want to move into getting more people to hand out $20s. Is that right?"

"You got it. I'm hoping to do a small workshop with five people who want to join the $20 club. I'm thankful your newspaper is willing to announce that," said Lynn. "But there are some restrictions."

"Tell me," Stephanie said.

"Anyone interested in attending the workshop should respond to this email, $20club@helping.com. I don't want my name or the hospital's name mentioned at all in your article or any announcement."

"I don't know if the newspaper is going to go along with that," Stephanie said.

"I get that, but those are the conditions. Obviously, your paper's announcement would be very helpful, but we also have other ways of recruiting participants. The confidentiality of the donors and recipients is of utmost importance to us."

"I know you mentioned I could not be a member of this group. Is that still true?" asked Stephanie.

"Yes. Again, the only publicity should be about the workshop with no names," Lynn said. "But, tell me about your interest in being in the group."

"I think being part of the group and listening to the motivation of the others would make the story more interesting. Human interest stuff," Stephanie responded.

"You are probably right about that," Lynn said. She would have preferred hearing something a little more about helping people but was glad she drew the line about not having Stephanie or any reporter be part of the group. Stephanie reminded Lynn of the "If it bleeds, it leads" slogan for reporters. That was the last thing she wanted to happen with this group.

Stephanie got up to leave. "I'll be back in touch, Lynn, with the paper's response. I can't promise anything."

"Good to meet you," Lynn said and then watched Stephanie drive away in the silver metallic Mercedes.

CHAPTER 14

The next morning at work, Lynn got a text from Peter.

I got an early case – no coffee this morning ☹. Lunch later? How about Saturday night for our dinner? Pick you up at 7:00?

Lynn texted back.

Yes, to everything! Cafeteria or the diner for lunch?

There was no answer back. Lynn assumed Peter had to go to the OR.

Lynn went out to check on the patients who had entered the ED.

"Hi, Beatrice," Lynn said to the day ED manager. "How's it going today?"

"It's busy, but we still seem to be managing. You want a report?" Beatrice asked.

"That would be great," Lynn replied.

"The guests that were still here from the night shift included a two-year-old who bit into a balloon yesterday evening. His trachea was partially obstructed, but Dr. Eddison was able to remove the balloon particle. We're just watching him for swelling and any signs of difficulty breathing. There is also a woman with a severe headache. She has a history of migraines, but Dr. Winters wanted to ensure she doesn't have something more serious. She ordered a scan.

Today we had a man fall off his roof when he was putting up two reindeer and a sleigh. Fortunately, he has a one-story house. He maybe has a fractured elbow and radius. We are still waiting for the results," Beatrice reported. "He wasn't sure if he was unconscious at all. We're checking his neuro signs, too. Christmas time can be dangerous."

"Seems like you have everything under control. We are anticipating flu cases. There is a rise now in the area. We have the signs up about getting a flu shot, and the new batch of handouts is in the back room. Let's spread them out in the waiting area and the patient rooms," said Lynn.

Lynn's phone rang. It was from Mike in IT.

"I'm heading back to my office," Lynn told Beatrice.

"Hi, Mike. Any results?" Lynn asked.

"Yes, if you have time, I'll come up and explain what happened."

"Can't wait to hear," Lynn said.

Tall and thin was just too inadequate to describe Mike, Lynn thought. He had to bend down to enter any room and barely took up more than 2/3s of any chair. He looked like he was in motion, even sitting down. Exuberance oozed out of every cell in his body when he talked about computer stuff.

"Ok, so here's what we know. Someone who has Dr. Brown's secretary's email address put that in the sender email that was sent to you. It's not that hard to do. Jawana probably sends emails all the time to various departments, so it will be hard to track the person from the email you received," explained Mike.

"I want you to think back to that email. When it showed up in your system, did the subject line say the meeting was canceled?" Jim asked.

Lynn sat trying to picture that email.

"Yes, it did," Lynn answered.

"Do you remember opening the email?"

"Not really. I didn't need to," Lynn said.

"Some email systems have what they call an "unsend" or "recall" feature. It works on unopened emails only. Someone could send you an email, and if you didn't open it, they could recall it. It would just be gone, then."

"Holy smokes! They sent this email to make it look like it came from Jawana and put the information in the subject line so I wouldn't need to open it. But then recalled it, so it was off my computer, which made me look like I lied about getting that message. That's scary!" Lynn responded.

"We are still trying to find where that email really came from, but so far, not much luck. It might have been from a burner phone. Is there anyone who wants to make you look like you make up excuses? Like you are untrustworthy?" Mike asked.

"You think maybe someone is trying to sabotage my reputation? I don't know anyone who would do that. I don't think."

"Think about it some more. This was a dirty trick. Let me know if you get any more. More are probably coming from what I have experienced with these kinds of cases," Mike said.

"Thanks, Mike. So glad to have you in my corner," Lynn said.

"You and your team have been so great every time my daughter has come in with an asthma attack. I know you have saved her life a few times when she just couldn't breathe. I'll do everything I can for you, too. Be careful out there," Mike said just as he was leaving.

Lynn's phone beeped because of a text message. It was from Peter.

Meet you in the cafeteria around 1:30

Lynn texted Peter back.

It's a date!

Lynn got to the cafeteria a little early. She paid for her lunch and sequestered herself in the corner booth where she and Peter usually met. Lynn could see the people at the cashiers from her seat. It was late for lunch, with few people going through the line. She spotted Peter wearing his usual green scrubs and white lab coat.

She was enjoying watching him. He seemed to always have this joie de vivre about him, filled with positive energy.

He had stolen her heart – she could feel joy whenever they were together. She watched him leave the cashier and look around until he found her. His smile was instant and broad as he headed toward their table.

"Hi," Peter said as he approached Lynn. He squeezed her hand. "So great to be with you."

They had agreed not to kiss in public while in the hospital to avoid feeding the buzzing hospital grapevine.

"Hi, yourself," said Lynn. "How was your case?"

"It was fine – a relatively easy knee replacement. Mrs. Francesco should go home tomorrow! The only problem we have now is getting OR time. With the fractures from falls this winter, the OR is extra busy. However, I'm not complaining," said Peter. "How's your day going?"

"Wait until you hear this story," Lynn said as she started to fill Peter in on Mike's explanations.

"OK, your story is so much better than mine. I lost out to Mike, a smart guy with a great story," said Peter, laughing.

CHAPTER 15

Lynn was at the conference room early that evening, setting up some slides for the first day of the $20 club workshop. Try as she might, she couldn't stop herself from chewing on her lip, something she always did when she was nervous. Walking around a little always helped.

"Hi," Lynn said, walking toward the two people who entered the room. "I'm Lynn Price, the coordinator of this $20 club.

"Paul Hastings," replied the young man. "Glad to meet you."

Lynn knew Paul was a graduate student from the description he had sent in. Even though Paul was casually dressed, Lynn recognized the expensive Cartier watch that elucidated his background when they shook hands. Lynn thought about when she lived with Alan and how he had looked at that watch, thinking it would help him look successful.

"I'm Wendy Anderson. I'm so happy to be doing this. Happy to meet you," she said, shaking Lynn's hand. "You are so lovely."

"We are delighted to have you participate.," Lynn replied as they shook hands. According to the list, Wendy was a high school teacher.

Two more potential participants entered the room. Lynn welcomed Abigail Taylor, listed as a homemaker, and Amanda Richey, a radiographer historically known as an X-ray technician.

Rushing in, almost out of breath, came Dennis Thompson, a police lieutenant. His application surprised Lynn, but she knew the police were looking into all different ways to connect with the community.

"Good morning, everyone. Happy to meet you. Before I start, I'd like to go around and get to know you a little better. Please introduce yourselves and tell us what interested you in giving out $20.00," said Lynn. "Wendy, would you start us off?" asked Lynn.

"Hi, I'm Wendy Anderson. I teach social sciences at Deer Park High School and have been there for eight years. Every Christmas, I see students who are so excited about Christmas talking about their much-anticipated gatherings, events, and presents. But there is always a core of students who don't say much. There's little enthusiasm for the holidays. I wonder sometimes if they are even going to get a decent meal. I recognize that $20 is not much money, but it could be a little pick up for those who have little to look forward to," said Wendy.

"Thanks, Wendy. Are you mostly looking to donate to teenagers?" asked Lynn.

"Either them or their parents. Either way is good for me," Wendy replied. I guess I'm a little like all of you. I have a good job, as does my husband. We are not millionaires, but we don't lack for anything. I hear stories about bad times, people just scraping by. I guess I want to know some of these people – not just read about them. I've learned that people are out there who could use an assist. These people are not impoverished and have pride in making it on their own. $20, as Wendy said, is not much money, but it could be a little boost and recognition that some people care about others.

"Got it," said Lynn. "Who would like to go next?"

"I will," said Amanda Richey. "Like Wendy, I see people when they come in for x-rays with varying enthusiasm for the holidays. The adults sometimes talk about barely getting by financially and feel bad that they can't do more for their families at Christmas. One woman began to cry when she told me her eight-year-old daughter wanted a doll like her friend had, but it cost $60.00. This woman said she couldn't afford it. Thirty dollars would have been a stretch for her. I felt so bad for her and so helpless. When I read the article in the paper, I thought, I could have slipped her a twenty."

"Thank you, Amanda. So, some of you are already seeing people who are getting by but don't have that little extra. Who wants to go next?" asked Lynn.

"I will," said Paul Hastings. "I'm in graduate school with other students who are scraping by. I'm fortunate to have parents who can financially support me during this time. I also worked in my father's business for a few years after college. I don't have financial issues, but some of my fellow students work one or two jobs and carry a full course schedule. I want to help, but I don't want them to feel like they are charity cases. They tolerate me buying coffee and doughnuts and an occasional lunch. I want to do more."

"Thanks, Paul. We will talk about how to hand out the $20 in a way that makes people feel seen and important but not less than. How about you, Abigail?"

"Hi, everyone. I'm in the fortunate position to be, shall we say, well off. Right now, I stay home and care for my four- and six-year-olds. My husband has an excellent job, and I have my own money. I donate to various charities but don't have contact with anyone. I don't want people to thank me or be so grateful. It's more about connecting with people and helping them out. I liked the part in the newspaper article where you talked about sometimes the connection with these people goes beyond just the $20s. You end up helping them with other issues. I feel like I can do that and would like to do that."

"That's great, Abigail. We will talk about that."

"Dennis, how about you?" Lynn asked.

"As I'm sure most of you knew, the local police are trying to get community people to see us as a support system instead of the Gestapo. We truly want to help. I thought this workshop could give me ideas."

"I agree. Here's a saying from Mordy Quotes, I think represents what this group is all about," Lynn said.

"Be someone who leaves a mark in people's lives, not a scar., who lifts people up, not casts them down, and who brings out the best in people and not the stress in them."

Before I start with the slides, I'd like to tell you a little story that I think captures what we want to do at the $20 club.

I love to stop at McBurger's when I'm traveling – the chicken nuggets and fries call to me," said Lynn creating smiles and light laughter. "On a recent trip, I stopped and handed the woman at the window a $20 tip. She told me her husband was out of work, which was so appreciated. A month or so later, I recognized her face in an ad for a moving company. I was moving into a new house and contacted that moving company. When we met to go over the moving plans, the woman remembered me. She said that right after I gave her the $20, her husband got this job offer but had to fax his application and resume to a distant company. He didn't have the $16 to do that until she gave him the $20. Using them for my move helped them with this new job. I also referred her and her husband to two real-estate agents I knew," explained Lynn.

"Wow, I never thought about tipping people at fast-food restaurants. Do they allow that?" asked Abigail.

"I wrote to McBurger's, and they said each franchise can set its own policies about tipping. I convinced local McBurger's to set up a tipping jar. At your next visit there, ask to talk to the manager and see what he or she says," said Lynn.

"I worked at the window of a fast-food place, whose name I won't mention, but not McBurger's," said Abigail. "It was so hard to understand the orders and get them right. There were lots of angry customers when I asked them to verify their orders. I hated it. For $8 an hour at that time, it wasn't worth it. That job made me go back to school."

"I taught in the community college system for a while. The average age of students there was close to 30. Most students got tired of unsatisfying and low-paying jobs. These jobs are great back-to-school incentives."

"I am so delighted to meet and know all of you. Let this adventure begin, as my mother called it," Lynn said.

CHAPTER 16

Lynn started her slide presentation.

Slide #1

Every day we have opportunities to be helpful to others around us. Most of the time, we need to notice those opportunities.

Slide #2

Here are some specific opportunities: A small financial boost of $20. Someone to listen. Immediate but noncritical aid information on topics within your area of expertise, donations of goods, and or referrals.

"Any comments on these opportunities?" Lynn asked the group.

"Most of the people I meet are students, many of whom are on a financial shoestring. $20 can buy recycled books for them," commented Paul.

"Many of us remember our student days that involved eating Ramen noodles and apples and taking part-time jobs. They were full of penny-pinching moments when we had pennies to pinch," said Lynn.

The group laughed and nodded their heads in agreement. "This next slide is a breakdown of the financial realities of many people."

> Slide #3
>
> The US household income is $62,657 to $46,886, depending upon age, race, and location. 50% of people are above the median, and 50% are below that level. Millions of working Americans are earning less than $30,000 each year.

"Also, they tend to be invisible. Here is a list of the type of jobs that are on the bottom of pay scales."

Lynn clicks on slide #4

Slide #4

Cashiers
Fast food attendants
Waiters and waitresses
Dishwashers
Ticket collectors
Aides in different areas
Laundry receptionists

"My favorite group is the bathroom attendants at airports. They make an average of $14.21 an hour, which is about $28,000 a year," said Lynn. "You do not need to be a billionaire, millionaire, major politician, or significant professional to add to the goodness of life for others."

Slide #5

- Anyone can contribute positive energy, achieve good results, and receive benefits such as the following:
- Emotional dividends
- Health benefits
- Reduced stress
- Live longer
- Increased happiness

"We've gone through the ins and outs of giving out the $20s. Kindness is choosing to do something that helps others or yourself, motivated by genuine warm feelings. You start it by finding the kindness place in your heart.

If you are stressed, angry, or in physical or emotional pain, feeling that kindness might be difficult. There are no time requirements for helping someone, although there are opportunities.

Sit for a minute, close your eyes, and feel that kindness place in your heart. It might remind you of a time when someone was kind to you." Silence spread across the room for 5 minutes.

"How did you all make out?" Lynn asked.

"I found this warm, fuzzy place," Abigail said. "It reminded me of going to this small hangout restaurant when I was in high school, drinking Coke with my friends. I loved the feeling of happy connection."

"I left the house this morning upset with my husband. He came home late after work last night and made himself a snack. The kitchen was a disaster this morning with dishes, pots, and pans all over, most of which still had food stuck in them. It was hard to feel kindness just now – squirting him with the kitchen sink hose was more on my mind," Amanda said.

"Excellent example, Amanda. Thanks for that. I would like to digress a little here. One of the acts of kindness we can do along with the $20s is to listen to our recipients and maybe help them with an issue. Amanda, is it OK if we talk to you more about what happened last night?"

"Sure. I'm still upset about it. Any advice is welcome," Amanda replied.

"Thank you. Amanda mentioned the word, advice. The one time, it is good to give advice is in emergencies if you know how to handle that situation. Otherwise, we want to send a message that we are supportive of this person and are there to help them work through an issue."

"Anyone up to trying that?" Lynn asked.

"I'll give it a try," volunteered Wendy.

"Wow, I can totally get upset about finding that mess in the kitchen. Tell me more about what upset you."

"I work all day, as you know, as an x-ray technologist. I come home and make supper for my family, which also includes my two kids. When Henry is not there, I leave him a plate to heat up and clean up the kitchen myself. When he comes home and does this, it makes me feel less than – like I'm his servant who cleans up after him. I feel disrespected," Amanda said.

"Besides squirting him with the kitchen hose, what else do you think would help in this situation?" asked Wendy.

"I could just leave the dishes for him to clean up and go to work after dropping off the kids at school."

"That sounds like you don't take on the role of servant," Wendy said.

"Yes, that's a good point. I could also talk to him about this. He's generally a good guy and helps a lot around the house and with the kids. We take turns taking them to school, for example. Holding on to my resentment isn't good plus squirting him with the water will just make another mess!" Amanda said.

The room filled with laughter.

"Wendy, great job! One other thing that you can do is to check in with the person whom you talked with to see how they are doing. In Amanda's situation, because she gave up on squirting her husband and her mood lightened, there's less of a need. You don't want this to be a therapy session, just friendly support."

"I do feel better. I did feel kindness from Wendy that was helpful. One of the important things I got, though, was that I don't have to carry out a role someone else laid out for me, like being a servant. I have control over not doing that," Amanda said.

"Yes! Good point. The people you will intervene with can make that same choice with support and some taking the time to listen."

Another thing to process is making sure we don't overdo it! It is one of the reasons I recommend giving out a maximum of five $20s bills. We don't want to go beyond our means. It is also easy to give away too much energy. Don't get depleted. Leave enough for you and your loved ones.

As promised, I will go out with you the first time and then be your backup if the recipient needs help. Questions?" Lynn asked.

"When do we start?" asked Abigail.

"Excellent question. Get your calendars out, and we'll set times to meet. I'm generally free in the evening after 5:30. This week, I'm also off from work on Friday during the daytime," Lynn responded.

CHAPTER 17

The next morning Lynn was back in her office after a good night's sleep. She started her day by reviewing her staffing for the next week. So far, she was short an RN for three shifts. Secretly she was hoping Peter would show up soon with coffee and pleasant conversation. Instead, her phone rang.

"Hi, Emma. How are you this morning?" Lynn asked her ICU Director colleague.

"I was great until I opened your snarky email. You have some nerve saying I had no clue how to run an ICU service. Who are you to suggest I hire a consultant to show me how to do a better job?" said Emma in a very aggravated voice.

"Emma, I am so sorry. I did not write any email that said those things about you. You know, I think you do such a super job working with us when we have critical patients," Lynn replied. Damn*! I can't believe more of this fake email is still coming*, Lynn thought.

"The email says it came from you. How can you say you didn't send it?" Emma replied.

"Someone is sending emails that look like they come from me. Mike, in IT, is helping me stop them. Would you kindly send me a copy of what you received? Jim in Security might need to check your computer if you don't mind," said Lynn.

"Really, that's what's happening? How do I know you are not just back peddling because I'm upset with what you sent," asked Emma.

OMG, Emma doesn't believe me. Suppose she tells other people this is what I said about her.

"Emma, listen to what Mike has to say. He's the expert. I'm also going to send an email out to the Directors or have Jim do that telling them someone is accessing my email system and making me look nasty and incompetent."

"OK, I'll wait since up to now, we have had a great working relationship. It will take me a while to recover from reading that email. I just forwarded it to you," Emma said and hung up.

"Jim, call me when you get a chance. There's another email floating around that looks like it came from me. It's very snarky and disturbing," Lynn said to Jim's answering system. "I'll text Mike, too."

"Knock, knock," said Peter holding his coffee offering. "I was going to ask how my gorgeous girlfriend was this morning, but the look on your face shows distress. What's happening?"

"Again, someone is sending emails that look like they come from me. This one was a snarky one to Emma Johnson, and God only knows who else. I just left messages for Jim in security and Mike in IT to call me. I wish I knew who had it in for me and is doing this."

Peter shut the door and gave Lynn a kiss and a hug, then sat down in front of her desk. "Let me see if I received anything from you," he said.

"Sure enough, there is an email from you. Let's see what it says. Hmmm. The gist is that you think we should take a break in our relationship. It's moving too fast for you. You are not sure I am the right person for you. WOW!" said Peter.

"You are under siege, my dear. I am happy you told me about crank emails going out before I read this. I would have been devastated."

Lynn looked at Peter with tears in her eyes. "What is happening here? Someone is trying to ruin not only my career but also our relationship. I don't know anyone who hates me that much."

Lynn could see Jim come up to the door with Mike. "Come in, Jim," Lynn said before he could knock.

"Apparently, whoever this is has sent numerous emails, Lynn, even me. I did take it upon myself to alert all those at the Director level and above in the hospital that your email account has been compromised, and you did not send negative or nasty emails."

"Thank you, thank you," Lynn said.

"If we can get to your computer, we'll change your email account, making sure it's more secure, and see if we can track down who is sending these messages. Once I'm in your account, I'll also send a notice to anyone you communicate with regularly that is not at the Director level or above, letting them know you are under siege here. I'm so sorry you are being attacked like this," Jim said.

"Come with me," Peter said, taking Lynn by the hand.

"Where are we going," Lynn asked.

"Home," Peter said.

CHAPTER 18

At home, Lynn cleaned the kitchen. The dishes were stacked up in the sink, and the trash was almost overflowing.

Then she got ready for her dinner with Peter. *What to wear?* She asked herself: s*omething pretty, maybe a little sexy, but not over the top.*

Lynn took out her maxi red dress. It had a deep V-neck, crouching from the V-neck to her waist, and a sweeping skirt. *Dressy but comfortable*, she thought.

At 7:00 pm, Peter was at her door.

"Holy smoke!" Peter said, followed by a wolf whistle. "You are stunning."

"Thank you," Lynn said. "You look spiffy yourself. Love the tie with just a dash of red, too. Proud to be with you!"

Lynn got her coat and put it on with Peter's help. His close presence in her house with complete privacy gave her goosebumps on the back of her neck and made her slightly lightheaded.

"We better get going," Peter said. "Otherwise, we may never leave."

They both looked at each other and laughed.

As they entered the Chateau restaurant with the ocean view, Lynn thought about what makes a restaurant romantic. She liked the quiet, soft music in the background, isolated seating, tasteful décor, and beautiful view. The Chateau had it all. Their table was near a window out on an extended porch that overlooked the ocean. It was a clear night with the moon shining brightly on the water.

Peter pulled back a chair for Lynn and, after she was seated, kissed her gently on the back of her neck. The kiss was electrifying.

"How am I going to make it through dinner with you?" Lynn asked.

"I understand. Think about poor me," said Peter. "I'm sitting across from this beautiful and irresistible woman." He reached over the table to hold her hands.

"Good evening," said the waiter, suddenly standing at their table. "I'm Phillip, and I'll be your waiter this evening. "Can I interest you in a bottle of wine or maybe champagne if this is a special occasion?"

"We will have a bottle of Dom Perigon," replied Peter. "Every night with my girlfriend is a special occasion."

"Well, thank you. That was very nice. You do know, I have my bad side, too," said Lynn. She was getting a little worried about the pedestal she was on in Peter's eyes.

"Yes, I do know about your bad side. I asked George about you," Peter said, his eyes twinkling.

"Oh, no! What did brother George say about me?" asked Lynn.

"He said you have many wonderful characteristics, like being lovely, kind, caring, smart, and honest, sometimes to a fault. You can get too involved with people you are helping, don't always laugh enough at his jokes, correct him when he is right, and sometimes pick terrible boyfriends, with me being the exception, of course," replied Peter.

"Oh, yes! I almost forgot – also, you poke him when he's just trying to have fun," added Peter.

"What can I say? He knows me well," said Lynn.

"I think you are terrific. It has been my pleasure to get to know you. Hanna loves you, too, and. She's a tough sell. You make me happy, Lynn. My life is so much better with you in it," Peter said.

"I thought that was you, Lynn," an uncommonly nice-looking man suddenly said as he approached their table. "This must be your brother, George, you were telling me about. Hi, I'm Bruce," the man said, reaching over to shake Peter's hand.

"Who are you?" asked Lynn loudly. "I have never met you before."

"Oh, you haven't told your brother about us. I'm sorry to have ruined that surprise. Lynn and I have been seeing each other for the past month. It's been great. She's wonderful," the man said to Peter.

"Will you please leave!" demanded Lynn. "I don't know who you are, and we certainly have not been seeing each other for the past month. Who put you up to this?"

"You heard the lady. Leave!" said Peter standing up now.

"Ok, ok. If that's the way you want to play this. I hope we are still on for our movie tomorrow," said Bruce.

"We are not on for anything except for the police if you don't leave this minute," said Lynn. Her voice was shaking, and tears were forming in her eyes.

Phillip had arrived at their table with the champagne.

"Is there a problem here?" he asked.

"Yes," said Peter. "This imposter is upsetting my girlfriend. Please show him to the door!"

Phillip firmly grabbed Bruce by the elbow away from the table.

"Truly, I never saw that man before in my life," Lynn said to Peter with tears in her eyes.

"What is happening to me? First, the phony email, and now this guy pretending to be someone I'm seeing. Someone has it in for me, and I'm scared."

"Just know, I have no doubt this fellow was a setup. Hold on! I'll be right back," Peter said, grabbing his phone.

He came back to the table, smiling.

"Where did you go? What do you do?" asked Lynn.

"I took Bruce's picture," said Peter. "Someone is setting you up, and I want to know who it is so all this can stop."

"I'm with you on that," said Lynn. "Send me that picture, too. I'll see what I can find out. He's not someone I remember seeing before."

Peter raised his champagne glass and said, "No one does this to my girlfriend and gets away with it!"

"So, how did someone know we were here?" Lynn asked. "Is one of us or both of us being followed? Should we make a list of all the people who knew we would be here? We can ask them if they told anyone."

After dinner, Lynn and Peter decided to continue the list-making at Peter's house. Lynn slipped into the casual pants and top she had left at Peter's another time. When it got to be around 1:00 am, Lynn fell asleep on the couch, drifting into delightful dreams about walks on ocean beaches.

CHAPTER 19

The next morning Lynn stayed for breakfast, enticed by Peter's buttermilk pancakes with blueberries in some and chocolate chips in others.

"Ms. Lynn, are you coming back later?" Hanna asked. "Or maybe we can come to your house."

Lynn looked over at Peter, who was shaking his head yes and smiling.

"I would love to have you come over to my house later. The toy basket is still there, and I think there are a few new toys in it. I could use some help sorting out the presents that are under my tree, too," Lynn said.

"OK, I can do that. I like sorting out presents, especially if there's one for me," said Hanna.

"That's what we need to find out," Lynn said.

"How about 5:00 o'clock for present sorting and around 6:00 for dinner?" Lynn asked Peter.

"Sounds great! Does that give you enough time to go out with your $20 donor?" Peter asked.

"I'm meeting the donor at 11:00 this morning, so I'll have plenty of time, but thanks for checking on that," said Lynn.

"That's great for me, too," said Hanna, who then scouted off to her toy room.

"Are you OK after last night's encounter with 'Bruce'?" asked Peter.

"It's a little worrisome," Lynn said. "I don't get what that was about. Here's this man I've never met, never even seen before, pretending like he and I had a relationship. Who does that?'

"Virginia, maybe," said Peter.

"What?' said Lynn.

"Sure, that's not beneath her," said Peter. "After we got divorced, she sent letters to this woman I had dated a few times. Virginia told her how rotten I was to her. I never did figure out how she knew about this woman and got her address."

"Yikes. We should fix her up with Alan. Then maybe she'll be happy and busy with her own life," Lynn said, laughing.

Peter was thinking.

"You know that's not a bad idea," said Peter.

"Really?" said Lynn. "I was joking."

"I got that, but we need to think more about that. It might be something that's a win for everyone. First, though, I need to find out if it was Virginia who sent that guy. I'm glad to have taken his picture. I'll send it to you, too. Let's hunt him down," said Peter.

"Thank you for being so trusting," Lynn said. "Someone else might have believed I really did know that fellow."

Peter looked at Lynn and said, "I trust you more than anyone else I know. I don't think you have a deceitful bone in your body. It's on the list of why I love you so much," Peter said.

Lynn and Peter kissed at the door as she left. She could hear Hanna say, "More mushy stuff," and laughed.

Lynn then headed out to meet Abigail at her favorite pizza place, The Pizza Pie, advertised as pizza that doesn't suck.

CHAPTER 20

Lynn had suggested going to restaurants, stores, grocery stores, and other places that Abigail frequented. The Pizza Pie was on her list of favorite places to be herself and relax.

Lynn joined Abigail at her table in the side section of the restaurant. It was void of other people.

"I ordered a large pizza and a Caesar salad for us. Your side of the pizza, as you requested, has extra cheese and mushrooms. Here's your bottle of red wine," said Abigail.

"Thanks for doing all this. What do I owe you?" asked Lynn.

"We're good," said Abigail. "OK, so tell me about getting ready to do a $20 handout. What are the rules?"

"I don't know if I'd call them rules, per se, more like guidelines," said Lynn. "First thing is to notice someone who could use a little boost at Christmas. Daily, we all see people who could use a lift. $20 isn't a lot of money, but for some, it can enable something special to happen, like buying a child a better Christmas present."

"Can you give me an example where it helped someone out?"

"I gave $20 as a tip to a woman working at McBurger's. Her husband was out of work but had a job opportunity. He needed to fax his application and work experiences to a corporate headquarters. It was 16 or 18 dollars to do the fax. They didn't have the money, except now the wife had the $20s. He got the job," said Lynn.

"For the most part, we pass by people every day who could use a boost, but they are invisible to us. We all have things to do and people to see, and we miss seeing them," said Lynn.

"Give me an example of that," said Abigail.

"The women who clean the ladies' rooms at the airports or other places are a good example. Maybe we put a quarter in the tip jar. One time, at the airport, I waited until the room was empty and handed the attendant $20. I had noticed that she looked sad, with slumped shoulders, no smile, and minimum energy. When I handed her the $20 and wished her Merry Christmas, she looked astounded, her eyes widened, her jaw dropped, and there was the beginning of tears in her eyes. 'Is this for me?' she asked, seemingly not believing the $20 was to be hers.

"Got it," said Abigail. "I'm looking around in this pizza place at the people. I don't see anyone." Just as those words came out, a young woman delivered the salad and plates to the table. "Your pizza will be out in a few minutes," said Meghan, according to her nametag.

"So, tell me, Meghan, is this really pizza that doesn't suck?" asked Lynn.

"It's great pizza, really," Meghan answered.

"Have you worked here long?" asked Lynn.

"I started here in August when I started school at the University. It's a great part-time job to help to buy books and food! We can eat here, for free, too," Meghan said, eyeing the number board. "I see your pizza is ready. I'll be right back."

"Wow!" said Abigail. "My first potential recipient was right in front of my nose, and I missed her."

"Don't beat yourself up. We all wear blinders a lot," said Lynn.

Abigail took $20 out of her purse. When Meghan came back with the pizza, she handed the $20 to her.

"Here's a little something for you. Put it in your pocket. I remember struggling during my college days. Good luck to you, and Merry Christmas," said Abigail.

"Thank you so much. Much appreciated," Meghan said, bursting into a wide smile.

"Good job, Abigail," said Lynn.

"I could relate. I got a scholarship for college, and my parents could pitch in a little, but I was always short," said Stephanie.

They both took a couple of bites of the pizza.

"They are right – this pizza doesn't suck. Actually, I think it's pretty good," said Abigail.

"Definitely," said Lynn as the cheese ran over the corner of her mouth.

"A couple of things," said Lynn. "Giving an extra tip to someone who gets tips is the easiest situation. In other cases, you are dealing more with people not wanting to be a charity case. Sometimes you must figure out how to give them money while respecting their dignity. I often will tell them I'm doing this for my mother, who started this idea, and they will be helping me out by taking the money. That's true, and it helps. You can always use me as an excuse."

"How would I do that?" asked Abigail.

"You can tell them you are taking a philanthropy course, and part of the clinical practice is to hand out $20s. In class, you need to report back to see if you were able to do that," Lynn said.

"Got it," said Abigail, laughing. "You get to be the heavy."

"Sometimes there's an opportunity in the grocery store. You see people shopping and putting stuff back on the shelf or in the refrigerated section, particularly where the meat is. If you have a conversation with them, what they are putting back is too expensive. Also, sometimes you are behind someone in the checkout lane, who can't afford to pay for everything they picked up, so they start putting stuff back," said Lynn. "They are very embarrassed, and occasionally, there are hecklers who complain because the check-out line is hung up.

"I have on occasion bent down and pretended I had found $20 on the floor. I ask the person if it's theirs. So far, they have always said no. I will say, 'I know it's not mine, I say, OK, I'll make an administrative decision and say it's yours then.' They typically laugh and take the money," said Lynn.

"It's a gift, not a handout, is the idea, right?" asked Abigail.

"Great way to put it. You got the idea," said Lynn.

"What else do I need to think about?" asked Abigail.

"My experience has been that these recipients might have life issues about which you end up helping them. It just happens. For example, you could come in here again and notice Meghan is not her usual happy self," said Lynn.

"Of course, I might say, Meghan, how are you doing? You look a little glum?" said Abigail.

"Yep, and whatever is bothering her might be something you can help with, or I can help with, too, as backup," said Lynn.

"Gotcha! Thanks, this was fun," said Abigail.

They both toasted with their wine cups enjoying the pizza that didn't suck!

CHAPTER 21

Back at home, Lynn decided to check on her mother. All seemed to have been going well since she was discharged from the hospital.

"Hi, Mom," said Lynn over the Phone. "How are you this morning?"

"I'm fine. I had a great breakfast, accompanied by a great talk with Dorika," said Dorothy.

"Super. How's Dorika doing?" asked Lynn.

"She's living a good life, thanks to you. I can't imagine the abuse she took from her husband. She and Randy, the superintendent of her building, are still happily dating. It's like you and Stan pulled her out of a snake pit, kept her safe, and now she's enjoying life, smiling a lot," answered Dorothy.

"I'm happy to hear that about Dorika. It would be best if you took some credit. You started this $20 gift idea. If I hadn't given Dorika $20, I would not have found out her husband was abusing her. Take a bow!" said Lynn.

"I am bowing," said Dorothy, laughing.

"So, how are you this morning?" asked Lynn. "Are you feeling OK, Mom?"

"I'm fine. Just a little tired," said Dorothy.

"Promise me you will call me right away if your fatigue gets worse," said Lynn.

"I promise," replied Dorothy. "Love you, honey."

"Love you, too, Mom."

Lynn made a mental note to check the date of Dorothy's next doctor's appointment. She also decided to call her brother, George.

"Hi," said George on the Phone. "What's doing, Sis?"

"I need another person's opinion," said Lynn.

"Are you suggesting I'm opinionated, and you want to dip into the barrel?

"No, I'm being nice today and saying I value your opinion. I'm worried about Mom. She's been more tired than usual. I'm going to check when her next doc appointment is, but I think maybe she needs to be sooner. Have you noticed any difference?" asked Lynn.

"No, not really, but you know me, I don't pay that much attention to health stuff. Maybe I'll ask Angie to see her – she's better than I am at noticing changes and getting Mom to talk about them. How's that sound?" asked George.

"Good idea, although you usually get Mom laughing – why don't you both go?" suggested Lynn.

"Sure, not a problem. We'll check on her, maybe tomorrow. How's everything else going?" asked George. "How're things with Dr. Pete?"

"All of that is very good, although something strange happened. We were out to dinner, and some fellow named Bruce came up to our table and implied he and I were dating. I never saw the man before in my life. Peter took his picture," strange things keep happening.

"You be careful. You know I tease you a lot, but I would feel terrible if something happened to you. Love you, Sis," George said.

"Love you, too, George!" Lynn responded. "I'll be careful."

CHAPTER 22

The next thing Lynn did was to text Peter, reminding him she was going to meet up with the ADA, who was prosecuting Reginald Smith, tomorrow morning.. She didn't want him to come to her office and not find her there.

Lynn was sitting in the waiting room of Michelle Thomas, just one of the ADAs prosecuting the case against Reginald Smith for his role in the trafficking of Sharon Vega. Lynn had been to court before, but mostly it was in support of patients or doctors. This was her first time as a witness to a crime. She could feel her heart racing a bit as she tapped her fingers nervously on the arms of the chair she was sitting on..

"Ms. Price, you can come in now," Michelle Thomas's secretary said to her standing near the door that Lynn assumed was Michelle's office.

Michelle was seated at a small table with a younger man sitting next to her. Lynn was invited to sit across from them. Michelle had added a warm smile to her invitation to be seated. That had helped Lynn feel a little more comfortable. Joseph Truman, on the other hand, looked even more nervous than Lynn felt, barely making eye contact with her.

"Hi, Lynn. We are happy to see you. This is attorney Joseph Truman, who has just joined the DA office," Michelle said.

"As you have been informed, this prep is to get you ready for your testimony about your experiences with Ms. Sharon Vega being dropped off at the door to the ED you manage. In court, Joe and I will be on your side during the questioning. For today, though, I will ask you questions similar to those I'll ask in court, but Joe will take on the role of the defense attorney. He will challenge some of your answers, like what the defense attorney might do. Do you have any questions about that?" asked Michelle.

"No, I've been to court enough times to have seen that type of interaction," Lynn said. "Are there any general guidelines for my answers?

"First of all, always be truthful. Somehow, untruths often get discovered and muddy up a case. Your testimony should be straightforward. Don't embellish your answers or add information beyond the question being asked. Unlike what you might see on TV, we bore people with facts as opposed to entertaining them with insights." Michelle laughed.

"Here we go. Ms. Price would you tell us about your position at Deer Park Memorial Hospital," Michelle directed.

"I'm the Director of the ED at Deer Park Memorial." Lynn stopped. "Should I talk about what my responsibilities are there?"

"Sure, that would be OK in this situation," Michelle responded.

"My main responsibilities are to see there is sufficient staff to provide care to the patients we see in the ED. I also am responsible for supplies being available to meet the needs of patients. In addition, I attend to the training of the staff and carry out their evaluations. I also meet with other hospital Directors to coordinate care."

"I do have a question. You refer to where you work as the ED instead of the more common ER description. When should either term be used?" Michelle asked.

"ER stands for the emergency room. We have moved way beyond just having an emergency room. We are a complete department with multiple rooms, including a trauma room. ED better describes the way hospitals operate these days," Lynn responded.

Michelle and Joe both shook their heads in understanding.

"What are the credentials that make you suitable for this position?" asked Michelle continuing the prep.

"I am a registered nurse with a bachelor's and master's degree in nursing. I also worked as an ICU and ED nurse for five years before taking this position." Lynn answered, feeling more relaxed.

"Was it in your capacity as this ED Director that you saw what happened to Sharon Vega outside your ED entrance?" Michelle asked.

"Yes, I was leaving my office to check on our supplies," Lynn answered.

"What did you experience on the morning when you saw Ms. Vega dumped from a car?" Michelle asked.

"As I walked by the glass entrance door to the ED, I first heard then saw a car pull up. The front passenger door opened, and a woman tumbled to the concrete in from of the ED door. The car quickly pulled away."

"What did you notice about the car?"

"It was a dark sedan with the beginning license number BKK-9, I think. It also had a fish on it," Lynn answered.

"Then what did you do?" Michelle asked.

"I yelled to the ED manager to bring a stretcher and an oxygen tank as I ran over to check the young woman. She was barely breathing with a weak thready pulse. My staff and I put her on a stretcher, gave her oxygen, and quickly wheeled her to the trauma room. Dr. Tom saw us and came with us to the Trauma room. The doctor and my staff began a resuscitation procedure," Lynn recounted with tears starting to fill her eyes.

"What were the results of the resuscitation?" asked Michelle.

"The patient died. She was too badly injured to respond to the resuscitation," Lynn answered regretfully.

"Very good, Lynn. That was excellent. Can I get you some water or a coffee before we see what Joe has come up with for possible questions on cross-examination?" Michelle asked.

"Water would be great," Lynn answered, welcoming a break. It had been harder to recall those events than Lynn had thought. That poor young woman had been so beaten up and thrown away like trash. It was inhumanity she hoped never to see again.

"OK, Joe. Let's start the possible cross by the defense," said Michelle.

Lynn instinctively braced herself. Even though this was a prep, she still felt tense. She knew from past experiences that the cross-examination could be brutal.

"Ms. Price, you said as you walked by the ED door, you heard a car and saw a woman land on the sidewalk. How do you know if the woman voluntarily left the car or if someone pushed her?" asked Joe.

"She was unconscious, so someone had to have pushed her. She could not have opened a car door herself," Lynn answered.

"Did you get a look at the driver?" Joe asked.

"No, I didn't see the driver's face. I got a brief glimpse of his right arm," Lynn said.

Michelle came to attention immediately. "I haven't heard you say that before. Joe, stop for a minute. When did you see his or her arm?" Michelle asked.

"He reached over to pull the door shut after Sharon Vega fell out of the car onto the sidewalk. He was a white male, probably left-handed," Lynn said.

Michelle was now on the edge of her seat. "You said it was a man who was left-handed. How did you know that?"

"He was wearing a large, gold men's watch on his right arm. Only left-handed people do that, as far as I know," Lynn responded. "Is that helpful?"

Michelle sat back in her chair.

"Joe, is Reginald Smith right-handed or left-handed?" Michelle asked.

Joe quickly looked through the report he was holding about the arrest of Reginald Smith. "It's not described in the arrest report."

"We better check that out," Michelle said.

Michelle looked at Lynn. "I think that's enough for to-day, Lynn. You may have just strengthened or bombed our case. Either way, what you saw will get us closer to the driv-er of that car, whomever he is. We will be in touch."

"I'm beginning to get nervous about this trial. Someone is sabotaging me at work. Could it be related to this case?" Lynn asked.

"Detective Gregowski mentioned that to me. So far, we have not put out the witness list, so your name is not known to the defense. If we need you in court, that will happen. Right now, we have a video of the car pulling up in front of the ED and then driving away, but we can't see Sharon being ejected from the car. You tie that piece together, and now seeing the driver's arm gives us more information. If you are called as a witness, we will need to put you in protective custody right before we send out the witness list," Michelle said. "These guys are violent and dangerous. However, if we get a confession, there will be no trial. Unfortunately, this is a wait-and-see situation."

Lynn was sure her face was now as white as a ghost. Being petrified did not even come close to describing how she felt.

Michelle added one more possible option.

"This guy we arrested could just have been a driver–gopher type guy for the organization. We can offer him a deal if he gives up some of the main players in this trafficking ring. We now have good evidence putting him at the scene, especially if he's left-handed. He may not go to trial if he takes a deal. Then we won't need your testimony. We will be pushing for that."

Lynn realized she had been holding her breath and now exhaled deeply. She looked at Michelle and Joe as she stood up to leave.

"I have seen the torment these traffickers have inflicted on people. I'll do whatever you need me to do to help put them away," Lynn said and left.

CHAPTER 23

Lynn was happy to be back at work the next morning after her court prep meeting. She was happy to be looking over her staffing schedule for the next week instead of thinking of being a trial witness when she heard a familiar tapping on her door.

"Good morning, Sweetie. How are you this morning? How was your court prep meeting?" Peter asked with a slightly worried tone in his voice. He had shut the door and reached out to Lynn to give her a hug. Lynn started to cry.

"Crying is good. It lets out those emotions," Peter said, somewhat surprised. "You have been under much pressure lately. Remember, I'm always here for you."

Lynn dried her eyes before taking a sip of the coffee Peter had brought.

"We have seen our share of the results of criminal activity in the ED, but I've never been this close to being in danger from some of them. Plus, I have this stuff going on with someone messing with my email account. Usually, my life is focused on helping patients with emergencies and supporting my staff here in the ED," Lynn said.

"Because you are so popular, you also have Dr. Brown's offer to think about, the possibility of being a nurse practitioner, your $20 club trainees, and me in your life," Peter said.

Lynn just nodded her head as she looked directly at Peter.

"How about we do this? I'll come to your house on Thursday with Chinese take-out, and we will review your situation and find some direction for you. If you want, make a list of your options with plus and minus signs or some other grading system. You're better at that than me," Peter suggested.

"I would so appreciate that. Thank you," Lynn said. She got up beyond her desk and fell into Peter's arms.

"There is just one more thing," Peter said.

"Yes, and what is that?" Lynn replied, smiling, still standing close to Peter.

"I need to be on that list with lots of pluses," Peter replied with a large grin.

"I wouldn't want it any other way," Lynn said.

"Love you!" Peter said, exiting her office.

Lynn started to say, "Love you, too," but Peter had already left.

I guess it is time I thought about all the stuff I have going on and what to do in my future life. Good idea, Peter, Lynn thought.

She was back reviewing next week's staffing schedule when her phone rang. It was Stan.

"Good morning, Stan. How are you doing today?" Lynn asked, her voice cheerier than before Peter's visit.

"Do you have a few minutes? I have some news about Mrs. Bustillo's unauthorized visitor. It's kind of a long and complicated story better told in person. I can meet you at our favorite restaurant in about an hour to fill you in, if that works for you," Stan said.

"Sure," said Lynn. "I'll see you then."

Lynn was thinking Stan saying they had a favorite restaurant together indicated a relationship they didn't really have. *Stop worrying*, Lynn said to herself. *Stan is always a perfect gentleman and a great friend.*

Lynn completed her staffing schedule and browsed the ED. Beatrice reviewed the patients who were present – a 62-year-old man with chest pain who was going to be admitted to the coronary care unit shortly and a 12-year-old girl with an asthma attack who was doing fine and would be sent home soon. The most worrisome was a 58-year-old woman with a 100-degree fever and persistent cough. Lynn saw that the lab had drawn blood already, and Dr. Archambault, an internist, was at her bedside. Dr. Carter, the infection control doctor, had been called in for a consult.

Beatrice had the staff wear precautionary gear with masks, gowns, and gloves. A large precaution sign hung on the patient's door.

"Good job, Beatrice, with this patient," Lynn said. "You all are the best staff I could ever want."

"Thanks," Beatrice said. "We do our best."

"I'm going to lunch to meet up with Stan to talk about Mrs. Bustillo's visitor. Apparently, he knows who that was and needs to discuss the situation with me," Lynn explained.

"Looking forward to hearing that story," Beatrice said, but there was a smile on her face.

"You are smiling, why?" asked Lynn.

"We all think Stan has a crush on you," Beatrice said, "even though he knows about Dr. Pete and you. He's always smiling more when you are around."

"Please discourage those types of rumors. We are just friends!" Lynn said.

"If you say so," Beatrice replied.

Stan was already waiting in a booth when Lynn arrived. He waved her over. She took a quick look at the menu and ordered a chef's salad and a cup of tea. Stan had already ordered his burger, medium rare with fries.

"It turns out the mysterious visitor is a long-lost grandson just wanting to meet Mrs. Bustillo., his grandmother. We picked up his fingerprints in Mrs. Bustillo's room. He was a partial match to Mrs. Bustillo and a fellow in prison named Robert Bustillo.

Robert Bustillo. turns out to be Mrs. Bustillo's son, who had a search warrant out for his arrest for using and selling drugs. He left town in a hurry taking his wife and 12-year-old son with him. Mrs. Bustillo's son was caught in Santa Fe, New Mexico, a few years later, where he was arrested for robbing a grocery store. He's still in prison.

His wife stayed in Santa Fe and established her life there. She had gone back to school to become a computer technician and was able to do well. Her son, Jonathon, grew up there.

The Santa Fe police gave me the wife's phone number and address. She told us Jonathon decided he wanted to come back here to reconnect with relatives, especially this grandmother. He's been living in a motel down near the beach but is running out of funds. He's looking for a job.

"Wow," Lynn said. "That's quite the story. Is the son in trouble?"

"No. He's never been arrested and was working as a pharmacy technician in Santa Fe. His boss had only good things to say about him," Stan answered.

"We just need someone to talk with Mrs. Bustillo to see if she wants to see this grandson. How is she doing, by the way?"

"She's doing well. She should be going home soon. Do you want to talk with her?" Lynn asked.

"I'm happy to if you will ask her if it is OK first," said Stan.

"I'll give you good references," Lynn said, smiling. "Let's go talk to Mrs. Bustillo. I'm thinking this is going to be wonderful news for her!

CHAPTER 24

Lynn and Stan went back to the hospital straight to Mrs. Bustillo's room. Lynn was pleased to see her sitting up in bed, her hair combed, and even some lipstick on.

"Good afternoon, Mrs. Bustillo. How are you feeling today?" Lynn asked.

"I'm feeling so much better. The doctor said I can go home tomorrow," Mrs. Bustillo replied. "It is hard to believe a near-death experience made me feel so good about living. What I still don't understand is being told to get back because I still have work to do. I am not sure what kind of work that entails."

"It just so happens we might be able to help you with that question. Mrs. Bustillo, I'm sure you remember me telling you I found a young man in your room and asked Stan Gregowski, our liaison detective, to investigate who that was. Stan has information about this mysterious person and would like to tell you who he is. Don't worry, I think you will like hearing about this young man," Lynn said.

"Now you have me curious. When can I meet up with this detective?" Mrs. Bustillo asked.

"He is here now; if this is a good time," Lynn responded.

"Absolutely! Send him in," Mrs. Bustillo said enthusiastically.

Lynn watched as Stan told Mrs. Bustillo about her grandson. There were tears in her eyes as the story unfolded.

"How can I reach him?" Mrs. Bustillo asked.

Stan wrote down Jonathon's phone number and address. Lynn and Stan weren't even out the door when Mrs. Bustillo. was on the phone.

"I love it when a plan comes together," Stan said, smiling. "We certainly are the A-team today."

"I'll treat you to a piece of key lime pie, which I hear is available in the cafeteria to celebrate," Lynn said. "I just need to let Beatrice know I'm back and to drop off my coat in my office."

The celebration mood changed dramatically as Lynn and Stan walked into her office. A tornado could not have done more damage.

"Don't go in your office," Stan warned. I'll have forensics come down to check fingerprints. I'm calling security, too."

Lynn quickly scanned her office. Her computer was still on her desk, which relieved her immensely. The file drawers were all open, with papers scattered around the floor. Most of the books in her small bookcase formed a floor maze between the bookcase and the desk. A Kleenex box that normally graced the top of her desk had been swept off, along with her pens and pencils and a stapler. The calendar was left on the desk, opened to today's date. The two chairs in front of her desk were tipped over but didn't look damaged.

When Lynn saw the writing on the wall as she turned to leave her office, she gasped. In large red letters, the message said,

This is just the beginning!

Who could be doing this? she asked herself. *What do they want?*

Stan and Jim Rogers from Security were coming toward her.

"I can't believe someone would do this," Lynn said. "I don't think I have enemies, but someone is out to make my life hell. My office has always been a safe and comfortable place for me – now it's trashed and violated."

"We will get this SOB. Don't worry," Stan said, with Jim nodding in agreement.

"I'm going to talk with the staff now to see if they saw anyone near your office," Jim said.

"I'll be here until the forensic team arrives. Are you going to be all right?" Stan asked.

Stan reached out as if to give Lynn a hug, but she turned slightly and started walking quickly toward Peter as he rushed to her. He held her close and then guided her to the bench outside her office.

"I was down the hall checking on a young man with a fractured ankle. Beatrice came and told me your office had been vandalized. Are you OK?" Peter asked.

"I'm scared, upset, and angry at the same time. I want this harassment to end, but don't even know who or why someone is doing this. I want my life back," Lynn said, close to tears.

"The most important thing is that you are safe, always. Stan and Jim will catch who is doing this, but they are escalating. I want you to stay with me until this is over. You shouldn't be alone," Peter said emphatically.

Before Lynn had time to answer, Stan and Jim were standing in front of them.

"The forensic team is on its way. I also ordered a police car to be in front of your house whenever you are home. There will be a policeman here in the ED 24/7, plus I'll be around a lot, too. We want to make sure you are safe," Stan said. "This could get dangerous."

Oh, great. I must choose which one of these two men will keep me safe. That's riskier than the villain who is doing this sabotaging! thought Lynn. *At least Peter is not wanting to pull out of the relationship with all this sabotage. But I need to get it together and deal with all this. I can't catastrophize it!*

"Let me think about this. Chances are, whoever this is knows where I live and knows that I spend time at Peter's house. How about this idea? My house has timed lights that go off and on depending on where I am in the house. That makes it look like I'm home. A police car in front of the house, even if no one is in it, would lead someone to think I'm there," Lynn suggested.

Stan nodded in agreement a little reluctantly.

"I can stay with my mother. A guard downstairs secures her apartment building. No one can use the elevator without a fob. The door to the stairs is always locked and in view of the guard. Plus, there are security cameras in the entrance and hallways," Lynn suggested. "We hid a woman there before, and my mother loved the adventure."

Both Stan and Peter nodded in agreement, with Peter looking disappointed.

"Peter, we had planned to get together and go over some of my career options and other stuff. Let's do that!" Lynn suggested.

"You are on! Tonight?" Peter asked.

"Tonight, I have my $20 group meeting, but tomorrow is good! In the meantime, I need key lime pie. Anyone coming with me?" Lynn asked.

CHAPTER 25

Lynn was glad to have the $20 group meeting to get her mind off someone attacking her until it hit her that the culprit could be someone in this $20s club. *My life is ruined,* she thought. *Everyone is a suspect.*

Abigail Taylor was the first to arrive.

"Hi, Abigail. Glad you could make it tonight. Are you ready to talk about your experiences giving out $20s?" Lynn asked.

"Of course. I even gave out another $20 to someone besides the person you and I saw together."

"That is great!" Lynn replied.

Lynn felt she could rule out Abigail as the saboteur. As far as Lynn knew, they had no connection besides this $20s club. Plus, she seemed so sincere during her encounter with the waitress at the pizza place.

Almost as a group, the remainder of the group came in. Lynn did a quick analysis of each of them as possibly wanting to do damage to her.

Paul Hastings was a graduate student from a wealthy family. Lynn realized she didn't know what he was studying in school. Wendy Anderson taught 4th grade at Deer Park Elementary. It's highly unlikely a grammar schoolteacher would be into this type of sabotage, Lynn thought. Amanda Richey, the X-ray technician, seems far-fetched. Dennis Thompson was a police officer. She knew very little about him other than that.

Lynn relaxed a little, feeling more confident but not entirely without suspicion. It wasn't someone in this group who was out to get her. She started the meeting.

"Hi, everyone. Good to see you again," Lynn began. "Tonight, as we had promised the last time we met, we would discuss your experiences handing out $20s. Again, if anyone would like me to accompany them for the first handout, I'd be happy to do that. Abigail and I went out on one adventure together, and she tells me she did a solo one. She's willing to discuss her experience. Does anyone else have a story to tell?" Lynn asked.

Lynn was pleased to see that everyone raised their hands.

"Remember, don't give out any names or identifying details. We are interested in the process and how it worked out. Abigail, would you come up to the front and tells us your adventures?" Lynn asked.

"Sure," Abigail said as she got up and walked to the front of the room.

"Lynn and I went to the pizza palace, which, as I'm sure most of you know, advertises pizza that doesn't suck. I had a conversation with the waitress who was a student at USC Wilmington. Lynn paid the bill with a 20% tip. In addition, I gave the waitress a $20 bill encouraging her to use it for schoolbooks or other supplies. That was easy. The waitress was thankful and had expected a tip.

But the next adventure was more difficult. I'm in the grocery store looking for short ribs. There's a woman, maybe in her 40s, also looking at the meat. She picks up a chuck roast but then puts it down. Then she looks over the prime rib roasts, picks one up, but then puts it back. She's up and down the aisle checking out the roasts. She comes near me, and I say something like, "Meat has gotten so expensive," Abigail says.

The woman nods at me and said, 'Tomorrow is my husband's 50th birthday. I wanted to cook a special dinner for him. I have four kids, 10 to 16. I need to get a nice roast that will feed all six of us, but the better roasts are so expensive."

"I'm thinking a $20 bill will help her buy a nicer roast, but how do I slip it to her? It dawned on me I could blame Lynn," Abigail said.

Everyone in the group laughed.

"I said, maybe we can do each other a favor. You need to spend a little extra to get a nicer roast, and I need to hand out a $20 bill as part of my volunteer training. If you will take this $20, I can go home and cook my supper."

"For real?" the woman asked.

"Oh, yes, I said. I need to get this assignment done for class tonight, and I need to cook dinner when I get home. So, you will be doing me a huge favor by taking this $20," Abigail recounted.

The woman agreed, took the $20, and then grabbed a rib roast.

"Yay!" shouted Amanda. "Great job!"

The group clapped in concert.

"Nice work, Abigail. "You gave away that $20 with great finesse. Blame me all you want!" Lynn said to the entire group.

"No, thank you for this $20 club. It's a great feeling knowing exactly where your money is helping," said Abigail.

"Anyone else ready to speak?" Lynn asked.

Paul volunteered.

"Figured I'd be helping poor college students, but instead, I gave $20 to the attendant of the port-a-potty at a college football game. He looked to be in his middle to late 30s, maybe doing this part-time to make some extra cash. He had on a wedding ring, so maybe he had a family. I just walked up to him, handed him $20, and said, 'Thanks for making these available here and keeping them clean!'

"He took the $20 and said it was nice to be appreciated!"

"You know, it felt so good to do that. In the past, I wouldn't have even noticed this guy. After this happened, I checked out the use of port-a-potties at sports events.

Someone wrote that sports couldn't happen without people like him and called the port-a-potty an unsung hero for outdoor sporting events. As a business major, I was amazed to read that the portable bathroom business is now a $17 billion dollar business. These guys and maybe gals are now essential workers!"

"Great job," Dennis said. "On the next sporting event, I'm looking for these attendants."

"Excellent work," Lynn said. "Let's take a stretch, and then we will have more presentations. If anyone wants to have me go with them to hand out their first $20, let me know now, and we can schedule a session. Drinks, cookies, and fruit are on the table."

CHAPTER 26

"Who else is ready to talk about their experiences now that we've had our break?" asked Lynn.

Amanda Richey raised her hand. "I've not been able to do this assignment yet. Can I make a time when we could do it together?"

"But of course," Lynn answered. "We can meet after this talk and set a date, time, and place,"

"Dennis, how about you? Do you have an experience that you can discuss?" Lynn asked.

"Wow, I sure do. I was in the checkout line at the Harris Teeter grocery store near my house. In front of me was a man in a wheelchair next to a woman whom I assumed was his wife. They both looked like they were in their 50s.

The checkout gal told them their bill was like $75.22. The wife takes out her wallet and tells the checkout gal she only has $69. She starts looking over her groceries for what she can put back. In the meantime, the woman behind me is complaining about the holdup at this line.

So, I want to do something, but I'm unsure what to do. Do I give the wife $10 to cover the groceries? Do I give her $20 to give them a little spending money? What do I say when I give the wife the money?" Dennis asked herself.

"Good for you to take the time to think it through. What did you do?" Lynn asked.

"Fortunately, I noticed a tattoo on the man's arm of a world globe and an eagle on top. I'm thinking maybe this fellow was a marine at one time. So, I said, 'Ma'am, from your husband's tattoo, it looks like he was once in the military, maybe the Marines.' The wife nodded yes.".

"Then I told her I have deep respect for anyone in the military, having served two tours myself."

"I took out my wallet when the fellow behind me tapped my shoulder, handing me a $20 bill. Soon the two people behind him also sent $20 bills forward. It was amazing. I turned to the husband and said,

"We in this line want to thank you for your service. All of us would like to pay for your groceries. It is the least we can do. Is that OK with you?"

"With tears in her eyes, the wife nodded her head, yes, as did her husband. I turned to the group and said, 'OK, they agreed." I handed the cashier $80 and told her to give the woman and her husband the change."

"I turned to the veteran in his wheelchair and said, "Thank you for your service. Have a wonderful evening."

"Good for you," Lynn said. "That's an amazing story."

"That's not even all of it. After the husband and wife left, I turned to the group and said, "Welcome to the $20 club. You are now an official member. I handed out the flyer about this program that I had in my pocket for them to look at. They all were very enthusiastic. You might get some calls. I hope it was OK to tell them they were members," Dennis said.

"Of course, it was fine. We are open to all people who are interested in helping others. You did a great job, Dennis, supporting this couple in an embarrassing financial situation, at the same time praising their contribution and not making them a charity case. Way to go!" Lynn said, clapping. The rest of the group started clapping, too."

"Wendy, what about you? Do you have a story to tell?" Lynn asked.

"Yes, I do. I was at a conference and flew into the Wilmington airport late, around 9:30. It was quiet, and the cleaning crews were working. I went to the restroom, where a tall, thin woman had started cleaning up. There were a few women there, and the place was messy. There was water on the floor, and the sinks had paper towels on them that had not been discarded. God only knows what the stalls looked like. My first thought was how lucky I was to be a schoolteacher and not have to do this kind of work. It must be tough.

The woman who was cleaning went about her job but, to me, seemed depressed. There were no smiles and no energy coming from her, although she was persistent in doing the cleaning. I waited until the other woman left and tapped her on the shoulder. I handed her a $20 bill and told her, "Thank you for your service. It is much appreciated."

"The woman turned toward me, surprised to see me handing her a $20," Wendy continued.

"Is this for me?" she asked.

"Absolutely," I said back.

"Thank you so much," she said, with a slight smile on her lips.

"I wished her a good evening and left to find my husband waiting to give me a ride home. I hoped this woman had a ride home, too," Wendy finished.

Another round of applause filled the room.

"Good job, Wendy. I'll bet it was great to see that little smile on that woman's face," Lynn said.

Wendy nodded yes.

"Wendy did a great job spotting someone that typically is invisible in our society. Thanking her for her work, which all of us know is so appreciated, also was an ego booster for this woman, too. You all did a good job Any questions or comments?" Lynn asked.

"What's our next goal? When do we meet again?" asked Paul.

"We meet in two weeks, on December 18th. That will be our last meeting, so we can party a little. Try to give out five $20s in total before then. Also, try to see if you can take one step further by offering some assistance or even advice to help a person. You could suggest a book, information, a way to get more customers, whatever you think might be helpful. See you then. Amanda, let's set a date for us to go out together."

After straightening out the room and shutting off the light, Lynn wondered about her upcoming session with Amanda. She was the only person who also worked in the hospital. As an x-ray technician, she was often on call at night. No one would have thought twice about seeing her in the hospital during off hours. How could she tell if she was a saboteur? Would she have a motive?

CHAPTER 27

The next morning, Lynn arrived at work in the ED at 6:30 am. She had trouble sleeping all night and, by 5:30 am, was wide awake. She hoped work would take her mind off being sabotaged. The night shift dealt with all the patients that had come in during the evening and night, either by sending them to a unit or discharging them. The ED was quiet.

Lynn prioritized her paperwork – statistics for the month of November, staffing for the Christmas and New Year holidays, and the supply orders for the month to prepare for colder weather.

"Lynn," shouted Beatrice as she entered her office. "We have multiple shooting victims headed our way!"

"Wow! I'll alert the OR and the surgical docs. I'm sure the police will be here shortly. Who is on triage?"

"Patty is doing triage. She's great at it," replied Beatrice.

"I'll be there to help with the families and whomever as soon as I finish the phone calls," Lynn replied.

Ten minutes later, ambulances started to arrive at the door. There had been a drive-by shooting at the front of the Deer Park high school as the students were entering the main building where the school busses dropped them off.

Lynn's job during these times was to make sure the staff had all the supplies and personnel they needed to handle the emergencies. She did that and also talked with the families, police, and liaison departments. That was above and beyond her responsibilities, but she had recognized early that assuming those responsibilities enabled her staff to care for the patients instead of always being distracted away from them by activities she could easily do. Plus, everyone knew she liked being involved.

"Here comes our first patient," Beatrice proclaimed. "He's a 16-year-old boy with a leg injury. It doesn't look like a bullet injury but more like a fall. Is Dr. Pete coming?"

"I'm here," Peter said. "I'll follow him to his room."

"Here come two more ambulances," Lynn said.

"I'm going out to meet the first one," Beatrice responded. "I'm onto the second one," Patty said.

Beatrice came into the ED running with a stretcher that Lynn could see was a teenage girl being resuscitated. Lynn could see blood spread over her abdomen.

"Trauma room," Lynn said to Beatrice.

Next, Patty came by Lynn, pushing a stretcher.

"Looks like this girl was shot in her arm. I'll take her to room 3 and assign Susan to her," Patty said.

Dr. Tom was at the door when Beatrice came in. He followed her to the trauma room. Lynn knew he would keep the resuscitation going until the trauma surgeon, Dr. Castillo, got there.

As the ambulance driver, Stephanie Wood, started walking away, Lynn stopped her to ask some questions.

"Any idea how many of these kids got shot or hurt?" Lynn asked.

"They were still looking for injured kids when I left. The last count I heard was six, maybe seven, that had been shot. One 17-year-old boy was pronounced dead at the scene. It was horrible. I need to go back to see if anyone else needs to be transported," Stephanie responded.

Lynn called the morgue to alert the pathologist, Steve Murphy, that at least one body from the shooting would be coming to him. As she looked to her left, Lynn sighed a sigh of relief. Humphrey Thomas, the chief of surgery, and his three residents were coming toward her.

"Where can we be the most help?" Dr. Thomas asked.

"There's a surgery likely in the trauma room, with a teenage girl being resuscitated who looked like she was shot in her abdomen," Lynn said. "Room 3 has a teenage girl who looked like she was shot in her arm."

"Dr. Phillips, you come with me to the trauma room. Dr. Anderson, you go to room 3 and check out the girl with the arm injury. Dr. Richardson, you stay here with Ms. Price and catch the patient in the next ambulance. I'll be around to check on everyone," Dr. Thomas ordered.

"Lynn, Dr. Caddell is coming in, too. I told him to come straight here. He specializes in head and neck trauma, although I'm hoping you don't have any of those. Page me if you need me," Dr. Thomas said with emphasis.

Lynn felt like she was finally breathing again. The doctors that got to the ED were some of the best on staff. For that, she raised her eyes to the skies and said a brief prayer of thanks.

Lynn knew that at least one more ambulance should be coming, and in five minutes, it showed up.

"Who do you have with you? She asked the driver as she went to open the back door.

"I think she's one of the teachers that was outside talking to a student. The story is that she pushed the student down to the ground and covered him. She got shot in the back, and I'm not sure exactly where," the driver said.

"There were a few more kids with minor injuries, but they are being transported to the urgent clinic down the street. I don't think more are coming your way, but I'd be prepared anyway in case someone gets more seriously ill from their minor injuries," the driver finished as he opened the door to release the next patient.

Mrs. Lafayette was positioned on her left side with an IV running in her veins. Lynn could see the pressure bandage covering the right shoulder area. Lynn was thankful the injury looked far enough away from the spinal to not have those injuries. She wondered if Peter was around or in the OR with the first patient he saw.

Patty triaged Mrs. Lafayette to room 4. Two orthopedic residents had come down to the ED, and they followed Mrs. Lafayette to her assigned room.

"Where is Dr. Pete?" Lynn asked Patty.

"I'm not sure, but I'll check," Patty said.

Another ambulance pulled up in front of the ED. The driver quickly ran to the back of the ambulance and helped with the next patient. He looked about 17, tall and thin, with a CRIPS tattoo on his right arm. He was getting oxygen but breathing on his own. He had a pressure dressing on his lower left abdomen with blood seeping through. She had heard the EMS call him Sam.

"See if Dr. Thomas and one of his surgical residents are free to look at Sam. He's bleeding through the pressure bandage," Lynn said to Patty, somewhat reluctantly. She generally didn't like advising the triage nurse, but in situations like this, with so many cases, expediency takes preference.

"How are you holding up?" asked a familiar voice as Peter approached Lynn.

"So far, so good, in this awful situation. I think Sam is the last of the patients from this shooting that we'll be getting. How about you? You going to the OR?" asked Lynn.

"The first case I saw, young Mr. Jackson Jones, has a torn ACL. It looks like he pivoted quickly to escape the gunshots and then fell. He's scheduled for surgery, but it's not urgent. He's alert and oriented, and we are waiting for his parents to come in and sign the consent form. He's only 16," Peter answered.

Mrs. Lafayette is another story. I'm guessing the shooter used a Bushmaster assault rifle and not just an ordinary .22 rifle. These damn assault weapons have so much greater mass and muzzle velocity. She's got some shattered bones in that scapular. Fortunately, the shot missed the subclavian and brachial arteries, but I don't want pieces of bone traveling. I'm taking her up to surgery now, and then I'll come back for Jackson. In the meantime, Stuart Wilson is staying with him. He's a little annoyed, by the way. Both residents wanted to go to surgery with Mrs. Lafayette. He lost the coin toss. They like the tougher surgeries!" said Peter, smiling.

"I can understand that. In their careers, they will see a lot of torn ACLs but not many gunshot wounds to the shoulder. Glad for their enthusiasm," Lynn said.

"See you later, my dear. In my mind, I'm kissing you goodbye for now," Peter said, smiling at Lynn while squeezing her hand.

In the middle of chaos, love still shines brightly," thought Lynn, happiness filling her, pushing away some of the stress. She knew, though, that parents and other relatives of the shooting victims will be showing up soon. She also knew the attacks on her were sapping her energy. She hoped she had enough strength to help the relatives.

CHAPTER 28

Lynn walked slowly back to her office to take a break now that all the patients were being seen and receiving their necessary care. For a moment, she couldn't tell what was more stressful, making sure the shooting victims all received treatment or the fear of more damage happening in her office.

Security had added a camera in the hall that covered the hallway and the door to her office. They had also added a keyless high-security door lock. Lynn was told these locks were made from hardened steel ball bearings and anti-drill plates.

Jim had told her there was no way in hell anyone was breaking into her office again.

She unlocked her door, held her breath, and entered her office. It was untouched.

She sat at her desk, drinking a cup of tea she had made in the ED. She browsed through her emails and texts. She only took the time to answer her friend Wanda agreeing to meet her in the cafeteria around 3:00 pm.

She wrote out the list of patients who had been admitted from the shooting.

A 16-Year-old boy with a torn ACL- Jackson Jones – waiting for parental consent and then to surgery with Dr. Pete.

A teenage girl with an abdominal bullet wound needing resuscitation was being taken care of by Dr. Castillo and one resident.

A teenage girl was shot in the arm – with a surgical resident, and Dr. Cadell took over her case.

Mrs. Lafayette – a teacher – was shot in her shoulder in the back in the OR with Dr. Pete.

A 17-year-old-boy, Sam, tall and thin, with a CRIPS tattoo on his right arm. He was getting oxygen but breathing on his own. He had a pressure dressing on his lower left abdomen with blood seeping through. Dr. Thomas and a resident were looking after him.

17-year-old pronounced dead at the scene – transferred to the morgue.

Her phone rang.

"Hi, Beatrice. What's up?" Lynn asked.

"We have one parent here already. Mrs. Jones, the mother of the 16-year-old with the torn ACL. She wants to talk with someone in administration. We know who that is!" Beatrice said with laughter in her voice.

"Before you go, I need some names. What's the name of the girl who was shot in the arm?" Lynn asked.

She's Gloria Jankowski. Dr. Cadell is talking to her parents and taking her to surgery to remove the bullet. She's doing fine." Beatrice said.

"What about the girl who was being resuscitated? How is she doing?" Lynn asked.

"That's Betsey Turner. She's on a ventilator. BP is stable. She got shot in the abdomen and the chest. She's got a chest tube in. Dr. Castilla talked to the parents on the phone. He's taking her to surgery to tie off any bleeders and remove the bullet. She might need a splenectomy. She's the most critical. She'll be up in the surgical ICU when the surgery is over," Beatrice finished.

"Do we know the name of the boy that died?" Lynn asked.

"I haven't heard anything about him," Beatrice said.

"I'll call Steve in the morgue. I need to know in case the parents come to the ED. I can't imagine sending your child to school and then hearing they were shot to death," said Lynn.

"Most be the worst thing that can happen to parents," Beatrice replied.

"I'll be right there as soon as I talk with Steve," Lynn replied.

"Hi, can I help you," a female voice answered the phone in the morgue.

"Hi, Sally. This is Lynn from the ED. I need to know the name of the boy who was shot and killed and sent to the morgue," Lynn said.

"Got it right here. His name is Tommy O'Brien. He's 17 years old," Sally said. "So sad."

"Do you know if the parents have been there yet?" Lynn asked.

"I don't think so. They would have stopped at my desk first," Sally responded.

"Ok, if they show up here in the ED, I'll walk them over to you," Lynn said.

Lynn walked over to the ED to find Mrs. Jones. As she walked near the nurse's station, Beatrice pointed to the woman sitting in the chair near the door to the waiting room. Mrs. Jones looked to be in her late 40s or early 50s, considerably overweight, and dressed in old, worn clothes.

"Hi, Mrs. Jones, I'm Lynn Price, the ED Director. I'm here to see if I can answer any questions for you," Lynn said.

"Thank you for coming to talk to me. The nurse told me my son needs surgery, but we don't have any insurance except Medicaid. I don't know if they will pay for this surgery. We have no money." Mrs. Jones explained.

"Did you show your Medicaid card to the intake staff?" Lynn asked.

"No, I haven't seen them yet. I just ran into the ED when I heard my son was hurt."

"Let's go over there. They will process all your information and contact Medicaid about the surgery. They are very good at the job. If they need Dr. Fry or me to talk with anyone, they will contact us. Dr. Fry is in surgery right now, but his plan was to operate on your son when that surgery is finished. He's a very good surgeon. Your son will be in good hands," Lynn said.

Lynn brought Mrs. Jones to Debra Hanson's window. Lynn knew if anyone could get services approved for Jackson Jones, she could do it.

"Beatrice, is there anyone else you would like me to speak with?" Lynn asked.

"So far, we are good. All the patients and parents are being taken care of. We all want to thank you for getting all that help here as fast as you did. That was a lifesaver," Beatrice said.

"Just doing my job so you all can do yours. So glad we got everyone taken care of," Lynn said. "I'm going to the cafeteria to get a bite. Page me if you need me."

Lynn gathered her late lunch from what food was left in the cafeteria. She spotted her friend, Wanda, sitting alone against the back wall. Wanda beckoned her to join her.

Lynn sat down near Wanda, and tears immediately filled her eyes.

"Are you OK?" Wanda asked.

"I barely got through helping with the gunshot victims in the ED this morning. My thoughts are always watching for the next attack and worrying about how awful they might be. We must find who is doing this before I get to where I can't function at all," Lynn said.

"How are going to do that?" Wanda asked.

CHAPTER 29

Back in her office, Lynn thought a lot about the question Wanda asked. How was she going to stop this saboteur? Her first step, she decided, was to talk to Stan and her brother, George. Stan should still be here investigating the shooters. Maybe he could meet for dinner at her house?

Before she could track down Stan, she heard a familiar knock on her door. A smile immediately brightened her face.

"Come in, oh champion of the wounded," Lynn said.

"You talking to me?" Peter asked in his best DeNiro imitation.

"That was very good! I didn't know you did imitations," Lynn said, laughing.

"There's a lot you don't know about me, Babe," Peter replied, walking over to kiss Lynn. "How are you after those busy, tense moments in the ED this morning?"

"I'm hanging in there," Lynn replied. "How were your surgeries?"

"Mrs. Lafayette is no longer in pieces – bone fragments and the bullet have been removed, and she's doing good on a morphine drip. In a couple of weeks and she will be acknowledged as the heroine who saved a student from getting shot. Jackson Jones has a repaired ACL, ready to enjoy more days of sports. Baseball is his game," Peter said. "However, I do have an ache."

"Are you OK? Did you get hurt?" Lynn asked.

"No, this is a heartache from not spending enough time with you. How about a nice dinner out tomorrow, Avec Moi? You up for that?" Peter asked.

Lynn laughed with a heart warmed by the unabashed affection from Peter.

"It's just what the doctor ordered," Lynn answered, tongue in cheek.

Peter smiled and laughed. "Pick you up at 8:00. You have made my day. Love you," he said, walking out the door.

Again, Lynn was about to say, love you too, but Peter was out the door and out of earshot.

Suddenly energized, she called George.

"Well, how is my favorite sister this morning?" George asked.

"I'm your only sister," Lynn replied.

"You still can be my favorite – I even looked it up," George said. "What's on your mind this morning?"

"I need help! This saboteur is draining my energy. We had five kids in from a shooting this morning that took all the energy I had. That's not like me. Usually, I'm hyped up on adrenaline. Can you meet with Stan and me at my house this evening to figure out ways to stop who is doing this?" Lynn asked.

"You bet you I'll be there. If you don't have them, ask Stan to bring the police reports he has. If you can write up all the events in as much detail as you can, that you experienced, that will be helpful. And Lynn," George stopped.

"Yes," Lynn replied.

"Don't invite Peter," George said.

"Really, why? I know he would want to help," Lynn answered.

"He and I got together with some college buddies the other night. He pulled me aside to say how happy he was seeing you. Off the record, he's got it bad for you. But anyway, he's also happy not to have all the chaos, disruption, and negativity his ex-wife, Virginia, brought into his life. He likes the peace and happiness he has with you," George told Lynn.

"I get it. You're afraid all this sabotaging will be too negative for him. He's been great with what's happened, though, even the fake stuff about me seeing someone else. He threw that guy out the door and took a picture of him for me," Lynn said.

"He's a great guy. I know. But this sabotaging is getting worse and more serious. Plus, he has Hanna to think about.

I wouldn't want my kids involved with serious threats. It's up to you, Kiddo. Just food for thought," George said.

"Dinner at 7:00 tonight, then?" Lynn asked.

"I'll be there with my appetite, which you know is huge, and my jimmy, screwdrivers, compass, measuring tape, and magnifying lens with me," George said.

"So, you are bringing your Sherlock Holmes kit you got when you were 11," Lynn said.

"But, of course," George answered. "I wonder if I still have the Sherlock Holmes cap."

"Love you, Bro," Lynn said, laughing.

"Right back at you," George replied as they hung up.

There was another knock on Lynn's door. To Lynn, the figure did not look familiar. She opened the door to see a delivery man with a dozen roses. Immediately, she thought Peter had sent them. The note said, "I loved our night together. See you soon, Hugs, Bruce." She immediately threw the roses in the trash.

Thank goodness Peter had left already, she thought.

Lynn left her office to check on her staff and to see if Stan was still in the ED.

"Beatrice," Lynn called. "How are we doing here?"

"I think we are back to our normal not-so-dull routine. All the shooting victims have left the ED. They all seem to have done well. Betsey Turner, the girl who was shot twice, did great. She's in the surgical ICU. Jackson Jones went home with his mother after his ACL repair. The others just need a few days on the surgical floors before they can go home," Beatrice said with a little bit of proud accomplishment in her voice.

"You and your team did such a great job! That was tense," Lynn said.

"You know we all include you as an important part of that team. So, thanks to you, too, we helped all those victims," Beatrice said. "Now back to reality with a patient with chest pain, we hope is angina, and a teenager with abrasions and bruises and a possible dislocated shoulder from falling off his electronic skateboard. I had no idea you can go 18 to 28 miles per hour on those things."

"It seems we are seeing more of those types of injuries. I'll check the stats, and maybe we can do an in-service on those types of injuries," Lynn suggested. "Have you seen Stan recently?"

"He was just here. I think he was talking to one of the ambulance drivers who were at the shooting scene," Beatrice answered.

Lynn spotted Stan at the entrance of the ED.

"Happy to get together with you and George tonight. Great idea," Stan happily replied to Lynn's request.

Lynn filled Stan in on the roses.

"Wow, someone is definitely out to ruin your life on many fronts," Stan said.

Lynn went back to her office, put the rose delivery out of her head, and started looking up ICD 10 codes for skateboard injuries which were in the V00.13 groups. That's a happening occurrence for those injuries to get their own codes, she thought. She also realized energy was flowing now, thanks to Peter's visit and the plans to find her attacker. From victim to a seeker, Lynn announced out loud.

CHAPTER 30

On the way home, Lynn stopped at the grocery store to buy ingredients to make chicken pot pie and serve it up with a side salad and then a store-bought key lime pie for dessert. She knew both men would enjoy that dinner.

After the dinner was in the oven, she got on her computer and made two lists: one list contained all the attacks that had been made on her, and the second list held the names or types of people who could be the perpetrator.

As she read through both lists, she could feel her energy dwindle again. *This was so hard,* she thought.

George knocked on her door and then just walked in.

"Why isn't your door locked?" he asked. "I could have been the Ted Bundy of North Carolina."

Lynn laughed at her brother.

"I obviously knew you were coming and would rescue me from any assailants, including Ted," Lynn said.

There was another knock on the door.

"Come on in, Stan," Lynn said.

"There you go, not locking your door and checking who is coming into your house. That's it. I'm hiring a bodyguard!" George said. "Stan, will you please tell my sister to keep her doors locked."

"Lynn, keep your doors locked," Stan said, going back to the front door to check what type of locks was on her door. He also automatically locked the door.

"To add to this discussion, I would also get better locks, like the one the security team put on your office door. Have someone also check your window locks. I'm going to text you the name of someone I recommend all the time to do that work," Stan said.

"See," George said. "Stan agrees with me. You backed out on staying with mom, where you would be safer. If you are going to stay here, you need safety precautions. I'm telling you; I'm going to hire a bodyguard for you."

"I knew she was coming home instead of her mother's apartment, so I ordered a police car to sweep and check her house once an hour. We also posted a security camera across the street on the poll," Stan said.

Lynn looked at George and Stan in utter amazement. She felt very fortunate to have these two men be that concerned with her safety but, at the same time, annoyed because they don't think she can take care of herself. She assured them she locks the doors ordinarily and even installed a video doorbell.

"Let's eat," Lynn said, deciding not to get into an argument. "We have a saboteur to catch."

After paying Lynn compliments about her dinner, the group sat around the cleared dining room table to plan their approach to catching whoever is sabotaging Lynn. She started by passing out her list of events that have occurred and possible suspects.

Events

Sent an email looking like it came from Dr. Brown's office saying a meeting was canceled.

Sent an email looking like it came from my office being snarking to key people and friends in the hospital.

A man named Bruce came up to Peter and me in a restaurant, thanking me for a beautiful time and saying he assumed Peter was George. Peter did take a picture of him after chasing him out of the restaurant.

A bouquet of red roses was delivered to me. It wasn't Peter who sent it. The note said, "I loved our night together. See you soon, Hugs, Bruce."

Entering my office and throwing books, papers, and furniture around. My calendar was open on the desk. It could be that he or she knows my schedule.

Possible suspects

Someone associated with the court case about the car driver who dumped the trafficked woman out in front of the ED.

Someone trying to break up Peter and me.

Someone trying to discredit me at the hospital, although I don't have anyone that I'm looking to fire or get reported.

Amanda Richey, who works as an X-ray tech, is one of my $20 club members. She's the only one who hasn't handed out $20 and has asked me to go with her for the first time.

George and Stan read over the list with an intensity Lynn had not seen in either of them before.

"You guys look like I'm headed for disaster," Lynn said.

"I'm thinking it is going to be worse before it gets better. These attacks are clearly escalating," George said.

"The most serious threats would come from whoever might be protecting the driver of the car. The people in these trafficking rings are ruthless. Is it for sure you are going to testify?" Stan asked.

The ADA is not sure. I do know she has not sent my name over as a witness yet. I'm the one, though, who can connect the car with the dumping of the woman in front of the ED. The police were looking for surveillance videos that put the car near the hospital at that time," Lynn said.

"Did you tell George what else you noticed about the driver? I can't say because it's confidential police business, but you can tell him if you want," Stan said.

"Should I trust George?" Lynn asked, smirking a little. Stan and Lynn both looked at George as if to determine his trustworthiness.

"Remember all those times I unlocked the door to the house when you were late coming home from a date? I covered for you, but I kept a list of who you were out with and how late you were," George replied.

"Aw, blackmail. I guess I must trust him," Lynn replied. "More wine, anyone?"

"What I told the police is I saw the arm of the driver reach out to shut the door to the car. He was white, and he had his watch on his right wrist," Lynn told George.

"Wow, so he's probably left-handed, and you can testify to that. Is he in custody?" George asked Stan.

Stan nodded.

"Is he left-handed?" Lynn asked.

"Yes. Do the police have anyone else who can identify him in any way as the driver of the car?" George asked.

"Not as far as I know, but I'm not assigned to that case, and it is still ongoing. Plus, I couldn't give you any additional police information. I only can talk about the car and the arm because Lynn told it to me directly and now to you."

"The ADA on the case said if she needed me to testify before she sent over my name as a witness, she would put me in safe custody," Lynn said.

"The only way the attacks on you are linked to this trial would be if there were a leak in the hospital, the police station, or the ADA's office. It would be a clear message, saying they can get to you if they want," George said.

"Does the ADA know about these attacks?" Stan asked Lynn.

"I haven't said anything to her. Should I?" Lynn asked.

"I can let her know. She can have someone investigate leaks. They are careful, but this will add to their surveillance," Stan answered.

"Good," George said. "We can leave Lynn's involvement with the trafficking victim as a possible source of the attacks to the ADA's office to investigate. Let's move on and look at who might want to discredit you in other ways. For a baby sister, you sure are trouble."

CHAPTER 31

Lynn, George, and Stan started working on the rest of Lynn's list.

"It looks like someone is attempting to break up you and Dr. Pete and make you look bad at work. The question in my mind is whether it is one person or two," George said.

"Oh, my God. You think two people could be terrorizing me?" Lynn exclaimed.

"I agree that could be a possibility. Let's examine who would want to break up, you and Dr. Pete. Any ideas?" Stan asked.

"Of course, there is Virginia, Peter's ex-wife. I don't know if there's anyone else in Peter's life that would do this," Lynn said.

"How about from your side? Any guy you dated would be jealous enough to do this?" Stan asked.

"Wow, I never even thought of that," Lynn said. "My last boyfriend, Allen, I don't think he cared enough to get some kind of revenge."

"What about a woman friend who would be jealous of you and maybe have an interest in Dr. Pete ?" Stan asked.

"Wanda is my best friend, but she's married. I also don't think she's the mean girl type," Lynn said. "There is a nurse in the ED that I always thought had a crush on Peter. Every time he has a case in the ED, she's fast on the draw to be the one to assist him. As far as I know, they never dated. But I'm not 100% sure of that. I don't think he has dated anyone since we have been together. Has he said anything to you, George?"

"I know he's crazy about you. He is a one-woman guy. He never even cheated on Virginia, and no one would blame him for doing that. It seems to me, though, he did go out on a few dates before you two got involved," George said.

"You two keep talking. Let me check my texts and emails from him way back when to see if a name of a woman comes up," George suggested.

"Lynn, is there anyone who might have a crush on you that would want to break you and Dr. Pete up?" Stan asked.

The only person Lynn could think of who might have a crush would be Stan, she thought to herself. That was not something she was going to address.

"Not anyone I can think of," Lynn answered. "I'm thinking this is more likely to be a woman than a man. What do you think?"

"I agree," Stan said. "Men tend to do things that are more physical – like messing up your office but the fake date and flowers – more likely a woman."

"I've got a name," George said excitedly. "Nancy Trevor! She's an X-ray technician at the hospital. Pete dated her a few times, but the relationship never really clicked for him. When he didn't follow up with calls for more dates, she pursued him with phone calls and notes. It took a while to get her to stop. It wasn't pretty. How would she know he was dating you?"

"The rumor mill in the hospital is strong. We have a lot of contact in the ED with the x-ray department, too," Lynn said.

"So, we have two suspects, maybe three with the ED nurse, that would be interested in breaking you and Peter up – Virginia and this Nancy person," George said. "Stan, how can we figure that piece out?"

"Lynn, do you have a copy of the picture of 'Bruce' that Dr. Pete took when you were out to dinner? I can run that through facial recognition. Maybe we will get a hit. Also, send me the date and the name of the florist who delivered the roses if you have that information still. We might be able to track the person who sent them that way," Stan suggested.

"I'm sending you the picture of Bruce! I'll check my calendar and trash bucket. The last I looked, the roses were still there. What a nightmare!" Lynn said.

Lynn had been enthusiastic about this attempt to find out who was terrorizing her, but now thinking there were at least two perpetrators was making her feel worse.

"Hey, stop feeling bad! We will find out who is doing this. You know I'll take them to the woodshed and beat them," George said.

"We don't have a woodshed," Lynn said, laughing.

"Whatever, no one gets to do this to my baby sister!" George said, banging his fist on the table.

"We have one more perpetrator to look at, whoever is sending these awful texts and messing up your office," Stan said. "I'd like to make a suggestion."

"Sure," both Lynn and George said at the same time.

"The hospital security put new locks on your office door, Lynn, and installed a security camera right outside your office. Plus, I have a police car patrolling around your house. Although I would suggest getting stronger locks on your house doors. The video camera on your front is good, but I'd get one for the back door, too. We need to have safety precautions in place," Stan said.

"Before we talk further about this in-hospital perpetrator, I'd like to talk with your IT people to see if they have any information about who sent those emails. The security department may also have some cameras that picked up people in the hallways around your office the night of your office break-in. Once I have that information, how about we meet again?" Stan suggested.

"Seems reasonable to me," George said. "I still would feel better if you were staying with Mom."

"I'll be fine here," Lynn said. "I'll order the more secure locks with videos tomorrow."

"I'll do that," George said. "I have lots of contacts with security people who do those installations,"

"Good work, guys," Stan said. "Thank you for dinner, Lynn. It was the best I've had in a long time."

"Thank you, two, for doing this. I'm feeling so much better," Lynn said.

"Me, too," George said.

Stan and George shook hands and walked out to their respective cars. George took out his cell phone and told Siri to call Henry.

"Henry, I have a job for you. I want 24-hour surveillance on my sister's house for the next week, starting tonight as soon as possible. Tell them to change cars, too. My sister is smart and will spot the same car around her house," George said.

"Yes, that's her address. Thanks!" George said, hanging up.

CHAPTER 32

The following day Lynn was back in her office. For the first time in weeks, she felt recharged instead of overwhelmed. She heard a familiar knock on her door. She unlocked it to let Peter in.

"Whoa! Are you locking your door even when you are in it? Yikes! Did you have another attack?" Peter asked.

"Nope, it's just a precaution. Stan and security recommended that until they find out who is doing these weird things," Lynn said.

"Good idea. I want you always to be as safe as possible. I never want to lose you," Peter said.

"Thank you for that," Lynn said. "I intend to be around to spend oodles of time with you. How's your day going?"

"Not bad. As you know, I don't operate on Fridays unless it's an emergency. I'm just doing rounds to discharge patients and check up on those staying here in our swank hotel. I have reservations for us at the Bridge tonight."

"I can't wait," Lynn said. "What about Hanna?"

"Virginia is taking her to visit with her grandparents this weekend. The weekend is ours alone. I'm hoping you can spend it with me," Peter said.

"Sounds like a wonderful plan. I do have a 10:00 am meeting tomorrow with one of my new $20 club members, which should take me until noon, I'm thinking. Other than that, I'm free to be with you," Lynn said.

"You have made my day, Sweetie. See you at 7:30," Peter said, then came over and kissed Lynn. "I'm beginning to like this locked-door situation!"

Smiling now, Lynn stayed in her office for a while, looking over weekend staffing. She then checked the supply room. All looked good for the weekend.

"Beatrice, how is everything going today?" Lynn asked.

"We are good. It's been quiet. One OB patient came through, but she has a way to go, yet. She's upstairs. We had one 10-year-old boy come in with a fractured arm. We are assessing him for abuse. Bethany recognized him from a few other visits. He has been in more than the typical number of times for a kid his age and general health. One of the social workers is coming to see him as soon as Dr. Tom looks him over," Beatrice said.

"Those abuse cases are so sad. Bethany did a good job. I'm so proud of you and the staff, Beatrice. Besides a raise, you all deserve a medal," Lynn said.

"Thanks, but we are doing our jobs as well as we can. Make sure you give yourself a raise and a medal. We all do our best because we know you are backing us up and pitching in. That goes a long way," Beatrice said.

"You know I love the work, too. I'm getting ready to take the weekend off. I think John will do fine with the coverage and supplies available this weekend," Lynn said.

"I hope you have planned some fun activities," Beatrice said with a smile. "I won't ask if Dr. Pete is involved, but we all love seeing you two together. He deserves a nice person, too. Evening shift had more than their share of demands and screams from Virginia."

"Weekend is looking good," Lynn answered, smiling back. "I see this tall, handsome man in my crystal ball coming to see me soon!"

On her way home, Lynn felt happy. She was looking forward to a nice weekend with Peter and just relaxing. Then the worrying came. Would there be another attack trying to break them up? Will it really work long-term between her and Peter?

"Wow! You look stunning," Peter said when Lynn answered the door. She was wearing a new dress from Chico's – the Travelers classic dress in the Wild Poppy! She had been saving this dress for Christmas but decided this was a special enough night to wear it!

She wanted the weekend to be about Lynn and Peter instead of Dr. Pete and Nursing Director Ms. Price. From the look on Peter's face, she thought they were off to a good start!

"You look quite handsome, yourself, Peter," Lynn replied.

"I can't even begin to tell you how happy I am to be with you," Peter said, helping Lynn with her coat.

Lynn had not been to the Bridge restaurant before and was blown over by the view and décor. The dining room contained seating for four in large padded semi-circular enclosures against the walls, cuddling tables with white tablecloths. In between the tables were arrangements of white and red poinsettias in gold vases. From all the scattered tables in the room, the clientele could see the vast expanse of the ocean, which tonight was covered with a darkening sky filled with collusions of sky bursts of reds and yellows from the setting sun. She and Peter were seated at a table for two near the windows.

"This has got to be the most elegant place I've been to. It's just lovely, Peter," Lynn said.

"I'm glad you like it. Sometimes when I'm feeling in the dumps about something, I'll come here for lunch by myself. It seems to lift my mood," Peter said. "I look at the ocean's vastness and think how small my problems are compared to so many others. It creates a perspective."

"I don't know that I have ever seen you in the dumps, so to speak. You are busy but always seem upbeat," Lynn replied.

"That's because when I'm with you, I feel happy. Mostly, feeling in the dumps happened when I was married to

Virginia. The screaming and bickering would get to me," Peter said.

"Enough about me. What makes you happy? What is important to you, Lynn? I don't know that I've ever asked you that," Peter said.

"Good evening. Welcome to the Bridge," a young man said to Peter and Lynn. "Can I interest you in a beverage?"

CHAPTER 33

"Cosmo for you?" Peter asked Lynn. She nodded her head yes. "I'll have a gin and tonic," Peter said.

"Let's look over the menu, and then I'll answer your question," Lynn said to Peter. "Everything on the menu looks amazing."

The drinks arrived. Lynn and Peter both ordered the stuffed flounder with a bottle of prosecco for dinner.

Peter held up his glass to toast Lynn. "I couldn't think of a better way to spend Friday evening," Peter said.

"Me, either," Lynn replied. "So, back to your question about what's important to me. Family, helping others, and being able to take care of myself are the broad picture. The family includes the immediate relatives, all of whom you know, and eventually getting married and having a family of my own."

"So far, so great. Go on," Peter said, encouraging the conversation.

"As you suggested, I need to think about where my passion is for my next career direction. All these attacks have diverted my attention," Lynn said sadly.

"You have time to decide what you are going to do about your career. Let's get you through whatever this sabotage stuff is. Then you will be able to relax and think about what you want to do," Peter suggested.

"Speaking of trying to get through something. Look at this flounder that was just delivered to us. Thank you, Walter," Lynn said.

"Would you like me to pour the prosecco?" Walter asked Peter.

"Definitely," Peter answered.

"This dish is wonderful to look at," Lynn said. "The crust on the fish is perfectly browned. The crab meat with spinach oozing out of the roll of fish. The fish sitting so elegantly on the serving of rice is perfect. The side dish of steamed vegetables couldn't be better."

"We aim to please, my lady," Peter said, raising his glass of prosecco.

After dinner, Lynn refused dessert but couldn't resist a bite of Peter's key lime pie.

"Lynn, I have a favor to ask of you," Peter said.

"Yes. Ask away. The mood is supportive of a favorable answer," Lynn said.

"Would you stay with me at my house this weekend? Separate rooms," Peter quickly added. "You can have the master bedroom, and I'll stay in Hanna's room. She said it was OK." Both Peter and Lynn smiled at the comment.

"I just would love to have a weekend that involves me waking up to you in my house. I hope you would like that, too," Peter said.

"Now that's an offer I can't refuse. I have that 10 am meeting tomorrow with one member of my $20 group. Other than maybe leaving early on Sunday to clean my house and go grocery shopping, I'm free. I am delighted to stay with you this weekend," Lynn answered.

Peter was smiling but also thinking.

"How about this? We can go over to your house sometime this weekend, our choice of when, and I'll help you clean and go grocery shopping. That way, you can stay over Sunday night, too," Peter suggested.

Lynn started to get nervous feelings. Having Peter help clean her house was maybe a bridge too far to be comfortable. It felt like an invasion.

"OK, I can see by the look on your face that it was too much," Peter said. "I just always want you to be happy and feel comfortable about us being a couple. I'm just so excited to be with you. But smaller steps look like they will be better."

"I don't know that I'm ready for you to see my house in its unclean state. That will happen, I'm sure. How about a compromise?" Lynn said.

"Do tell," Peter said, leaning forward toward Lynn.

"Let's go grocery shopping together, but I'll do the cleaning sometime later during the week. That way, I can stay over on Sunday night, too," Lynn said.

"I believe we have a deal," Peter responded, smiling happily.

CHAPTER 34

"You definitely pack light and quickly," Peter said to Lynn as they entered his house. "Good to know."

"I see where this is going. You are checking out what living with me would be like. Am I right?" asked Lynn.

"Do I have to admit to that? That's just a small part of the bigger picture. Mostly, I like your company," Peter responded.

"Good save," Lynn said, laughing.

"Let's get you comfortable in the bedroom," Peter said. "Somehow, that didn't sound quite right."

"I know what you mean, I think. You did a good job early on establishing our boundaries by saying we will have separate bedrooms. I'm good with that. Sex can wait until we know where we are headed in this relationship. Right now, we are still testing the waters. Agree?" asked Lynn.

"I agree. I honestly see us heading toward a more permanent relationship, but it is good to see if that will work. So far, we are doing well, in my estimation. We even negotiated this weekend well. It's been fun, even," Peter said.

"So, shall we meet by the fireplace after I get comfortable in the bedroom?" Lynn asked.

"I've even got marshmallows!" Peter answered.

After a relaxing, pleasant evening, Lynn slept the best she had slept in a long time. The next morning she was up and showered before she met Peter in the kitchen.

"Who is cooking breakfast?" Lynn asked.

"A coin toss?" asked Peter. "Heads, you make breakfast, and tails, I don't make breakfast.

Lynn laughed. "Ok, I'll make breakfast. That was a smooth move. Now I know to watch out for them!"

"Busted! But it is better for both of us if you cook breakfast and most meals. I can make great linguini with clams and a salad which is for dinner tonight, but that and one other dish is the extent of my culinary expertise," said Peter. "Also, how about when you cook, I clean up?"

"Perfect," Lynn said.

After a breakfast of scrambled eggs, bacon, a peeled clementine, and biscuits, Lynn headed out to meet up with Amanda. A little more passionate kiss than usual took place at the door right before she left.

Amanda was already waiting at Lucky Sam's coffee shop. She had ordered a pumpkin spice latte for Lynn, one of Lynn's favorites.

"Good morning, Amanda," Lynn said brightly. "I hope your day is going well."

"It's a sunny, crisp day. I love it," Amanda replied.

"We had talked about going over to the campus and seeing if you can find a college student needing a boost. You still want to do that?" Lynn asked.

"That would be fine, except I think I have found someone in this coffee shop. See that young man behind me, working on his computer?" Amanda asked.

"Yes, I can see him," Lynn replied.

"When I was in line for our coffees, he spent a few extra minutes counting out his change to add to his two one-dollar bills to pay for his cup of black coffee. He seemed to barely have enough change with nothing left in the bill section of his wallet," Amanda said. "I can remember those days."

"Sounds like a good $20 recipient. What are your thoughts about how to give him $20?" Lynn asked.

"I had a few thoughts. I could drop $20 on the floor near him and say it looks like he dropped it. I could blame you by saying this is part of some training. I could just say I noticed him counting his change at the checkout, and I remember the days when I did that and had at most an apple and a box of animal crackers for lunch. Here's a $20 to help you with a better lunch," Amanda said.

"Nice options," Lynn said. "What are the pluses and minuses of doing any of them?"

"If I said I found $20 near him, he might give the money to the cashier in case someone comes to claim it. That won't help. He might question what kind of training involves giving out $20. Maybe the honest one is the best one. What do you think?" Amanda asked.

"I think you are right. You might want to do that before he leaves. It looks like he is packing up his computer," Lynn said.

Amanda got up, $20 in hand.

"I just wanted to say hi and tell you that I remember the days when I was a student and had to scrape by to pay for an apple and a box of animal crackers for lunch. Since I completed my education, I'm in a good financial place. I want to pay my situation forward to you and wish you good luck in school," Amanda said to the young man, handing him $20.

"I don't know what to say. I'm not used to people handing out money. Usually, they want some from me. This is a life raft for me. I'm on my last 25 cents until my check from my parents comes in tomorrow. They do the best they can, but we are not rich. I have a part-time job but barely have time for that and keeping up with my schoolwork," the young man said. "I was about to take some ketchup packets and mix them with water for supper. Now I can eat something decent. Thanks a lot!"

"Glad to help. When you are successful, you can pay it forward to some worthy student, too," Amanda said.

"I'm going to be a veterinarian. I'll remember your act of kindness always."

Amanda came back to the table she shared with Lynn. There were tears in her eyes.

"Good for you, Amanda. Nicely done. It is amazing what even just $20 can do for someone at the right time," Lynn said. "Suppose you wanted to help this young man beyond giving him the $20. What are your thoughts about that?"

"Good question. It would be great to have a fund for students when things get tight. Here's another thought – maybe he could use a job that pays better but doesn't require more hours and maybe even better hours given his school schedule," Amanda replied.

"Good ideas. It's the adage, 'Give a man a fish, and he will eat for a day. Teach a man how to fish, and you feed him for a lifetime.' Giving him $20 helps him immediately have at least one good meal. Helping him find a better job keeps him fed long-term," said Lynn.

"What resources do you have that could help him find a better job?" Lynn asked.

"I have two dogs. I take them to a vet, whom I also help occasionally when they need x-rays done on dogs. The vet does the x-rays, but I help with the positioning. They are often looking for help," Amanda said.

"Excellent. When you hand out your next $20, think about what resources you have that might help that person even more. It's not required, but you never know what you can say or do that helps a person substantially improve his or her life. We all have resources, as you just described one of yours," Lynn said.

"I get it. Sounds good. By the way, if you don't mind me mentioning it, I heard about someone messing up your office. I think I might have seen him or her," Amanda said. "I was on call one evening late when I saw someone walking down the hall toward your office. Whomever it was, entered your office. I was curious because the person didn't look like your silhouette. When I walked by the office, I heard a noise and tried to look through your glass door but couldn't see much through the translucent glass."

"Amanda, would you be willing to talk to detective Stan Gregowski about what you saw? He's investigating the break-in," Lynn asked.

"Sure, give him my phone number, and we can set up a time. I'm happy to help. I love being a member of this $20 club. I'm paying what you have done to help others forward, to help you as best I can."

CHAPTER 35

"I must say grocery shopping with you was great fun, except when you showed me up on the self-checkout lane. I can see another race is in our future," Peter said, helping Lynn put away her groceries.

"That wasn't a fair contest. You have someone do your grocery shopping for you. I have more experience with the self-checking lane. You got some good stuff for your kitchen. I noticed the clams and the linguini and salad fixings. Is that for dinner?" Lynn asked.

"Yep. As I said, it's only one of the two showoff meals I can make," Peter said.

"Are you hungry for lunch? I can make grilled ham and cheese sandwiches with chips," Lynn offered.

"I'm sold. I want to hear how your session went this morning, too," Peter replied.

"Sit at the counter, and I'll tell you all about it while I make the sandwiches," Lynn said.

"The woman I met with this morning works at the hospital. I can't tell you more than that about her. She was the only group member who hadn't done at least one $20 give-away the second time we met. She did a great job handing out $20 to a college kid who looked like he was on his last quarter, literally," Lynn started.

"She claims to have seen a person near my office one evening a while back and says she's willing to talk with Stan about it," Lynn said, being careful not to talk about the actual break-in.

"It doesn't seem like she got a good look at the person, but she might have noticed something helpful," Lynn said.

"That's good news, isn't it? You don't sound enthusiastic," Peter commented.

Peter and Lynn took their sandwiches and drinks to the kitchen table.

"I'm worried what she is saying she saw might be a distraction away from what really happened. I just have this gut feeling she's in on the attacks. I know that sounds crazy since I don't have any proof," Lynn said.

"When something like that happens to me, I suspect I subconsciously picked up some information that hasn't hit the Wernicke's area in the temporal lobe of my brain. I remember this patient that I cared for who came into the hospital very beat up. Her sister, who had come to visit, found her unconscious on the living room floor. She called 911 and told the police she thought it was a robbery because a set of Baccarat Mille Nuits candlesticks was missing. Virginia told me they would go for over $500," Peter explained with a small grimace.

"However, when I talked to the husband, he said something about how horrible it was for her to be beaten up in her own kitchen. At first, what he said didn't click with me, but I suspected there was no robber. After I thought about it, I wondered how he would know the robber hit her in the kitchen, not in the living room where she was found. I mentioned this to the detective on the case when he came to talk to the patient. Sure enough, the police found her blood in the kitchen and other evidence that linked the husband to the beating," Peter explained.

"I get it. Something this woman from the $20 club said or did something that set up a warning signal, but I can't put it together yet," Lynn suggested.

"At least that's how I understand how that can happen. By the way, you make a great ham and cheese sandwich. Thanks for this!" Peter said. "All of a sudden, it will click, and you'll understand the information in a context. At least, that's how it works for me and a few others who have said something similar," Peter said.

"Sound reasonable. In the meantime, let's finish lunch and get your stuff home into the refrigerator," Lynn suggested.

"All the food is put away," Lynn said while finishing up in the kitchen at Peter's hours.

"Do you mind if I take a short nap before dinner? I think worrying again about these attacks drained me a little," Lynn asked.

"But of course. No hurry about dinner. We can eat on your schedule," Peter said.

Lynn once again went into Peter's bedroom. She was surprised at how comfortable she felt in his room. He had a king-sized bed with remotes to move any part of the two sections of the bed up or down. The overfilled comforter set had a small amount of embroidery in neutral colors on the sides of a light, blue-based fabric with coordinated pillow covers and bed skirts. To Lynn, it seemed simple but inviting.

She undressed except for her underwear and crawled into the side of the bed she had slept on last night. She wondered how it might feel with Peter next to her. Suddenly, she felt something near her feet that she hadn't felt the night before. Pulling back the covers, she discovered a short, black lacey negligee.

"What the hell," Lynn said softly. "I can't believe this is happening."

"Peter," Lynn shouted, reaching for her bathrobe.

"What's the matter? You OK?" Peter asked, running into the bedroom.

Lynn held up the black negligee. "I found this in the sheets," Lynn said emphatically.

"Virginia!" Peter yelled. "I can't believe she did that again."

"How would Virginia have done this," Lynn asked. "What do you mean she did it again?"

"While you were at your meeting, Virginia called and asked if she could come over and pick up some special clothes of Hanna's. Her mother wants to take them all out to fancy dinner tonight. I said sure. She was in the back where the bedrooms are. She brought out one of Hanna's outfits and left. No yelling or screaming even. I didn't think much about it at the time," Peter said.

"First of all, be assured no one wearing that negligee has been in that bed with me. Virginia did this once before, after the divorce, when she thought I was sleeping with this woman I had dinner with a few times. Except that time, it was a red negligee," Peter explained.

"I'm sorry, Lynn, to bring this type of craziness into your life. Please believe I only want to make you happy," Peter said.

"I believe you, Peter. Do you think she's the one who orchestrated the fellow Bruce who interrupted our dinner and later sent the roses?" Lynn asked.

"For sure, she did this. You didn't say you noticed anything in the bed last night, right? The only people in that bedroom since last night were you and probably her. I didn't go into the bedroom at all," Peter said. "I think it's reasonable to assume she hired this Bruce fellow."

"I'm sorry, but I don't know if I can handle this, too," Lynn said. "Even when we were out to dinner, I kept waiting for someone to show up and make some insinuation about me. Now someone, probably Virginia, is trying to insinuate you were sleeping with someone recently."

Panicked, Peter asked, "What are you trying to say?"

"I think before we can move our relationship forward, you need to take care of Virginia, and I need to find out who is sabotaging me at work. I'm too stressed with all this. I think I should go home," Lynn said.

"I know we both care a lot about each other and want to make this relationship work, but there's too much in the way. Can we put us on hold until all this sabotage is over on both sides?" Lynn asked.

"You know I want to keep seeing you, but I think you are right. Virginia will keep being a problem if I don't do something about her," Peter said. "I do need to say what is happening to you at the hospital is not upsetting me other than wanting to help you. I have lots of energy to help find out who is doing that," Peter said.

"Thanks for that," Lynn responded. "When you stop Virginia from her intrusions, let's start seeing each other again. I'm overwhelmed with people trying to ruin my life."

"OK. Know that now you are safe in my house. Virginia won't try anything else today. Will you just stay until tomorrow morning? It would mean a lot to me," Peter said.

If Lynn had any doubt about how she felt about Peter, the doubt vanished at that moment. She just loved him too much to turn down his request.

"OK, tomorrow we start fighting our attackers," Lynn said. "Right now, I'm going back for my nap."

Peter was on his phone after Lynn went into the bedroom. "Tony, I have another issue with Virginia and need your help. When can we meet?" Peter asked. "Tomorrow around 2:00? See you then."

CHAPTER 36

Entering the kitchen after taking her nap, Lynn was impressed with Peter's culinary skills. The table was set with a small vase of flowers. The pasta and clams were cooking, but the salad was ready, along with a breadbasket.

"Wow!" Lynn said. "You cut an impressive figure in the kitchen."

"Well, thank you, my dear. It's been a while since I made a decent dish in the kitchen, but it's returning to me. May I pour you a glass of Chardonnay?"

"You certainly may," Lynn said. "I'm sorry, I was so out of sorts."

"I understand. You are trying to work and do good things but getting attacked from multiple sides. Unfortunately, someone from my life past is contributing to those attacks. I'm so sorry about that," Peter said.

Lynn moved the salad bowl and the breadbasket to the table. Peter brought over the two clams linguine-filled dishes.

"See, we make a great team," Peter said, smiling.

"Yes, we do," Lynn replied. "Thanks for this great dinner."

"I aim to please," Peter replied.

After dinner, Lynn and Peter snuggled together on the couch.

"I've been thinking about all this and realize I haven't been totally honest. I didn't tell you someone broke into my office and messed it up!"

"What! When did that happen? Why wouldn't you tell me that?" Peter asked.

"George said not to," Lynn replied. "Apparently, you had told him at your gathering with former classmates how happy you were to see me. You also were happy not to have all that negativity Virginia had brought into your life. He thought you would see what was happening to me as more negativity."

"Makes sense," Peter said. "But the negativity I constantly talked about had been directed toward me. I will always want to know if anything bad is happening to you so that I can help. I know you are strong and can fight your battles, but I can at least provide some protective gear, always."

"You are the best guy ever," Lynn said. "There's more I need to tell you. Stan, George, and I met to figure out who might be doing all these attacks and how to stop them. What would you think about joining us now that you feel Virginia is behind at least the efforts to break us up?"

Peter didn't answer right away.

"How about this? I think you are right in saying I need to deal with Virginia before you and I can move forward. I've called my lawyer and set up a time to get together. It seems best to just let me and my lawyer get rid of that piece of negativity. Virginia is my problem, and I don't want her to be yours," Peter said.

"All right, that makes sense," Lynn responded.

"Just know, whatever I can do to help you with what's going on at the hospital, I'm there. I'm so sorry, Lynn, all this is happening to you." Peter said, reaching for Lynn's hand.

Tears ran down Lynn's face. Peter reached and took Lynn in his arms. "It will be better soon," Peter said. "Tell George and Stan I'm on the team, too, fixing my part of the problem. No one will win this fight against the four of us."

The next morning, Lynn and Peter reluctantly said goodbye, knowing each was faced with stopping people from attacking Lynn. For their relationship to work, these attacks had to stop. It was like the Sword of Damocles was hanging over their heads.

Once home, Lynn called George.

"Good morning, George. Do you have some time to get together today?" Lynn asked her brother.

"Sure, what's up?" George asked.

"The short version is that Peter and I found out it was Virginia who is trying to break up Peter and me. We can cross that issue off the list. I need to fill you in on the other details about Peter. I might need your help," Lynn said.

"Hey, Angie," George said to his wife. "Lynn is coming over for dinner tonight. You go enough food – you know she doesn't eat much."

"Angie says you are so welcome to come for dinner. If we get short of food, she's going to take some out of my serving since I need to lose weight, anyway," George said. "See what I live with! Can you make it over by 6:00 or sooner?"

Lynn laughed. "Thank Angie for me. I will be there a little sooner so we can talk. OK?"

"See you then!" George said. "We are always happy to see you, you know."

Lynn then sent a text to Stan.

"Hi, Stan. Peter and I have definite proof that Virginia is behind the escapades that were aimed at breaking up Peter and me. Yesterday she tried something she had done before to Peter. He knew instantly it was her. Peter said he would meet up with his lawyer and take care of her through legal means. We have something that should have her fingerprints on it. I can fill you in with more details when we meet again," Lynn wrote.

"That's good to know. I'll see you on Thursday when we are scheduled to meet again. Tell Peter I'm happy to help him if I can," Stan said.

"That's funny because he said to tell you the same thing," Lynn responded. "I'm so grateful to have all of you helping with these attacks."

"We all love you, Lynn, and are happy to help," Stan commented.

"Thanks, Stan," Lynn returned Stan's message with a happy face emoji.

We all love you? Lynn asked herself. *What does that mean coming from Stan?"*

CHAPTER 37

"*I'm not going to think about Stan or anything right now,*" Lynn said to herself. *"I'm cleaning and doing the laundry to take my mind off everything else."*

When she finished, Lynn drove to her brother's house. When she knocked on George's door, it opened, and George's three children enthusiastically greeted her.

"She's here!" Bernie shouted to George and Angie.

"Bernie, I'm so happy to see you! How are you?" Lynn asked.

"Some things are good, and some things not so good," Bernie replied.

"Let's talk more later," Lynn said, smiling. "Right now, I have to peel Eloise and Edison off my legs."

"I am so happy to see all of you. How are you two?" She asked Eloise and Edison.

"We are doing a puzzle," said Eloise.

"Yep. It's a big puzzle with lots of pieces," Edison said.

"I need to see this puzzle. In the meantime, would you take me to your parents?" Lynn asked.

"We know where they are. We can take you there," Bernie replied.

"They are just in the kitchen," Eloise prompted. She rolled her eyes. "It's no secret place."

"Yaa, it's not a secret," Edison chimed in.

"I see the mob squad got you," George said, laughing. "At least you know they are happy to see you."

"That includes me, too," Angie said.

"OK, kids. Go finish your puzzle while I talk with your Auntie," George said. "Let's go in the den. There's some protection from the noise and intrusions there."

"Spill, what's going on?" George asked.

"Peter invited me to spend the weekend with him," Lynn started.

"That's my boy," George interrupted.

"Don't get too excited," Lynn said. "We had separate rooms."

"Baby steps are good, too," George commented.

Lynn gave him a look that would cause a growling bear to run.

"I'd like to talk uninterrupted for a few minutes," Lynn said. "Here's the story. On Saturday, I met up with one of my new $20 members to help with a handout. When I returned to Peter's house, we chatted, and I decided to nap. After I got into Peter's bed, I felt something and pulled out a short, black, sexy negligee."

A knowing look came over George's face. "The old negligee trick," George said. "Don't tell me. Peter recognized that as one of Virginia's attempts to make him look like a womanizer."

"Yep. Peter said while I was gone, Virginia called and come over for some clothes for Hanna. She must have planted the negligee, then. I sort of fell apart because of all the attacks. We agreed that Peter and I would cool it a while until he straightened out Virginia. He's meeting with his lawyer," Lynn said. "We can cross off the whodunit about who is doing the visits and gifts from the secret boyfriend."

"I'm sorry to hear Virginia is being true to herself. What a piece of work she is. But you and Peter are right. It's his problem, and if he can't get her legally or otherwise to back off, your relationship with him will always be anxious. I get that," George said. "Maybe I should go talk with her, too. I know people who can scare you know what out of her."

"George!" Lynn said emphatically. "As Mom used to say, "No roughhousing!"

"All right. All right. I'll just check in with Peter and see if there is anything I can do to help him," George said a little reluctantly. "I'm sorry, but Virginia has spent years making Peter's life, and now yours, miserable. She needs to be taught a lesson."

"I agree with that but work with Peter. I'm sure he'll be happy to have you on his side," Lynn said. "However, I don't want to bail either of you out of jail."

"All right, party pooper. I'll rein it in."

"Thank you. You're a good brother," Lynn said.

"Let's get you a glass of wine and a good dinner. It's the least we can do," George said.

"Auntie Lynn, Auntie Lynn. Come help us with this puzzle. It's all about whales, but they are all the same color," complained Bernie.

"But they are different sizes. That helps," Edison chimed in. "Come help us."

On the way home, Lynn was happy about her time with George and his family, but then the sadness about where she was with her relationship with Peter overtook her. She wondered if he would be bringing her coffee tomorrow at work or was that over, too.

CHAPTER 38

When Lynn arrived at work the next day, she was nervous for the first time since she was made director of the ED. She was on guard for the next attack, be it about her relationship with Peter or her competency at work.

"Good morning, Lynn," Beatrice said, stepping into her office. "How was your weekend?"

"It was good for the most part," Lynn said.

"Sorry to hear it wasn't wonderful all the time," Beatrice said.

Lynn debated saying anything to Beatrice about the negligee but voted against it. Better that the staff doesn't talk about her personal life, she decided.

"How's everything on the unit?" Lynn asked to change the subject."

"Not too bad. Earlier, we had a patient who miscarried and went to the OR. I think she got here in time before she lost too much blood. It was sad because it was her third miscarriage," Beatrice said.

"Now we just have a person with a fractured hand. Dr. Phillips is here checking him out. Another patient came in with respiratory distress. We are not sure what's causing it – no history of asthma. He's going to the ICU to be safe," Beatrice continued.

"Let's hope it's a quiet day for all of us," Lynn said.

"I think Stan is looking for you. You want me to send him in?" Beatrice asked.

"Sure," Lynn replied.

Lynn was working on her reports when she heard a knock on her door. She could tell by the shape of the figure it was Stan and not Peter.

"Hi, Stan. Come on in." Lynn said.

"How did you know it was me?" Stan asked. "Do you have x-ray vision I don't know about?"

"I can't make out faces clearly, but I can recognize figures of familiar people. So no to the x-ray vision, which is too bad," Lynn said.

"I have some news about the trial. So far, the lawyers don't need you to testify. The footage from the camera is very good. Because of what you said about the driver of the car being white and left-handed, they checked to see his arm as he shot the car door. The arm and the watch are very clear. They also picked up some fingerprints on the victim's clothes. They have plenty of evidence identifying this driver," Stan said.

"I'm so thankful not to have to go to court. I have enough with all this sabotage stuff," Lynn said, relieved.

"I'm just cautioning you, though, if things go sideways in court, you still might be asked to testify. It's unlikely, but still possible. The good news, though, is your name has not been submitted as a possible witness," Stan added.

"That's good to hear," Lynn said.

"We hope so. These types of cases are not always air-tight. Sometimes there are unfortunate leaks," Stan said reluctantly.

"I'll settle for so far, so good, then," Lynn said, laughing.

"I was happy to hear the good news about Virginia being pretty much identified as the person who is trying to break up you and Dr. Pete. That's a good find," Stan said trying to find encouraging words.

"That's true. Peter is meeting with his lawyer today to get some resolution with Virginia. If those attacks stop and I don't end up going to court, life will be better. All that's left really is to figure out who is sending these emails under my name and messing up my office," Lynn added. Saying those words seem to lessen the anxiety that was constantly with her.

"The security team here and I are keeping an eye on your office. IT is trying to track down who sent those emails. We only have one fingerprint from your office after the break-in that's not identified," Stan added. "I think whoever messed up your office wore gloves."

"Thanks, Stan. I so appreciate this update. Keep me posted," Lynn said.

"You know I'm always happy to help you in any way I can," Stan said. "See you in the grocery stores."

Lynn laughed. Since she and Stan lived in adjacent neighborhoods, it wasn't unusual to bump into each other in grocery stores. Her thoughts wandered a little. She asked herself if she would go out with Stan if she and Peter couldn't make it work. Stan's wife had died, so there are no complications there. In her heart, Lynn knew she did not have the right feelings for Stan to be dating him. Then she wondered if that was because of her feelings for Peter. At that juncture, she stopped thinking about her romantic life and got back to work.

A knock on her door was followed by a tall, good-looking doctor coming to see her with cups of coffee in both hands.

CHAPTER 39

While Lynn was happy to see Dr. James Buchanan, Peter's chief resident, disappointment passed through her.

"Hi, James. How are you? Dr. Pete giving you the coffee run this morning?" Lynn asked.

"Yes. He's tied up in surgery with a trauma patient but didn't want you to miss your coffee. He also said to give you this note," James said, passing a small envelope to her.

Hi Sweetie,

I know we agreed not to see each other, but that's so much harder to do than I even imagined. I read this comment by Tommaso Ferraris last night.

They told me that to make her fall in love, I had to make her laugh. But every time she laughs, I'm the one who falls in love.

It so made me think of you. It's not just your laugh that makes me fall in love with you more; it's everything about you.

I'd like to set a dinner date for Saturday night with you. I had a meeting with my lawyer yesterday, even though it was Sunday, and I'm scheduled to meet again with him today. He has some great ideas for getting Virginia to stop these phony impersonations and any other attempts to question our relationships. He says she will stop or be in jail by the end of the week.

Love you,
Peter

Lynn took out her notepad.

Hi Peter,
A definite yes for Saturday. Miss you, too. My joy in coming to work comes from knowing I'll be seeing you.

Love,
Lynn

Lynn put her note in an envelope and handed it to James.

"Thanks for the coffee and the note. Peter must trust you a lot to ask you to do this delivery," Lynn said.

"He's been so good to me; I'd do anything for him. You two deserve a good life without malignant interference. I wish you both the best," James replied.

Lynn tried getting back to her papers. Peter's note had lifted some of the sadness from not seeing him.

Beatrice stuck her head into Lynn's office.

"Lots of incoming patients," she said. "Looks like food poisoning from one of the restaurants near the shore. We can use your help."

Suddenly energized, Lynn followed Beatrice to the admissions area to help with nearly 12 patients who were complaining of nausea and vomiting.

"Where did all these patients eat?" asked Lynn.

"As far as we can tell, they had a birthday celebration last night. This morning, these patients came in with stomach pains, nausea and vomiting, diarrhea, and fevers. The lab is running tests to see what kind of bacteria is causing these symptoms," Beatrice said.

"How are we doing for ED space?" Lynn asked Beatrice.

"We were lucky it was quiet before this group started coming in," Beatrice said. "We're putting the sickest and oldest patients closest to the nurses' station. Also, we have room for everyone else. Dr. Tom ordered IVs for everyone so the patients don't get dehydrated. We could use some more help, though, to monitor the sicker patients."

"I'll call the administration and have them send us some extra help," Lynn said, reaching for her phone.

"Hi, Jenny. This is Lynn Price in the ED. We are now swamped with patients who seem to have food poisoning. We could use at least two more nurses down here."

"I'll get right on it," Jenny, the assistant to the staffing director, said.

"Thanks!" Lynn said. She spotted Michael Durand, the owner of Waters Edge, talking with the ED receptionist.

"Hi, Michael. Good to see you. We have about 12 people here who were at your restaurant last night. Any clue as to what might have happened?" Lynn asked.

"I can tell you exactly what happened, unfortunately. We just hired a new sous chef whom our chef did not adequately supervise. The sous chef cut up raw chicken on a cutting board but then, without washing the board or knife, cut up carrots and celery on it. The chicken was then cooked, but the carrots and celery were not and were on the salad," Michael said.

"Possibly, we are looking at Salmonella poisoning then," Lynn said. "Thanks for that info, Michael. I'll pass it on to Dr. Tom, who is here this morning."

As Lynn went looking for Dr. Tom, she was thankful Michael Durand had the integrity to speak up. So many owners would not have been so honest about how the food poisoning got transmitted.

"Tom," Lynn said, calling to Dr. Tom. "Michael Durand thinks contaminated raw chicken juice got on carrots and celery used on the salads. Our best guess is Salmonella until we get lab confirmation."

"That's good to know. We have one elderly patient and one patient who is severely dehydrated from diarrhea that I will start on antibiotics immediately," Dr. Tom replied.

Lynn answered her phone while looking at two registered nurses entering the ED.

"Two nurses coming to help out," Jenny said on the phone.

"They just walked in. You are a lifesaver, Jenny," Lynn replied.

"Glad to be able to help," Jenny said.

Lynn went up to the two nurses, both of whom Lynn was happy to see had worked in the ED before. She walked them over to get directions from Beatrice.

Lynn could see the look of relief on Beatrice's face knowing two more nurses would be helping. She gave Lynn a thumbs up!

Lynn heard loud retching sounds and ran quickly to the end rooms with the sicker patients. An elderly woman was in bed vomiting over an emesis basin.

"I'm here, Mrs. Delmar," Lynn said. "I'm putting a clean emesis basin into your hands and taking the full one out. I'll be right back as soon as I dump out this basin."

Lynn learned long ago to take deep breaths and turn away from vomit to prevent her from becoming nauseous. Before flushing it, she quickly checked the nature of the vomit, pieces of undigested fish, and undistinguishable vegetables. Her stomach felt queasy.

She returned to Mrs. Delmar's side, pushed her call bell, and gave her a sip of the water. Exhausted, Lynn helped Mrs. Delmar get into a comfortable sitting position. Lynn checked to see that her IV to keep her hydrated was running well.

Beatrice had come in with one of the new nurses.

"Thanks, Lynn," Beatrice said. She turned toward Mrs. Delmar.

"Mrs. Delmar, this is Rachel Robinson, a nurse who will stay with you now. Dr. Tom will be in to see you again soon," Beatrice explained.

Mrs. Delmar looked over to Lynn and mouthed the words, thank you.

"That's what we do," Lynn said, quoting Obama's words after sinking a basketball. That brought a smile to Mrs. Delmar's lips.

"I'm going to talk with family members to make sure they are handling all this OK," Lynn said to Beatrice.

"That's also what you do," Beatrice said, smiling.

CHAPTER 40

Lynn started her rounds talking with the families of the patients who had food poisoning. This type of situation was always difficult with friends and family members. The relatives could be a help and comfort if the patient was not too sick, but obstructive if the patient was very ill and needed much care. Her job, as Lynn defined it, was to ask scared relatives and friends to come to talk with her out in the hall if they were getting in the way.

She started her rounds. She pulled three overzealous relatives out of the treatment rooms in the next two hours. She informed Beatrice and Dr. Tom that the lab results indicated salmonella caused the food poisoning.

By noon, all the patients had stopped having GI symptoms and were having lab work done to make sure they were well enough to go home.

During the busy time, while Lynn was focused on these patients and her staff, there were no thoughts about other aspects of her life. As soon as the ED was under control and the patients were getting better, an ache attacked Lynn.

Thoughts of the attacks on her, the separation of her and Peter, came back into focus. She noticed she was even anxious about going back to her office. *Will I survive all this?* Lynn asked herself.

Fortunately, her office was just as she had left it. She started checking her email. No signs of issues there. Relieved, she plowed through the paperwork that needed to be done and prepared for the final meeting of the $20 club that evening.

After a quick snack, she met up with her group.

"Hi, everyone. Good to see you all. I hope you have had some great experiences. Tonight is more of a wrap-up session, as I mentioned in the email I sent out. I would like to hear from each of you about how these experiences with your recipients affected you, as well as any new stories you might want to share and, of course, any questions you may have.

In honor of this being our last session, we have champagne, orange juice, and cake on the table in the back of the room. Help yourselves.

I want to thank you all for attending this workshop. It has been my pleasure to get to know you all and to be with some of you in the field," Lynn said.

"Who would like to begin?" Lynn asked.

"I would like to start," Amanda said.

"You are on, Amanda," Lynn responded.

"Lynn and I met at a coffee shop.. There was a young man sitting at a table next to us with his computer. He was in front of me, buying a cup of coffee with his last nickels and quarters. His wallet was empty. Lynn and I talked about the best approach that might be my empathizing with him. I told him I remembered my student days preparing to be an X-ray technician when I was chronically short of cash. I told this young man, now that I was employed, I'm paying it forward so he can have a good meal tonight," Amanda described. "He thanked me and said he planned on taking some ketchup packages and mixing them with water for his dinner that night."

Amanda took a moment to halt the tears in her eyes. "The other four people I gave $20s to were equally appreciative. I truly learned how a little kindness at the right time can be so helpful to others," Amanda said.

"Thank you, Amanda. That's a great story," Lynn said.

"I'd like to go next," Paul said. "I had the best time ever handing out these $20s bills. I also had an opportunity to help someone beyond the $20.

"Do tell," Lynn said.

"I was on the train going to Raleigh recently while my car was in the shop. There was a young guy sitting next to me, looking at information about Duke University. He told me he was going there for an interview. I told him congratulations, that was such a great school. He said, "Yes, but I don't think I will get in." He continued pointing out the worn and pretty ugly clothes he was wearing. "How can I make a good impression wearing these clothes?" he said.

"He told me he was eligible for a scholarship, but his family was poor. They could barely afford the bus fare and the room at the YMCA he was staying at that night.

"I texted my father to get his OK to take this fellow to the men's store where my family has an account. My father said, "but of course, and bring him home to stay here overnight." James and I went to this men's store and got him the best look we could without being over the top, which would threaten his scholarship. I also slipped him $20 for whatever he needed. I'm waiting to hear if he got in."

"The way I see it now, here's this capable fellow who could do good things with his life. All he needed was a little help that my family could easily afford."

"I had something similar happen," Abigail said. "I was talking to a mother at our parent's group. She told me she was very proud of her daughter, Tory, who was a graduate student. She was worried about her because she was sleeping on the floor in her apartment in a sleeping bag. I convinced my husband our daughter needed a new bed, and that Tory could have the old one, which incidentally was still in good shape," said Abigail.

"Who would like to speak next?" Lynn asked of Wendy and Dennis.

"I gave out all my $20s, but one interaction was the best. As an 8th-grade teacher, I hear students talk about what is going on in their lives. Our school has an 8th-grade party and dance for the holidays. The kids usually dress up for it. One smart and sweet girl in my class had her eye on a dress at the local boutique. Her parents couldn't afford it. They were $25 short. They were still looking for a dress their daughter liked that they could afford. I was trying to find a way to give the family the extra $25. I figured I could be flexible to add the extra $5.

I went and talked to the woman, Paula, who owns the boutique whom I know well. We came up with a plan. I gave her the extra $25. She called the mother and told her they were starting a sale, which was true. The dress her daughter wanted was going to be reduced by $25. That was a little of a stretch. Paula said if the mother still wanted the dress, she would put it aside for her. The mother was at the shop in 15 minutes. She was so happy to be able to buy the dress her daughter liked so much. There were tears in her eyes as she thanked Paula.

"Good for you, Wendy. That's such a great story. Thank you for sharing," Lynn said. "Dennis, what about you?"

"As a policeman, I am trained to spot problems, particularly crimes or situations that can lead to crimes. In general, looking for the bad guys. Doing that, I didn't see much else. You asked how this has affected us. I now see those who have been invisible to me for years. Last weekend, I took my remaining four $20s and found these people. I was looking for a picture frame at Goodwill when I saw this woman adding up what she was putting in her cart. Things came in and out of the cart depending on what she saw and how much it cost. I told her I hadn't worn the coat I had on for a while and found $20 in a pocket. I believe it was there to bring good cheer to someone. Happy holidays, I said and handed her the $20.

Next, I went to McBurger's for a coffee. I told the woman to keep the change from a $20 and whispered to put it in her pocket.

Then, I went to the hardware store for a special screwdriver. A young man, maybe 16 or 17, was taking tools on and off the shelves, checking the prices. I asked if he was looking for something special. He said his father does odd jobs fixing things in houses. His tools are very old and worn. He had $25 to buy him something but wasn't sure what. I told him I'm always fixing things around my house. I use a Craftsman tool kit like this one that I took off the shelf. Look, it comes with an extra $20, I said, as I twisted $20 around the handle.

"Thanks, mister," the young man said, smiling. Off he went to the checkout counter.

"I stopped at Milly's diner for a sandwich. I have been there hundreds of times. A young girl – 16 or 17 – took my order. I noticed her tapping her watch now and then. "Watch not working well?" I asked.

"I think it's giving up the ghost. It's old and charging it doesn't work anymore, but I need it to get to work and school on time. I handed her a $20 tip. Use this toward a new watch, I said.

"Wow!" Lynn said. "You were on a roll."

"What was astonishing to me was how different I reacted to situations that I've probably seen hundreds of times before. All the places I mentioned could have had people with similar stories when I was there before. I just didn't see them. And now, thanks to this workshop, I'm front and center, looking and seeing. Thank you, Lynn," Dennis said.

The group stood up and started clapping for Lynn.

"Thank you," Lynn said. "I'm returning the praise to you who have done great deeds and achieved major insights. I raise my champagne glass to all you members of the $20s club! Happy holidays!"

CHAPTER 41

The next day when Lynn entered her office, she was overwhelmed by the smell of flatulence. It was so strong that it hurt her nose. She could barely stand being in the office. She tried to check her desk, the bookcase, and her closet. The smell seemed stronger in the closet, but she had to exit her office to take a deep breath.

She called the security office and texted Stan while she waited in the hallway.

Henry Bukowski from security came rushing up to her.

"I cannot believe someone got into your office with all the precautions we have taken," Henry said. "Let me check it out."

Stan texted back. "I'll be there in 15 minutes."

Henry came out of the office, coughing.

"I'm going to need a mask to do a thorough check of your office. Whatever someone planted, it is disgusting. I need a mask. I'm going to also run through the footage from the last couple of nights in front of your door. I'll be right back," Henry said.

Stan was hurrying toward her. He also went into her office.

"Oh, my God. How disgusting that smell is. Did you notice any odd smell before today?" Stan asked Lynn.

"I thought I smelled something yesterday, but nothing like this," Lynn replied.

"Someone might have planted whatever this is a few days ago that ripened. Shrimp is particularly disgusting when left out for a few days. We had a case like that when a man died eating shrimp but wasn't found for a few days later," Stan said.

"Why would someone want my office to smell bad?" Lynn asked. "Is there anything to gain from that?"

"Since this odor is like flatulence, you might start hearing rumors that you sit in your office expelling a lot of gas. It's another attempt to make you look unprofessional," Stan said.

Henry arrived with an odor-control face mask with a charcoal cloth that neutralizes smells. Jim also came with him. He was carrying a similar mask. They both entered Lynn's office.

"How about I buy you a cup of coffee?" Stan suggested.

By now, Beatrice and Dr. Tom were in the hallway with Lynn.

"Go, Lynn," Beatrice said. "It's pretty quiet here."

"We can manage," Dr. Tom said.

Maybe it was her imagination, but Lynn thought more eyes than usual were on her as she entered the cafeteria. She grabbed a table in a remote corner of the cafeteria while Stan got the coffee. She so wished it was Peter bringing her the coffee. She missed him much more than she had anticipated.

"Is this ever going to end?" Lynn asked Stan as he place the cups of coffee on the table.

"Sure. We will catch who is doing this. Unfortunately, it just takes time. Depending on what Henry and Jim find, we will check and then interview anyone who was near the office when whatever is causing the smell was placed. It's going to take a little time to figure out how long it took the object to decompose enough to smell that bad," Stan explained.

"We also might find some fingerprints or maybe even saliva if they made it look like your half-eaten lunch," Stan said.

Lynn's phone buzzed, indicating a text message. Henry sent a picture of a half-eaten shrimp plate. The shrimp looked slimy and soft. Henry's note said the shrimp had a strong foul, and rotten smell.

"Let's hope housekeeping can get rid of the smell soon," Stan said. "I know this is hard on you, but the more attacks there are, the more opportunities we have to catch him or her."

"I hope that is soon. Whoever this is, is destroying my credibility and my nerves. I'm afraid to even enter my office," Lynn said, close to tears.

"I'm going down to the security office to look over the videos. It probably took a few days for the shrimp to get spoiled. I'm guessing the plate was planted over the weekend sometime," Stan said. "I'll get back to you soon."

Lynn walked back to her office just in time to see two staff from the housekeeping department go in. She went to check on Beatrice and the ED patients. At least that part of her life was untouched so far!

"We have a problem," Beatrice said to Lynn. "The patient in room 4 has had a botched abortion. Wanda and Dr. Acosta are in there now with her."

As Lynn approached room 4, Wanda exited that room.

"So, how is it going in there?" Lynn asked.

"Not good. Mrs. Lockwood went to some back alley fake doctor for an abortion. She didn't know she was pregnant until she missed two periods and did a pregnancy test. She was too far along to have an abortion in her state," Wanda explained.

"We are just inundated with women from other states," Lynn said.

"Mrs. Lockwood has lost a lot of blood and may still be bleeding," Wanda said.

"What about the fetus? Was it removed?" Lynn asked.

"Dr. Acosta is not sure. There is no fetal heartbeat, but he needs to check the uterus," Wanda said.

"I'll tell the OR to get ready," Lynn said. "Would you make sure Dr. Acosta's notes are clear about what procedures he performs? I'll talk to Beatrice, too, about the nurse's notes also documenting her bleeding and her low blood pressure."

Wanda nodded. "Gotcha. We will have Mrs. Lockwood go straight to the surgical ICU after the surgery. I'll keep you posted."

Lynn called down to medical records to look up how many patients who had botched abortions elsewhere came to this hospital. Everyone knew that restricting legal abortions would lead to more back-alley procedures and an increase in the death rates of these women.

Lynn checked her office and found that housekeeping was gone, as was the yellow police tape. Whatever the housekeepers had done to clear the odor, it had worked. With trepidation that she might find something else out of place in the office, she went in.

As soon as she sat behind her desk, sadness overcame her. She was constantly on guard that another attack would occur. Plus, she missed Peter coming in smiling with his two cups of coffee. He gave her strength and happiness. She hadn't heard how his meetings with his lawyer had gone. She was counting on hearing all about keeping Virginia from interfering with their lives on Saturday when Peter had invited her to dinner.

Will they ever have a life together again? Lynn wondered.

CHAPTER 42

Lynn heard her phone buzz.

"Hi, George. How's everything going?" Lynn asked her brother.

"How am I? How are you? Stan told me about the smelly food in your office. Someone sure wants you to leave your position. How about taking a break and coming over for dinner? The kids have been asking for you," George replied.

"That sounds great. I'll be over as soon as I finish some paperwork. Our librarian here found a new book to read to the kids, too. See you soon."

Lynn was greeted at George's house by three youngsters grabbing her arms and legs as she tried to get into the house.

"Hi, Lynn," Angie said. "Glad you could make it over."

"Thanks for inviting me. I'm happy to be with family and not thinking about all the awful stuff that's going on," Lynn replied.

"Dad said you have a new story to read to us tonight," Bernie said enthusiastically.

"What's the name of the book?" Eloise asked.

"Yes, what's the name?" Edison echoed.

"I'll tell you about the name after your finish your dinner. I'll read the story after you are in your pajamas and in bed. Is that a deal?" Lynn asked.

"OK. Can you give us a hint now?" Edison asked.

"OK. Just a hint. It's about an eight-year-old boy and his six your old brother and sister," Lynn said.

"Wow, that's just like us," Eloise said.

"Yes, but I'm closer to nine years old than eight years old," Bernie added.

George loved the interchange between his sister and his children. He was happy to bring some joy to her. The bodyguard he had hired to watch Lynn and her house had to be off tonight until 9:00 pm. He wanted to make sure she was safe.

"Angie, this is the beef stew I have ever eaten. It is so good!" Lynn said.

"We have dessert too that Eloise and I made," Edison piped up.

"Homemade dessert, too. I feel like a princess in this house," Lynn said.

"We are finished with our dinner, Auntie Lynn. Tell us the name of the book, please," Bernie asked.

"It's called Christmas shopping with Grandma," Lynn said.

"That's a great title!" Bernie said.

"If you want to hear the story, you better finish up and get ready for bed – including brushing your teeth," Angie said.

There was a mad scramble upstairs to the bedrooms.

George just shook his head and laughed.

"They don't get that excited when Angie or I read them stories. You sure have the magic touch," George said.

"You know how much I love your kids and love reading to them. The librarian keeps an eye out for good stories, too," Lynn replied.

Angie followed the kids upstairs to make sure they brushed their teeth and put clean pajamas on.

"So how you, Sis? Are you doing OK with all this nonsense?" George asked.

"Honestly, I'm barely hanging in. Peter doesn't drop by my office anymore, and I miss him. I'm on edge, waiting for the next attack. It's hard to focus on other things in my life. Thank you for inviting me over. It's a nice break," Lynn said.

"You know you are my favorite sister," George said.

"I know. I've heard that before. It always makes me wonder if you had another sister if you would still say that," Lynn said, laughing.

"I would just tell each of you that each was my favorite sister when we were alone," said George. "Simple."

"Ready for story time," Bernie hollered from the top of the stairs.

"I'm coming," Lynn replied.

The twins were snuggled in their beds, and Bernie sat next to Lynn on the couch.

"Here are the characters – Here's Grandma Kathy, and here are her three grandchildren, Tommy, Suzy, and Joey," Lynn said, pointing to the figures in the book as she started to read.

"The grandchildren and the grandmother live in New York City. You can see the picture of the Statue of Liberty and the Empire State Building in the background.

Lynn starts to read the story.

"Are you ready to go Christmas shopping for Mom and Dad?" Grandma Kathy asked.

"We sure are. But what are we looking for?" Suzy asked.

We are looking for something that will make them happy. Your mom and dad do so much for you and everyone else; it is nice to do something for them," Grandma said.

Lynn showed her niece and nephews the pictures in the book of the mom and dad cooking meals, driving them to school, and helping with homework.

"That's what our mom and dad do, too," Joey said.

"Good point, Joey," Lynn said and continues reading.

"Let's go to Bloomingdales," Suzy said. "They have everything."

"That's a great idea," Grandma said.

"I've heard of Bloomingdales," Eloise said. "Mom likes to go shopping there when she goes to New York City."

"You have to watch out for the perfume ladies, though," Edison added.

Lynn laughed. "Let's see how the shopping turns out. Here are Suzy, Joey, and Tommy walking with grandma past the windows at Bloomingdales. In real life, the figures are moving. Check out the giant gold bear. He's spectacular," Lynn pointed out in the picture in the book.

Lynn starts reading the book again.

"Do you think Mom would like some new jewelry?" Grandma asked as they entered the jewelry section of Bloomies.

"If it's very pretty, she might," Suzy said.

"Wow, look at all the jewelry," Tommy said. "It's hard to pick something. There is so much to look at."

"We'll keep that in mind," said Grandma. "Let's take the escalator up to the next floor. Maybe we can find a scarf or some gloves."

Lynn stops reading for a minute.

"See how carefully everyone steps onto the escalator. Have you ridden on an escalator?" Lynn asked.

"I have," Tommy proudly said. "It was a little bit scary. I thought my foot might get caught."

"Really? That can happen?" asked Joey.

"Your feet, especially with shoes on, are too big to get caught on an escalator. You will see people picking up their dogs, though, so their paws don't get caught," explained Lynn.

Lynn turned the page.

"It looks like they are in the women's section of the store," Eloise said. "There are many scarves there. I like the one with the ballet shoes on it."

Lynn continues to read the story.

"How do we know which scarf would be good for Mom?" Lucy said. I know which one I would like."

"What colors does your mom wear most of the time?" Grandma asked.

There was a picture of Tommy, Joey, and Suzy deep in thought on the page.

"I don't know," Suzy said. "Maybe blue."

"I think she wears clothes that have red in them," Tommy said.

"No, I think she likes yellow," Joey added.

"Wow! We need to know what color someone would like before we can buy them clothes," Grandma added. "Let's go up to the Christmas decorations section. That might be easier."

"Buying presents that people like is not easy," said Tommy. "That's what mom and dad do for us at Christmas."

"It takes paying attention to the people we love. I know that's what your mom and dad do when they buy you presents," Grandma said.

Lynn looked over at her niece and nephews to see them all asleep. She kissed each one good night and quietly left the room.

"How did it go?" George asked.

"They all fell asleep. The story is to be continued," Lynn said, smiling.

CHAPTER 43

The next morning the ED seemed quiet. Lynn checked in with Beatrice to see how many patients they had.

"Good morning, Lynn. So far, we are slow, with only three patients. We have an eight-year-old girl with an asthma attack. She came in wheezing with severe shortness of breath. The albuterol worked well. She's symptom-free, but we are just watching her to make sure the attack is over. Her vital signs are normal, and she should go home soon.

Then, we have a 78-year-old woman who fell early this morning on her way to the bathroom. She has a sprained wrist that she fell on to lessen the fall, but she complained about being dizzy before she fell. She's getting a cardiac workup. We had an OB patient come in earlier, but she's already been transferred to OB. That's about it for us this morning," Beatrice said.

"How was the night shift?" Lynn asked.

"As usual, they were busy. One patient was coded because of a heart attack around 2:00 am. The staff successfully revived him. He went to the OR and then will go to the coronary ICU. The rest of the cases were minor issues," Beatrice said.

"Good work! That reminds me, we need to start working on staff evaluations. They will start being due in January," Lynn said.

"I'll send you the list of employees and their employment dates. Let me know when you want to begin," Beatrice said.

Lynn decided to take a walk around the unit and end with a check on the crash cart. The parents were with Lisa Driscoll, the eight-year-old girl with asthma, who was talking without signs of breathlessness. That's always a good sign with an asthmatic, Lynn thought. Mrs. Olsen, the 78-year-old woman, was getting ready to go to x-ray for an ultrasound.

Lynn went to check on the two crash carts, usually called EDCCs, instead of Emergency Department Crash Carts. She quickly checked the resuscitation equipment that should be on top of each cart. Then she checked each drawer to make sure they contained the necessary medications. Unlike other units, the ED had two carts, so they would be prepared for more than one patient needing to be resuscitated. From what Lynn could tell, the medications in the cart that was used last night had been fully restocked by the pharmacy. The other cart still had a breakaway plastic lock on it.

In the ED, Lynn had one cart secured with the breakaway plastic lock, but the other one was unlocked for quick use but kept in a place of constant surveillance behind the nursing station.

Lynn's responsibility included having both carts checked on a regular basis to make sure the equipment works correctly and that all the medications are current and not out of date.

"How's everything looking?" Beatrice asked Lynn.

"All looks good. It looks like the pharmacy restocked any medications that were used. I checked the dates the carts were totally checked, and they are up to date. Now back to paperwork," Lynn said.

Back in her office, Lynn again missed not having Peter drop in with two cups of coffee. She hoped he had good news to share on Saturday night.

A few hours later, Beatrice knocked frantically on her door.

"Come in, Beatrice. What's going on?" Lynn asked.

"The pharmacy technician and now the supervisor are here doing their weekly crash cart checks. There's medication missing," Beatrice said.

Lynn raced to talk to the pharmacy supervisor, Bill Rodriguez.

"What's missing?" Lynn asked.

"The good news is the locked cart is fine. We just replaced two meds that will be outdated next week. The other cart is missing its supply of diazepam. As you know, that's not a typical med for a crash cart, but it is useful for severely anxious patients," explained Bill.

"We have used it on occasion. I know your pharmacist refilled the meds this morning on that cart. I checked the meds myself after I came on duty. It must have gone missing after 10:00 am. We could start there to see if anyone noticed someone hanging around the cart," Lynn said.

"Beatrice, call security and have them send someone up here," Lynn ordered.

"Why would anyone take the diazepam?" Lynn asked Bill. "It's just valium that most people could get a prescription for."

"Could be many reasons. Their prescribing doctor cut someone off. They don't want anyone in their local pharmacy to know they are taking the drug. Kids do stuff like that for fun, but not usually off a crash cart. This is someone who works here. Only a few people know this cart has that medication, too," Bill answered. "Here comes someone from security."

"So, what's happening up here?" Jim Rogers from security asked.

"Bill sent someone to do a routine inspection of the crash carts. They found the diazepam, better known as Valium, missing. The pharmacist that was working last night restocked the cart after a code, and then I checked it around 9:30 am to make sure it was fully prepared for another code.

I didn't find anything missing. I would have noticed the empty space quickly," Lynn explained.

"I think we have surveillance cameras in this area. I'm going to go pull them up and will be back to let you know what we see," Jim said.

"Let me know what you find out," Bill said, then left with his pharmacist.

"This unit sure is a hot spot for attacks," Jim said, turning to Lynn.

"That's for sure. It's very discouraging and depressing," Lynn said.

Jim looked at Lynn surprisingly and maybe a little suspiciously.

Lynn laughed. "No, I didn't take the diazepam. I need my wits about me to keep working here," Lynn said.

"I'll be in touch soon," Jim said.

Lynn went back to her office and called Wanda.

Do you have time for lunch?

Lynn texted.

Now I'm under suspicion of taking drugs from a crash cart. These attacks are getting worse, Lynn thought.

CHAPTER 44

I'll meet you at 1:00 in the cafeteria near the wall.

Wanda texted back.

Lynn went back to her office despondent. Will this ever end? She asked herself.

She tried to concentrate on her paperwork, but it was difficult. She so missed not being able to talk with Peter about all this. She needed to stop thinking about Peter and focus on work.

Her phone buzzed, indicating she had gotten a text. It was from Jim in security.

Can you meet me in my office around 2:30? I have something to show you.

Sure. I'll be there. Lynn answered.

I'm so hoping it is good news, Lynn thought.

In the cafeteria, Lynn grabbed a chicken salad sandwich and a glass of iced tea. Since it was the end of lunchtime, there were plenty of seats against the wall.

Lynn looked around at the people in the cafeteria and wondered if it was one of them who was harassing her. She can't imagine anyone disliking her enough to do all this to her. Maybe she should sign up for the nurse practitioner program and leave her job and this hospital. She could work for George and take care of all his employees. Easy peasy, she thought, but also maybe boring.

"I'm here," Wanda exclaimed, dropping into the seat next to her. "I haven't heard the details, but it sounds like some mystery was occurring in your department. What's going on?"

"Some diazepam was missing from one of our crash carts, and I'm the chief suspect!" Lynn said.

"What? How could anyone think you could take that drug from the crash cart?" Wanda asked.

"I checked the cart this morning because the night shift had a code last night. The pharmacist happened to do their scheduled check of all the meds on both carts and found the diazepam missing after I had checked it off as being present," Lynn explained.

"When security came up, I made the mistake of saying all these attacks were getting to be discouraging and depressing. He gave me a look – like we know who has been discouraged and depressed," Lynn explained further.

"Yes, but security also knows a very sneaky perpetrator keeps attacking you!" Wanda said.

Lynn laughed.

"Perpetrator, huh? Are you still watching those Blue Bloods reruns?" Lynn asked.

"It comes in handy," Wanda said, smiling. "I have a small idea of what an investigation looks like."

"Wanda, what would I do without you? You are such a great friend," Lynn said. "This has been one of the worse experiences in my life."

"Look at it this way. You found out who was trying to break up you and Peter. That part is being dealt with by Peter and his lawyer and whoever else they need to bring in to stop Virginia. That will be resolved – we can count on that," Wanda said with certainty.

"But, we don't…" Lynn started to say when Wanda interrupted.

"No, don't go there. You and I both know Peter. He can be trusted to always do the right thing. Remember when the mayor's assistant was beating up his wife? Peter was called in to fix her fractured arm that was twisted. The mayor begged Peter not to report the injury to the police. I think he even offered him some perks with the city healthcare system," Wanda said.

"I do remember that situation, although I hadn't heard the mayor offered Peter a bribe," Lynn said.

"Peter turned him down flat and reported the incident to the police as domestic abuse. He follows through and does the right thing. You need to have confidence that he will take care of Virginia. I wonder if she would like a new start in Alaska?" Wanda said.

"I do know Peter is not mean – so Alaska might be mean," Lynn said smiling.

"So, do you think those attacks against you and Peter having a relationship might stop and will continue to stay stopped?" asked Wanda.

"Peter and I are having dinner on Saturday. He's going to fill me in on what he and his lawyer have come up with," Lynn explained. "I hope it's good news."

"I'm happy you will see Peter this weekend. I know the distance has been hard," Wanda said.

Lynn was almost in tears.

"Cheer up. This person, I feel it's a guy, will get caught soon. Mike, from IT and Jim from security, along with Stan, are working diligently. Super locks and surveillance equipment surround you. This creep is not Superman. He's going to slip up and get caught. They always do – at least on Blue Bloods."

Lynn and Wanda both laughed.

"Speaking of crimes, what's the story about the trafficking court case? Are you going to be asked to testify?" Wanda asked.

"So far, no. I'm on standby, and it's not even a plane flight to some exotic land," Lynn said.

Wand laughed.

"Now we are getting somewhere. My wonderful friend's sense of humor is coming back," Wanda smiled.

"So far, they have the surveillance footage of the car, the victim being tossed out, and the guy's watch on his right arm when he reached over to shut the car door. The fellow they arrested is left-handed and owns that type of watch which he wears on his right arm, in addition to owning the car. I think they are trying to get him to give up higher-ups in this human trafficking ring for a reduced sentence," Lynn explained. "I don't have anything else to add. They called Dr. Tom to testify about the woman's condition and how she died in the ED."

"They would do that on Blue Bloods, too," Wanda added.

Both Lynn and Wanda laughed loud enough to draw attention to them.

"We better get going before they throw us out," Lynn said. "Thank you, my friend, for helping me be more optimistic. Talking with you was better than any antidepressant on the market. Thanks for being there."

"Always, my friend. Now go to your meeting with Jim in security and then let me know the good news," Wanda said.

"Speaking of which, I just got a notice from security that my car alarm went off. I'll check that first," Lynn said. "It's always something, isn't it?"

CHAPTER 45

Lynn's car was fine and still locked. *Someone just bumped into it*, she thought.

Talking with Wanda had lifted Lynn's spirits. She could now see progress being made to flesh out and stop these perpetrators. As she approached the security office, however, anxiety crept in again. The car alarm didn't help.

"Hi, Tracy," Lynn said to the receptionist in the security office. "I'm here to see Jim."

"He's with Stan in his office. Go on in," Tracy replied.

Lynn was surprised to see Stan sitting at Jim's desk, looking over what looked like surveillance tapes.

"Good to see you, Lynn. Come here and have a seat. We want to show you a glimpse of your attacker," Stan said.

Lynn took a deep, relaxing breath. *Can this really be true?* she asked herself.

"I'm starting to the point where you checked the crash cart this morning," Stan said. "You finished around 9:40. Now you see people at the nurses' station mulling around. Sometimes it's hard to see the crash cart behind them or who all these people are until they face the surveillance camera."

Lynn was watching to see whom she recognized. So far, they were the nurses who typically worked on the unit.

"I want you to look at this navy, light blue, and white checked shirt. It looks like a man's shirt, but we never see his face," Stan explained.

"I'm switching surveillance areas now to the hall in front of your office. There you go, leaving your office. Now, we see this man, with his back to the camera, wearing a dark navy or black baseball hat, wearing a navy, light blue, and white checked shirt, knocking on your office door. When there's no answer, he stays a little bit longer in front of your door."

"I see that," Lynn says.

"We can't see what he's doing because he shifted his body to cover any activity. A few minutes later, he leaves," Stan continues.

"So, what was he doing in front of my office?" Lynn asked.

"Give us one more scene, and we will tell you what we suspect," Jim added to the information.

"Here, he is outside near your car. He has on the same checked shirt and the baseball cap. Again, his back is toward the surveillance camera. If you remember, we had you park there because of those cameras. He tries to break into your car, but the siren goes off. He hightails it out of there.

Now we see you checking your car, which appeared to be still secured," Stan continued.

"Wow!" Lynn said. "If I'm getting this picture, this guy in the checked shirt shows up near the crash cart. Maybe he steals the diazepam, although we can't see that. Then he tries to break into my office, maybe to plant the diazepam there? That doesn't work, so he tries to break into my car to maybe stash the diazepam there, but the car alarm goes off."

"If you ever get tired of working in the ED, we could use your insights here in security," Jim says.

"Oh, no. We want her on the police force," Stan says.

"Is what I said what you two are thinking?" Lynn asked.

"Right on the money," Stan said. "If we searched your office and found the diazepam there, it would be a huge investigation. Even if you were found innocent, the fact that you were investigated would tarnish your reputation. That seems to be what this persistent fellow is trying to do."

"What's next? How do we find this guy?" Lynn asked.

"We now know he works in the hospital and knows his way around the ED. He also has way better-than-average computer skills. From our calculations, he's about 5'10" tall, with an average build. Do you have any male nurses who work in the ED?" Jim asked.

"We have two full-time male nurses and two part-time fellows. The two full-time guys are taller, over six feet tall. They wear scrubs to work, also, as do the part-timers. The part-timers are in their 50s and are retired Navy Corpsmen. I can't think of any reason any of these men would get something out of sabotaging me. But then, this has never happened to me before. I'll send you their names and background information," Lynn said.

"Great! That's a start," Jim said.

"Here's the not-so-good news. He has tried twice to pin the theft of the diazepam on you. He may try again. If he's getting desperate, he may get dangerous," Stan said.

"Wow! Really? Do you think he might attack me?" Lynn asked.

"We think he might try to break into your house and plant the diazepam there. We have alerted your brother that this might happen," Stan said. "That way, he can alert the guys who are watching your house when you are there."

"What? Does my brother have someone watching my house?" Lynn asked.

"Oh, oh," Stan said. "I thought you knew. When you refused to stay with your mom or with him, he hired these fellows to make sure you were safe always."

"The stick beating is in order," Lynn said quietly, almost to herself.

"Did you say stick beating?" Stan asked.

"It's a family thing. When my mother was not feeling well, George wanted to call me, but my mother was reluctant to bother me. George told her I would beat him with a stick if he didn't tell me about her. She knew he was joking but gave in and let him call me," Lynn said.

"You think he's a little overprotective?" Stan asked.

"A little would be OK. Excessive is not OK. He already had Fort Knox locks installed on all my house doors. I now have extensive alarms on all doors and windows that go off if a fly comes nearby. There are also surveillance cameras on all sides of my house. I knew about all that but not about the bodyguards," Lynn said.

"I'm guessing, though, this guy who is trying to discredit you doesn't know about any of the protection that's set up at your house," Jim said. "It might be good if he tried to break in. Chances are he would try something after you left for work in the morning."

"We could set a trap," Stan said. "Let's do a video call with your brother and see what we can devise.

"Works for me," Lynn said. "I'm getting very tired of all these attacks. Let's do it. First, let me have a word or two with my brother."

CHAPTER 46

When Lynn was back at her office, she called George.

"Good morning, Sis. How's your day going?" George asked.

"I was meeting with Stan and Jim from Security about this perpetrator. In the conversation, I found out you have hired someone to bodyguard me! I have my stick ready to beat you!" Lynn said.

"I'm only protecting my little sister. Who could get upset about that?" George said in his most innocent-sounding voice.

"You are impossible, but I still love you," Lynn said, laughing. "You know that innocent voice always makes me laugh."

"That's what I was going for," George said, laughing himself. "It's your fault I hired the bodyguards. You wouldn't stay with mom or me, and if I had asked you about the bodyguards, you would have said no. You gave me no choice. I'm innocent here!"

"Seems to me I've heard these innocent pleads before," Lynn replied. "Please, please do not do something like this again. Promise!!!"

"OK, if you insist. I won't ever hire bodyguards without letting you know again," George said.

"I also want you to promise never will you do anything that involves me without first letting me know. It's not just bodyguards," Lynn said.

"All right. I promise not to do anything that involves you without letting you know first. Man, you create a hard bargain," George replied reluctantly.

"So, what's going on with finding this perpetrator? Do we get to find and torture him?" George asked.

"George, you promised to behave. Just find – no torture," Lynn replied.

"OK," George said in the same voice 8-year-old Bernie uses.

"Impossible," Lynn said. "Here is what is going on. This morning, after a code last night, I checked the crash cart they used after the pharmacist refilled it. All the equipment and meds were there. A few hours later, a pharmacist came to check both crash carts for outdated meds and so forth. The diazepam, better known as valium, was missing. I became a suspect right away."

"Trouble follows you, my dear sister. Yikes!" George said.

"Fortunately, both Stan and Jim knew about this perpetrator and checked the surveillance tapes of the crash cart with the missing diazepam, my office hallway, and my care," Lynn explained.

"They are really good guys," George said.

"For sure. Stan and Jim saw a guy wearing a plaid shirt on the surveillance films near the crash cart. They also picked him up on different cameras, trying to enter my office and trying to break into my car. He was unsuccessful in all attempts," Lynn said. "They think he might be getting desperate."

"Do they think he might try planting the valium in your house? Do they want to do a sting using my bodyguards?" George asked.

"I'm not sure exactly what they want to do, but they want to zoom with you about how to carry out a trap. You in? Although I know that's a silly question," Lynn said.

"I'll be in touch after I talk to Stan and Jim. Here I thought it would just be a dull day at the office," George said.

"You are the only person I know who runs a multi-million-dollar business and finds it dull," Lynn replied.

"I hire good people. The business runs itself now. I need something more exciting upon which to apply my creative energy!" George replied.

"Just remember your promise to me not to apply those creative ideas to my life without letting me know!" Lynn said emphatically. "You know I love you."

"OK, OK. Such a killjoy, but I love you, too." George said and hung up.

Lynn looked over her to-do list for the day. Most of it was paperwork she decided to put off.

She heard Beatrice knock on the door.

"Come on in, Beatrice. How's it going on the unit?"

"It's stable. All the patients are stable or being discharged home or transferred to one of the units. Tonight, being Friday night, will be crazy as usual. When they make this hospital a Level 1 trauma center, it will be a different place," Beatrice said.

"How did you hear the administration want to make it a level 1 trauma center?" Lynn asked.

"There always have been rumors they might want to do that but lately people are talking about hiring someone to run it. I think the administration wants patients who are not true emergencies to go to the acute care clinics instead of here. Our ED will only have full blown emergency cases – tough ones at that," Beatrice said.

"I thought that was being kept on the quiet," Lynn said. "Can you think back to where you heard that much detail?"

"I'm not sure. You know what a rumor mill this hospital is. Let me give that some thought. Is that important?" Beatrice asked.

"It might be. Are you ready to leave and enjoy your weekend? What's on your schedule for fun?" Lynn asked.

She wanted to get off the topic of the plans for developing a Level 1 trauma center before she got asked if she's in line for position as director.

"I know Christmas shopping is on the schedule. The kids want to talk to Santa, too. I love those pictures. They are growing up so fast, soon they will have nothing to do with Santa," Beatrice said.

"Oh, I don't know about that. George and I had our pictures taken with Santa for our parents when we were both in college. It was a hoot," Lynn said.

"What an idea for my parents. I'm going to see if my sister and brother will do that with me. Thanks for that tip," Beatrice said. "Have a fun weekend."

Lynn decided to leave, also. It had been a long but optimistic day. She decided to ride the optimism and go shopping for a dress to wear to dinner with Peter.

I hope he has good news about stopping Virginia and her antics, she thought.

CHAPTER 47

Lynn woke up Saturday morning full of energy. Finally, this is the day she and Peter will be together again; at least, that's what she hoped for. She was drinking her coffee in the kitchen when her phone dinged.

Are we still on for dinner tonight? the text from Peter read.

Definitely! I can't wait to see you, Lynn answered.

I am so happy to hear that. I miss you. I'll pick you up at 7:00 if that works for you. I have good news, too. Peter texted back.

7:00 is great. See you then. Looking forward to hearing the good news. I have some, too.

Lynn started cleaning her house when her phone rang!

"Hi, George. What's happening?" Lynn asked.

"The kids want to know when you will finish the story you were reading. Can you do dinner tonight?" George asked.

"I have a date tonight," Lynn said.

"What? Have you met someone else already? I know you're gorgeous, but man, that's fast," George said.

"Wouldn't you be surprised to know whom I'm having dinner with this evening," Lynn replied.

"Now you are just getting even with me for my body-guards. You know I was just keeping you safe," George said. "Isn't forgiveness a virtue?"

"All right, I'll let it go," Lynn said. She tried to control laughing out loud.

"Nice to be off the hot seat," George said. "So, who is the lucky fellow taking you to dinner tonight?"

"It's Peter. That was our agreement about when to see each other. He's met with his lawyer, and we will talk about what the lawyer says. I'll also be able to fill him in on what Stan and Jim saw on the surveillance films. Did you guys come up with a plan to catch that guy?" Lynn asked.

"We did the zoom meeting. We have a tentative plan but need to work out some extra details. We will catch him. Don't you worry," George said assuredly. "We are the modern A-team!"

Lynn laughed. "I can see it all now. If you say, 'I love it when a plan comes together,' I'm taking out my stick. Seriously, though, be careful. This guy could be getting desperate and dangerous," Lynn said.

"We will be careful. Don't worry. How about coming over for dinner tomorrow night? You can fill us in on what's happening on Peter's end and finish reading the story to the kids. They will be excited," George said.

"Sounds good. What can I bring?" Lynn asked.

"You are always welcome to bring Peter. I would like that," George said.

"I'll see how it goes tonight. That's a maybe," Lynn said.

"All right, Sis. I hope it goes well. I know it's been tough on both of you. I don't like seeing both of you so unhappy. Good luck!" George said.

"One way or another, I'll fill you in tomorrow at your house," Lynn said. "Thanks for being there for me."

"I'm always here for you, Sis," George said.

At 7:00 pm, when Peter rang her doorbell, Lynn's house was clean, and she was dressed for the date. She bought a satin smocked-cuff blouse in plum berry at Chico's with her straight black skirt.

"Wow!" Peter said after Lynn opened the door. "You look amazing. It's been too long not seeing you."

He hesitated to kiss Lynn until she took his hand and came toward him. They both welcomed the kiss.

"I'm ready. I just need my coat," Lynn said.

They held hands, walking to the car.

"Before I get into your car, can I be assured the guy who calls himself Bruce won't visit us in the restaurant?" Lynn asked.

"I'm hoping he is in jail by now. But yes, you can be assured he won't be there according to what the lawyers have said," Peter responded.

"Thank you and your lawyers. I hope never to go through all this again," Lynn said.

Peter reached over to squeeze her hand.

"Much better days are coming," Peter said.

"Mexican food near the beach. Great choice. I love this place," Lynn said as they drove closer to the restaurant.

"I thought about something a little more romantic, but I remembered you like Mexican food. I also thought we could both use a romantic place that was fun," Peter said.

The receptionist took Peter and Lynn to a table for four near the windows overlooking the ocean. She quickly removed the extra two settings.

"Do you know someone who works here?" Lynn asked.

"As a matter of fact, I operated on the owner's son, who had a leg fracture. The kid is doing great, too. The owner told me I always will have the best table in the house whenever I come here. So, here we are," Peter said.

"You are definitely the man to know and to hang out with," Lynn said, laughing.

Their waiter came over with a bottle of champagne that he opened, then poured Peter and Lynn a glass, leaving the rest of the bottle in the wine cooler.

"Here's to us seeing each other again. I can't begin to tell you how happy I am to be out to dinner with you. This separation has been torture. Here's to us," Peter said, toasting with his glass.

"I so miss you dropping by my office with your coffee cups. None of my days seem as happy without seeing you first," Lynn said.

"I always knew the coffee got me into your office with deep appreciation," Peter said, smiling.

Lynn ordered her fish tacos which meant they were filled with cod and topped with salsa, avocado, cotija cheese, and a yogurt Ranch dressing. Peter ordered the burritos stuffed with black beans, Mexican rice, guacamole, sour cream, and ground beef. After dinner and more champagne, Peter asked Lynn if she was ready to hear what the lawyer had to say.

"I'm primed and ready," she said, laughing, thinking it's been a while since she was so happy.

CHAPTER 48

Peter began describing his arrangement with his lawyer.

"Of course, I told my lawyer and his private investigator all the shenanigans Virginia had pulled, not only with you and me but also with another woman that I had had a few dates with before we started going out," Peter said.

"We talked for a while. The investigator came over and picked up the black negligee. I had thrown out the red one a long time ago. I also sent them both the picture of 'Bruce.' I wrote out the times, dates, and locations of each event. I also included the information about the roses you were sent from 'Bruce'. He was happy you had kept and given me the card that came with the flowers," Peter explained.

"Sounds good. What happened then?" Lynn asked.

"I met with them later in the week. They found Virginia's fingerprints on the negligee. 'Bruce' is really Donald Olson, Virginia's cousin's husband. Apparently, this cousin was struggling financially, and Virginia offered to pay her husband $5,000 to carry out this subterfuge," Peter said with a hint of anger.

"Wow! she was serious with that amount of money," Lynn said.

"She's a woman who wants what she wants and will go to extremes to get it," Peter said.

"The lawyer filed for a restraining order against Virginia. She is charged with harassment leading to emotional distress, embarrassment, and harassing a new partner. Because I am a physician in the community, this type of behavior makes me look bad and can not only affect me emotionally, and it also can reduce the confidence people have in me to practice my profession," Peter said.

"All of that is certainly true. It's true for me, too," Lynn said.

"I tried keeping your name out of it. The lawyer didn't think your name needed to be mentioned," Peter added. "However, if you want to get involved, we can include you, too."

"The other good news is this lawyer is also the one who handled my divorce. He has all the background information about Virginia and me from before the divorce," Peter explained.

"Feel free to use my name. I'll provide whatever support you need. What does the restraining order do?" Lynn asked. "Don't you need to see each other when you drop off and pick up Hanna?"

"That's a little tricky. Usually, the restraining order says no direct contact and not being within x number of feet from each other. I or my designee can pick up and drop off Hanna, but Virginia can't come anywhere near my house, my office, or any place like the hospital where she knows I will be," Peter explained.

"If I remember correctly from working with patients, when they filed for a restraining order, the defendant, in this case, Virginia, will get a copy and the date for the court hearing. It may take a few days for the court hearing. Is that what's happening?" Lynn asked.

"Yes, the court hearing is set for next Monday at 10:00 am. What I also found out is that if someone is charged and convicted of harassment, the first offense is a Class A1 misdemeanor, which can be up to one year in prison. If there's a restraining order and the person keeps up the harassment, the charge becomes a felony. There's some incentive for Virginia to stay away," Peter said. "The other incentive is that some court cases make it into the press, especially if it includes information about a celebrity. The last thing Virginia wants is her name being muddied and her friends finding out about it."

"I'm sorry, Peter, you are going through this, too. You deserve better," Lynn said.

"I have better," Peter said, reaching over the table to hold Lynn's hand. "You are the best thing that has happened to me in years. Now tell me your news."

"I don't know if you heard through the hospital grapevine that some diazepam was missing from one of our crash carts. I was the last one to inspect the cart because of a code the night before. The pharmacist had replaced all the meds before I did my inspection. Then the pharmacist came back later to do the typical med inspection to replace any outdated meds. That's when they found the diazepam was missing," Lynn explained.

"Was the finger being pointed at you? Let's see, you are anxious, maybe depressed a little, and diazepam would be helpful?" Peter asked.

"Yep, you got the message. Fortunately, security and Stan, and most of the people in the ED know I was being harassed. Jim in security and Stan looked at the surveillance cameras around the crash cart, my office, and my car. They called me downstairs to look at what they found," Lynn said.

"Good for them. That was wise. I know they changed the locks on your office doors and put surveillance cameras in the hall. What did they do to your car?" Peter asked.

"I now park in a place in front of surveillance cameras," Lynn said.

"OK, I got it. Good for those guys to be on top of everything," Peter said. "Ordinarily, I love a good mystery, but being one of the characters takes away from the fun. What did they find on the tapes?"

Lynn laughed. She thought how great it was to be even just conversing with Peter.

"This crash cart was right behind the nurses' station. In the first video, you see the nurses going back and forth.

Also, they spotted a guy with a navy, light blue, and white checkered shirt there. There's only a glimpse of that shirt. The second video shows a guy with a baseball cap, a jacket, and a glimpse of the same shirt trying to break into my office. He is unsuccessful. Then the same person, apparently, tries to break into my car, but the alarm goes off. You never can see the fellow's face, but they figure he's about 5'10" with an average build," Lynn explained.

"Peter, what's the matter? You look ashen," Lynn asked.

"I have a navy, light blue, and white checkered shirt that Virginia bought me a few years ago," Peter explained.

"What! How is that possible? I know you weren't on the videos because you are a lot taller, and you wouldn't steal anything from a crash cart," Lynn said. "Unless they think I needed the medication, and if you wrote me a prescription, that would make you look like you were inappropriately treating me."

"But maybe, just maybe, someone wants us to think it was me, especially if they didn't know about the surveillance around your office and your car. Is it OK to stop at my house so you can look at my shirt?" Peter asked. "Let's see if you think it's the same design as the shirt in the videos."

"It will be my pleasure," Lynn said.

CHAPTER 49

"It is getting cold. This is supposed to be the warm south," Lynn said as they approached Peter's house.

"Let's get into the house. I'll start a fire in the fireplace," Peter said.

Both Lynn and Peter quickly ran into the house out of the cold. As promised, there was soon a substantial fire in the fireplace that made one feel snuggly and warm.

"Here's my checkered shirt," Peter said. "Does it look like the one you saw in the videos?"

"The videos only show a small section of the shirt, but it looks like the same design, except your shirt, has this red line on it. I don't remember that from the videos. Let me look at the label," Lynn said.

"Virginia only bought me shirts from Montgomery's downtown. She wanted me to look stylish all the time. Somehow, she thought the shirts from there would help. I am who I am. Being stylish isn't exactly my strong suit." Peter smiled. "I'm glad you don't worry about me being stylish."

"You always dress well. More important though is I feel like you are my best friend," Lynn said, looking at Peter. "I hated not seeing you."

"Taking the break was tough. I barely got through the days. I had to drag myself to work every day," Peter said with his head hung down and the saddest face Lynn had seen him make.

"Are you sure you are not at least part Russian? That's an awful lot of Russian angst," Lynn laughed.

"OK. To cheer you and me up, I'll make hot chocolate with marshmallows. Let's sit on the couch before the fire," Peter replied with a smile.

"It seems like we are making progress identifying whoever is tormenting you and me," Peter said. "What do you think?"

"I agree. Let's see what we know and what's being done. We know someone who works in the hospital is the one sabotaging me. He's wearing a shirt like the one you own. Is the shirt part of his plot, or is it incidental? We certainly could be getting suspicious of everything," Lynn said.

"Paranoia is easy to acquire in these circumstances. Someone could go to Montgomery's and see if they will tell us who bought a shirt like that one recently," Peter suggested. "If it turns out to be Virginia, we will know she's working with this guy on the video. George said something like that when he had a zoom meeting with Stan and Jim."

"By the way, George invited me to come to dinner tomorrow evening. When I asked if I could bring something, he suggested I bring you. What do you think?" Lynn asked. "This hot chocolate is delicious, by the way. It is just right for a cold evening like this."

"Dinner with you and George tomorrow sounds great. We can hash through some of this stuff with him. I think he's a little bored, too," Peter said.

"A little bored? He's jumping at all opportunities that provide some excitement. I must warn you; he now thinks he's like George Pepard, the A-team captain, getting involved with finding out who is harassing me. Did you know he hired someone to guard my house when I was home?" Lynn asked.

"No, I hadn't heard that," Peter laughed. "I can see him doing that. He is very protective of you. He's always been a good guy as long as I have known him," Peter said. "How are you doing now with all this stuff?"

"Better now that I feel protected and some of the investigations are falling into place. I certainly feel less nervous being out with you now that you and your lawyer are restraining Virginia. Thank you for doing that," Lynn said.

"As hard as it was to stop seeing you, I'm glad you needed her to be stopped. I can't have her harassing me and anyone I date for the rest of my life. We got divorced because she was always screaming and yelling at me. When she did that at the hospital, it was also embarrassing. She's got to be stopped," Peter said with emphasis.

"I'm glad you feel that way. I also feel good that I probably won't have to testify in court and that Stan, the guys in the security office, and my brother are working on catching the guy at the hospital. I have a problem with one thing at the hospital," Lynn said.

"What can I help you with?" Peter said.

"Have you heard the rumors about the hospital administrators wanting the hospital to become a Type 1 trauma center?" Lynn asked.

"Yep. Everyone is talking about it," Peter answered.

"Remember me telling you Dr. Brown called me into his office to talk to me about these changes they want to make? I have until after the first to let him know if I am interested in the job to cover the ED and the outpatient clinics," Lynn explained.

"I remember you saying something about it. Are you thinking of taking that job?" Peter asked.

"I'm not sure yet but in the meantime, maybe whoever is trying to make me look bad is someone who wants that job," Lynn said. "Or at least doesn't want me to have it."

Lynn thought the look on Peter's face could have been illustrated by having a lightbulb above it.

"That makes so much sense," Peter said. "You would be the most likely candidate, but someone might easily think he would be the next candidate if you were eliminated from the running. Are you thinking it might be Jim Walker?"

"He fits the description of the guy on the video, and he has a degree in computer science," Lynn said. "But he's kind of a laid-back guy. I'm not sure he even likes the job he has now. I also don't think he has emergency department experience."

Lynn stopped to take a few bites of her French toast and a sip of her coffee.

"Dr. Brown asked me to keep this quiet, but it seems that the rumor mill has picked up on knowing about going for the Level I trauma center," Lynn added.

"Maybe, I'm not reading you correctly, but you don't seem overly enthusiastic about being that big-time director," Peter said.

"Right now, I still have some opportunities to talk with patients. Moving a level or two up the administrative ranks might take those opportunities away from me. That job will involve more paperwork, more supervision of staff, and calculating more statistics about what kind of patients we are seeing in both areas. I can do those things, but I'm not sure my heart will be in it," Lynn said.

"That's a big decision you need to make. Can we talk more about it tomorrow over breakfast?" Peter asked.

"Is that your way of asking me to stay over?" Lynn responded.

"Separate rooms!" Peter said quickly. "I'll even check the bedroom to ensure nothing is hidden in the sheets. I miss you so much. I would love to wake up knowing you are still here tomorrow morning."

"That sounds wonderful to me, too," Lynn said.

CHAPTER 50

Lynn woke up the next morning to the smell of French toast and coffee. *What a way to start the day*, she thought.

"Good morning, Sunshine," Peter said when Lynn came into the kitchen area. "I hope you slept well."

"I was out as soon as my head hit the pillow. I haven't been this relaxed in months; it seems like," Lynn said.

"That's a good sign. I'm feeling better just being able to spend time with you. When I'm with you, everything feels like it's in place. It's so easy being together," Peter said. "I never knew this was even possible."

"I'm glad because it was a miserable time without you dropping in and us spending time together. It is better together," Lynn said.

"So, does that mean we can keep seeing each other from now on," Peter asked.

"I sure would like that," Lynn said.

Peter came over and took Lynn into his arms. They held each other for a few minutes until Lynn suggested the French toast might be burning.

"Boy, that was close!" Peter said, putting the rescued French toast on each of their plates. "I have something to ask you."

"Ask away," Lynn said.

"I'm going to New York for a few days for a training program. A doctor at a hospital in New York City is giving a course on bio-printed bones and joints. We should be able to use 3D-printed implants that fit better than the ones we are using now. I want to see what that involves and talk to other docs about using that technology. I, of course, would love to have you come to the city with me," Peter said. "It seems to me both of us could use a break from all this tension we have been experiencing."

"Hum. Christmas shopping in New York sounds delightful. How far would we be from Bloomies?" Lynn asked.

"We can stay close by if you want. I can always take a taxi, uber, or subway to the hospital. There's Hotel 57, that's only a few blocks from Bloomies. We also would be close to the Metropolitan Art Museum and other cool places to see," Peter said.

"When are you scheduled to go to this workshop?" Lynn asked.

"It starts next Friday and Saturday," Peter explained. "We could leave Thursday night to get there the night before and come back on Saturday or Sunday, depending on if we want to spend an extra day in the city," Peter explained.

"That sounds so delightful. My only possible hiccup would be the trial of the guy who tossed the abused woman out of the car in front of the ED. I'm not scheduled to be a witness, but they asked me to stand by in case they need me. Let me ask Stan tomorrow how that's going and if they have a trial date yet," Lynn said.

"OK, let me know as soon as you know, and I'll make plane reservations. How's the French toast?" Peter asked.

"It's delicious, as is the coffee. But coffee is always good when you bring it," Lynn said.

"Thank you so much," Peter said with a bow as he got up to refresh their coffee cups. "What time are we expected at George's house?"

"Let me text him to let him know you have agreed to come, too. He'll be happy about that," Lynn said.

"Peter? Who is this Peter that you want to bring to my house?" George responded.

"Tell him I'm some poor down-and-out fellow you feel sorry for," Peter said after Lynn showed him George's text.

"Oh, him," George said. "OK, we will let him in. Can you guys get here around 6:00?"

"We will be there with the proverbial bells on," Lynn said.

"Happy for you guys," George said.

"How about I drop you off at your house, so you can get ready for tonight and do what you need to do? I can pick you up before we go to George's," Peter offered.

"Perfect," Lynn said.

When Lynn got home, she decided to call Stan. Somehow having Stan living in an adjacent neighborhood made it OK to call him on a Sunday.

"Stan, I know it's the weekend, but I'm tentatively planning to go away this Thursday and want to know when the trial date will be. Give me a call if you have the time and inclination," Lynn said to Stan's phone.

Lynn was cleaning her kitchen and making a grocery list when her phone rang. It was Stan.

"Hi, Stan. Sorry to bother you on a Sunday," Lynn said.

"Not a problem. I was just planning Christmas activities with some relatives. There's a lot that has happened with the human trafficking case, but I'm not comfortable talking on the phone about it. I know you are OK going away for a long weekend. If you want to meet up now, I can fill you in on the details," Stan said.

As much as Lynn wanted to know what was going on with that case, she had read enough romance novels to know that meeting up with another guy when you were involved with someone else did not usually turn out to be a good idea.

She knew the chances that Peter would see her with Stan out for coffee and even care was slim, but why take a chance? she thought.

"I'm heading over to my brother's house soon. Can we meet tomorrow? I'm very interested in knowing what's going on," Lynn said to Stan.

"Great. I'll see you tomorrow," Stan said. "How about your office around 1:00? This needs to be said in a quiet place."

"That sounds fine. See you then," Lynn said.

CHAPTER 51

W*hat to wear, what to wear?* Lynn said to herself. Going to her brother's house was informal, but she also wanted to look good now that she and Peter are seeing each other again.

She looked at her bed, which now had two dresses, three pairs of pants with matching tops, and two skirts hiding somewhere under the clothes.

I don't know what to wear, she said to herself.

Finally, she settled on her festive light blue and navy Fair Isle pullover sweater and her jeans. She saw the sweater as being feminine, with a soft and drapey feel. The jeans, she thought, added a little sex appeal.

"Wow! you look great," Peter said as he came into her house, followed by a wolf whistle.

"Just the reaction I was going for," Lynn admitted as they both laughed and kissed.

"I have some good news," Lynn said in the car.

"Tell me," Peter said.

"I talked to Stan, and he said there is no trial date set for this week. He hinted that there may not be a trial. I'm meeting with him tomorrow in my office to hear more details," Lynn explained.

"So, you can come with me to New York?" Peter asked.

"I will happily be your companion for those days," Lynn said. "I'm even OK with staying until Sunday if that's what you want."

"That is excellent news. I'll make flight and hotel reservations. Thank you for coming with me. It will make the weekend enjoyable," Peter said as he squeezed Lynn's hand.

"This is great for me, too. I can get a lot of my Christmas shopping done in Bloomies, one of my favorite NYC stores," Lynn said. "They also have the best-frozen yogurt I've ever tasted."

"You probably know more about restaurants in NYC than I do," Peter suggested. "Feel free to make dinner reservations for Friday and Saturday if you want. Fancy places are fine."

"See if you think this might be fun. There are several restaurants where TV shows and movies have taken place. You can sit there and picture the scenes from the shows," Lynn suggested. "Most are not fancy but unique."

Peter looked over at Lynn with an expression she had not seen before. She couldn't tell what it meant. It was like being surprised and pained at the same time.

"I'm happy to find high-class restaurants if that suits you better," she said. "There are plenty of those in New York."

"I'm constantly amazed at how easy and how much fun it is being with you. Virginia would have insisted on going to the most elegant and expensive restaurant so she could be seen with celebrities. It would have been hell if I couldn't make that happen," Peter explained. "Life was always stressful, no matter where we were and what we did. With you, life is fun and loving. Thank you for that."

"I'm just being me. OK, so what are your favorite TV shows and movies that happened here in the city? I'll see what I can do about getting reservations at those restaurants," Lynn said.

"Let me think," Peter said. "I think Seinfeld was filmed here. Wasn't When Harry Met Sally filmed here, too?"

"Yes, those two were filmed in the city. The Rainbow Room is also a place mentioned in Friends, Will and Grace, and How I met your mother. Serendipity 3 is a dessert restaurant where the movie Serendipity with John Cusack and Kate Beckinsale was filmed. It's on 60th street, close to where we will be staying," Lynn suggested.

"Whatever you pick, I know they will be fine," Peter said.

George was standing outside near the front door when Lynn and Peter arrived.

"Glad you two could make it," George said. He and Peter did their usual weird, complicated college handshake.

"You two are strange sometimes," Angie said as they entered the house. "Don't you think, Lynn?"

"Yes, I do, but you can't help but love them. Pathetic can be appealing," Lynn said.

"Hey," Peter and George said in unison.

"I prefer creative," George said.

"Me, too, and engaging," Peter added.

"We have wine and champagne on the counter," Angie said. "Help yourselves."

"Aunty Lynn and Dr. Pete are here," Bernie yelled out to his siblings. The three of them ran to Lynn and Peter with open arms for hugs.

"Come see the puzzle we are putting together," Edison said, grabbing Lynn's hand.

"We could use some help," Eloise added, pleading with Peter.

After a delicious meal of a rib roast, a Caprese salad, mashed potatoes, and asparagus, the children went to finish their puzzles.

"OK, guys, what has happened? You two look happy. Something is going on," George said.

Lynn gestured with her hand extended to Peter to begin.

"I have met with my lawyer, and he's filed a restraining order against Virginia. We are going to court tomorrow to finish that filing. Virginia and her lawyer will be there. The good news is they found Virginia's fingerprints on the black negligee that she stuffed in between the sheets in my bed.

They also located the fake 'Bruce,' who is Virginia's cousin's husband. To avoid a court case, he's willing to testify. Virginia hired him to follow me and approach us when Lynn and I are together," Peter explained.

"All right! That's good stuff," George said.

"Have you talked with Stan and Jim about the checkered shirt guy?" Lynn asked George.

"Yes, he filled me in on those videos. They are getting close to finding this guy," George says. "We are still working on a way to trap him."

"We have something to add to that," Peter said. "I have a checkered shirt like the one Lynn said the suspect was wearing. Lynn said mine had a red stripe through it that she didn't think was on those videos. Here's a picture of my shirt. Virginia bought it for me just before our divorce."

"Oh, oh. Should we add Peter here to the suspect list?" George asked Lynn.

"George, stop teasing Peter," Angie piped in.

"No, not Peter, but maybe Virginia is in cahoots with someone in the hospital and bought him a shirt like Peter's to throw suspicion on him," Lynn said.

"I think you two should run away somewhere without a forwarding address. You deserve better," George said.

"We are going to New York City at the end of the week," Peter said, holding Lynn's hand.

"Aunty, Lynn. Aunty, Lynn. Will you come and read us the rest of the story you started?" Bernie asked, standing next to his brother and sister near the entrance to the living room. All were dressed in their pajamas.

"I'll be right there," Lynn said. "I'll be back in a bit," Lynn said to the adults.

"Have fun. Peter and I can reminisce about the old days," George said, "and maybe the future ones.

CHAPTER 52

"Where did we leave off in the book?" Lynn asked. The three children were all snuggled in on two of the three twin beds.

"I think we should start all over because I've forgotten parts of the story," Eloise suggested.

"I don't want to listen to the beginning again. I remember where we left off. The three kids, like us, were shopping in Bloomies with their grandmother for a gift for their mother. So far, they haven't bought anything because they didn't know what colors their mom likes and what things she likes. That's important to know when you are buying someone a gift. They were going up the escalator to the Christmas decorations part of the store," Bernie said with great assuredness.

"Sounds right, Bernie. Good job! Here's the picture of the decorations section of the store," Lynn said.

"There's a lot of stuff there," Edison commented.

Lynn started reading.

"What kind of decorations does your mom like?" Grandmother asked.

"Mom likes elf stuff. We have some elf stuff in the house," Timothy said.

"Great!" Grandmother said. "Anyone else know something she likes?"

"She likes snow globes," Suzy said. "She's always shaking the one she has of a gazebo."

"She also likes those funny-looking people. Most of the time, you can only see their noses. They have a pointy hat," Joey said.

"The gnomes. You are right she likes gnomes. We are off to a good start," Grandmother said.

Lynn turns the page. It looks like here is where they start finding things.

"Here is the elf section," Grandmother said. "Timothy, do you see anything your mom might like here?"

"She has some stuffed elves already. I don't think she would like a shirt with elves on it. Here's a package of two wine glasses with elves on them. I know she and dad don't have them," Timothy said. "What do you think, Grandmother?"

"I think the elf wine glasses would be perfect," Grandmother said.

Lynn turns the page. "Look at all those snow globes on this page," Eloise said. "I like this page."

"Now, Suzy, let's see if we can find a snow globe that your mom would like," Grandmother said.

"Here's one with a Christmas tree in it. Here's another one with Santa and another one with a snowman. But what would Mom like, right Grandmother?" Suzy asked.

"You are right on target," Grandmother said.

"Here is one with three snowmen. It looks like two boy snowmen and one girl. They look like us. I think Mom would like that," Suzy said.

"Then, let's put that one in our basket," Grandmother said.

"But where are the gnomes?" Joey asked.

Lynn turned the page.

"They are cute and strange at the same time," Joey said. "They have gnomes on the shower curtains. That's weird. Here are two gnomes that look a little alike, but mom has something like them. Here are some dish towels with gnomes on them. Mom doesn't have them, and she's always in the kitchen. That will be cheery for her."

"Excellent idea," Grandma said. "Put them in the basket, and now we can pay for these gifts and then go and get a snack."

Lynn turns the page, with grandmother and the three children sitting at a table drinking hot chocolate with marshmallows and eating Christmas cookies and ice cream.

"This is delicious," Suzy said. "Who knew Christmas shopping could be such fun?"

"It's work, though," Timothy said. "You need to do homework first and find out what people like before you can buy them a gift."

The grandmother is smiling broadly on the page.

"Yes, what he said," Joey said, pointing to Timothy. "But also, it feels good inside to buy something special for someone else."

"You know what else feels good?" Grandmother asked.

"What?" All three grandchildren asked in unison.

"Going Christmas shopping with my grandchildren. It's a wonderful time."

"The end," Lynn said, turning to the last page, which has a picture of the grandmother and the three children saying Merry Christmas to all and to all a good night.

"I like that story," Eloise said. "Will you read it again the next time you come visit?"

"I'll be happy, too," Lynn said. "But I have a question for you three."

"What's the question?" Bernie asked a little suspiciously.

"Dr. Pete is attending a training program in New York City at the end of this week. He invited me to come with him," Lynn explained.

"Are you Dr. Pete's girlfriend?" Bernie asked.

"You might say that," Lynn replied.

"OK, just checking," Bernie said. "I like Dr. Pete. He and dad are good friends, but they do that strange handshake. Grown-ups do strange things sometimes."

Lynn laughed.

"I so agree with you, Bernie. We are staying on the upper East side in New York City in a hotel near Bloomies. I'll show you where that is in a minute on a map. You know what I was thinking?" Lynn asked.

Bernie, Edison, and Eloise were quiet for a minute.

"You could take us with you to New York City?" Bernie asked.

"That's a good idea for a future trip, but not this trip," Lynn said.

"I know," Edison said. "You could buy Mom the same presents the kids bought in the book."

"That's exactly what I was thinking," Lynn said. "Does your mom like elves, snow globes, and gnomes?"

"I know she likes snow globes, so those would be good," Eloise said.

"She does the elves on the shelf every year. I'll bet she likes elves," Bernie said.

"She doesn't have any gnomes, but.... she did talk about how much she liked Mrs. Ardmore's gnomes," Edison said.

"I say go for it," Bernie said. "What's the worst that can happen?"

Lynn smiled at Bernie's comments since she had heard her brother say those exact words many times. That acorn is listening to that tree, she thought.

"What he said," Edison agreed. Eloise shook her head yes.

All four piled their hands on top of each other.

With smiles on their faces, the three children drifted off to sleep.

Lynn and Peter said their goodbyes to George and Angie, thanking them for dinner. George gave Lynn a thumbs-up and a big smile. She knew he was happy seeing Peter and her together.

CHAPTER 53

"How was your chat with George?" Lynn asked Peter on the drive back to her house.

"It was fine. It's good to catch up with George and Angie and discuss future plans. They are good people and fun, too. They have seen me through some dark days," Peter said.

"Me, too," Lynn said. Lynn wondered what dark days Peter was talking about. Maybe, getting divorced from Virginia.

"However, it looks like our days are getting brighter," Peter said, reaching to hold Lynn's hand. "As you know, I won't be at work tomorrow morning because I'll be in court. I don't know how long that's going to last. I'm also on call tomorrow night," Peter explained.

"I'm going to have my usual Monday, whatever that is. Give me a call when you can, and we will go over our respective days," Lynn said. "How does that sound?"

"Wonderful. I love the feeling of being connected with you," Peter said. "It just seems to work without any hassle."

"Maybe I'm just on my good behavior," Lynn said in a teasing tone.

"George did say something about you beating him with a stick now and then," Peter said, trying to control a smile.

"He started the stick-beating approach by mentioning to my mother that I would do it to him. All I said to him was it sounded like a good idea on some occasions," Lynn said, smiling. "You are too nice to beat with a stick. Tickling with a feather might be better."

"We will have to try that out sometime," Peter said, smiling.

Peter and Lynn parted company after a kiss at her door and promising to be in touch the next day. They knew there were still hurdles to climb, but now they were together again, hopeful but not yet with complete confidence that the togetherness would last.

The next morning Lynn was up early and feeling energized. It was the best she had felt in over a week.

"How was the weekend?" Lynn asked Beatrice the next morning when she arrived at the ED.

"The ED was busy this weekend. We had four drug overdoses, one of which was an attempted suicide. Holiday time is joyous for some and the entrance to the pit of depression for others," Beatrice said. "We had one frostbite case, two asthma attacks, five cases of the flu, and four slip and falls, two of which had fractures. In addition, we had nonurgent cases of high blood pressure, bloody noses, and diabetic over and under doses of insulin.

"That was busy. The holiday season has begun. Who is here now, this beautiful Monday morning?" Lynn asked.

Beatrice looked at Lynn carefully. "You look happier this morning. How was your weekend before we get into patients?"

"It was a good weekend. I got to finish a lovely Christmas story to my brother's three kids," Lynn said.

"Ok, if that's all you are giving me, but I know other good things probably happened," Beatrice said. "Back to the ED. This morning we have another attempted suicide. It's a 38-year-old married woman. She's alert and oriented; right now, the doctor, husband, and patient are discussing follow-up care. The patient wants to go home, but the husband favors a psychiatric admission. He's afraid she'll try again if she doesn't get help."

"That's so tough. I should start the report on suicide attempts so far this year. It always peaks in April, May, and June. Usually, November and December are lower. I need to check if that's still happening this year," Lynn said.

"That's surprising. I'd think suicide attempts would be happening more near the holidays," Beatrice said.

"The theory is that depressed people are surrounded more by others who are down because of the weather in the winter. They can also hibernate more and not face many interactions except for the holidays. They don't even need to go shopping because of online ordering. In the spring, the people who are depressed because of the weather perk up, while the others stay depressed. The social pressures increase in the spring, which can lead to stress. They see others enjoying life and feel theirs is just filled with unhappiness," Lynn explained.

"We don't seem to have too many suicide attempts," Beatrice said.

"That's also where the theories break down a little. We have milder weather almost all year round, so you would think we would have more suicides, but we are in the bottom 20% of the states with suicide deaths. That's why it's good to keep our own statistics," Lynn said, "to know exactly what we see in the ED."

"Make sense. The other patients we have are an elderly gentleman who is going for surgery for a fractured patella. He fell this morning. I noticed Dr. Pete is not around today," Beatrice said.

"Yes, he told me he's not going to be here this morning," Lynn said, smiling at Beatrice's attempt to get an update on their relationship.

"I see. You two are talking again," Beatrice said. "I'm glad."

"Me, too," Lynn said. "Do me a favor and keep it off the grapevine?"

"Lips are sealed," Beatrice said, running a pretend zipper across her mouth.

"Stan is meeting with me at 1:00. "I'd like to avoid any interruptions, if possible," Lynn said.

"You got it," Beatrice said and went back to check on her patients.

Lynn pulled out her to-do list. Even though it was only December, she liked to get a head start on her annual statistics. She didn't mind doing them but wondered how she would feel doing much more of them. She knew this new job would have even more paperwork if she decided to take it. She recognized she wasn't jumping for joy about this new opportunity. She knew she needed to pay attention to those feelings.

CHAPTER 54

"I so appreciate you are always on time," Lynn said to Stan when he showed up for their 1:00 pm meeting.

"Being on time was drilled into me by my parents and the nuns at Catholic school. I think once I added being late as one of my sins in the confessional," Stan said.

Lynn laughed.

"Here's the story about the trial. As you know, this is confidential. I know Jim did a sweep of your office to make sure there were no listening devices. We have learned that Reginald Smith, the driver of the car who dropped off Sharon Vega at the entrance to the ED, was trying to help her. He was ordered to finish her off and then bury her. He thought maybe she could have been saved by bringing her here.

"So, he was trying to do something good," Lynn said.

"That's what he says. I know I'm getting cynical; while I am optimistic, I'm not 100% convinced he's telling the truth. But we now have some information about others who are involved in this trafficking ring. That's the current focus.

The ADA has agreed not to charge Reginald Smith. He's in protective custody and is scheduled for witness protection as soon as we arrest those involved in this trafficking ring. We won't need you as a witness. You are off the hook, my dear," Stan said happily.

"Thank you, Stan. I was willing to testify, but I'm relieved not to have to do that. That's one potential scary event I can cross off my list," Lynn said.

"You for sure have enough on your plate. I understand Peter and his lawyer are in court today about the restraining order against Virginia. She's relentless," Stan said. "I hope that goes well for you two."

"Thanks, Stan. I appreciate all you have done to advise Peter and help with this guy here. I do have something I need to give you," Lynn said, pulling out Peter's plaid shirt from the paper bag under her desk.

"That looks like the plaid shirt we've seen on the video," Stan said.

"Yes, it does. This one seems to have a thin red line going through it, though. I don't remember if the shirt on the video has a red line going through it, although we don't have complete pictures of that shirt. What's interesting is that Virginia bought this shirt for Peter before their divorce," Lynn said.

"So, the plot thickens. Maybe Virginia is involved with whoever is sabotaging you?" Stan said. "We know Peter wasn't the one stealing the diazepam because he was operating at the time."

"You checked him out?" Lynn said, surprised.

"Of course. We checked out your staff, too. By we, I mean the security team and me," Stan clarified.

"Does Peter know where Virginia bought this shirt?" Stan asked.

"Yes, at Montgomery's," Lynn said.

"We could see if someone bought this shirt there recently. Maybe a high-end store, like Montgomery's, has surveillance cameras near the cash register," Stan said. "I just had a thought about not calling these registers 'cash registers. They should be called credit care registers."

"Good point," Lynn said, laughing.

"It's always a pleasure to see you laugh," Stan said. "I know all this has been tough."

"That's for sure. In my lifetime, I have never had people attack me like Virginia and whomever this fellow is. It's just a lot of upheaval in my life," Lynn said.

"Right now, we are going through hospital pictures looking for someone wearing that checkered shirt. We are staking out your house, with George's help, 25/7. If this fellow tries to enter your house, we will catch him. Unfortunately, we are sure he will try again to plant the diazepam, so you look guilty of taking that medication off the crash cart," Stan said. "I wish we had better news, but we will catch him."

"Thanks for all you are trying to do. I couldn't ask for a better investigation," Lynn said.

"Thanks," Stan said as he got up to leave. "Call me anytime if anything else occurs."

"Will do for sure," Lynn said.

Lynn texted Peter.

I hope all is good with you. Stan just left. The good news is that I'm off the hook about testifying in the trial for the trafficked woman. I'm thankful that's resolved.

Lynn waited a few minutes, but there was no answer from Peter.

She went through her to-do list and decided to get something to eat from the coffee shop. She took a few minutes to double-lock her office door.

"Ow!" Lynn said as someone knocked into her. She grabbed his arm to blunt her fall, accidentally scratching his hand.

"What's wrong with you?" she yelled as her assailant scurried away. She immediately called Stan and then the security office.

"Someone just slammed into me," she said. "I might have his DNA under my fingernails."

"What happened?" Jim from security asked.

"I was locking my door when this guy slammed into me. I accidentally scratched his hand," Lynn said.

"Lynn, are you OK?" Stan asked as he hurried near Lynn.

"I'm fine," Lynn said, "but this fellow isn't," showing both Jim and Stan the blood on her fingers.

Stan was on the phone calling for a forensic team to come to the hospital.

"I want you to show us how he slammed into you," Stan said. "I'm going to use a few different moves on Jim."

"Don't worry, Jim, I'm not going to follow through with the moves completely," Stan said.

"For which I am grateful," Jim responded.

Stan attempted several moves, demonstrating pushing with his body against Jim.

On the third attempt, Lynn identified the move.

"That's it," Lynn said. "That's what he did."

"Soccer!" both Jim and Stan said in unison.

"Maybe even football," Stan said. "Whomever this guy is, he probably played soccer or football in high school. That will help. We see if we can match the DNA under your fingernails and look for someone with arm scratches."

"Yay, progress," Jim said.

"Maybe we should also look for pictures of Virginia with some guy here, too. Let's see if Virginia is working with someone here," Stan said.

Jim nodded his head in agreement.

"Lynn, can we check your pockets and purse to see if there's any diazepam planted there," Jim said. "If there is, then he's not likely to consider a home invasion."

CHAPTER 55

"Look what I found," Stan said, holding up what looked like medication. "Is this from the crash cart?"

"That's what the diazepam looks like. The bump was an attempt to plant that medication on me," Lynn said. After thinking about the attack, she asked, "Doesn't it seem like a waste of time?" Lynn asked. "I would have found that early on and discarded it to avoid looking like the one who stole it," Lynn suggested.

"That's so true. Planting the diazepam in your office or car would have been more likely to have been found in a search and not by you," Stan said. "It might be that the fellow who bumped into you was ordered to plant the diazepam, and this is the only way he could get that done. That might mean whoever is doing these attacks is not the mastermind of these assaults. He is just carrying out orders."

"Oh, great," Lynn said. "We need to find not only the puppet but the puppeteer as well."

"I'm betting if we find the puppet, we will have fewer problems finding the puppeteer. The fellow doing the actual assault may be being blackmailed," Stan said. "This is still progress. We will get to the bottom of these attacks soon."

Lynn heard her phone beep with a text. It was from Peter.

The hearing went well – the judge ordered the restraining order. Virginia is spending the night in jail and paying a $5,000 fine. Apparently, judges don't like being screamed at and called names. I think being called an ignoramus was over the top for this judge. She gave Virginia three warnings and then charged her with contempt when she wouldn't stop yelling.

I have custody of Hanna which will be fine, except I have a problem tonight. Mrs. Appleton can only stay until 6:00 pm, and I already have an OR case from being on call.

Can I impose on you to come to the house to be with Hanna around 5:30 until I get home? You know I'd love to have you stay over, too.

Lynn answered.

Glad to hear about the restraining order. I feel very safe with Virginia in jail. Wow! Happy to meet up with Hanna around 5:30. I'll bring pizza, salad, and tiramisu.

Also, you might hear I've been attacked again. I'm fine. Will fill you in later. Love you!

Lynn turned to Jim and Stan, smiling.

"Sometimes I just know there is a God," she said.

"Apparently, being called an ignoramus and being screamed at by Virginia didn't sit well with the judge who ordered the restraining order. Virginia gets to pay a fine and spend the night in lock up. We are all safe tonight," Lynn said.

Stan and Jim laughed heartedly. If they hadn't had a direct confrontation with Virginia in the hospital, they knew people who had.

"I guess she finally met up with someone who put her in her place," Jim said. "Pun intended!"

"Can we keep this just between us? I just don't want Peter to be embarrassed. If he wants to tell people, that's fine with me, but I don't want this to get out because of me. OK?" Lynn asked.

"Fine with me," Stan said.

"Me, too," Jim said. "I'm just glad Dr. Pete got the restraining order. He's a good guy and a great doctor. He fixed my 10-year-old nephew's fractured tibia and was terrific with Henry, who runs around without any problems. Dr. Pete deserves better than being screamed at all the time."

"I think we all agree on that," Stan said. "No one will hear about Virginia spending the night in jail from us. It is going to be hard not to smile, though, when someone mentions her name."

Lynn couldn't help but laugh, too.

After Stan and Jim left, Lynn checked on the patients in the ED. The staff was on top of all that needed to be done, so she ordered the pizza and headed out to be at Peter's house by 5:30.

Lynn put in the new code to open Peter's door. There was a sense of relief to know Virginia did not have that code and that there was a restraining order prohibiting her from coming near Peter, his house, and anyone whom he was dating. It was an extra bonus to know she was in jail for the night.

"Hi, Mrs. Appleton. Good to see you," Lynn said upon entering the house. Hanna came running to greet her.

"Good to see you, too, Hanna. Your dad told me you like pizza with pineapple on it. Is that true?" Lynn asked.

"No pineapple on pizza," Hanna said. "Is that really what you brought?" Hanna asked.

"No. I wouldn't do that. We have two pizzas. One has extra cheese with ground beef. The other has extra cheese with mushrooms and ground beef. Does that work for you?" Lynn asked.

"The pizza without the mushrooms is perfect for me. Did you bring dessert?" Hanna asked.

"But of course. What is your favorite dessert?" Lynn asked.

"You know I like brownies when we cook them, but I like the tera something from restaurants. You didn't happen to bring that, did you?" Hanna asked.

"Let's check this container to see if it's what you like," Lynn said.

"That's it! That's what I like. I knew you wouldn't let me down, Ms. Lynn," Hanna exclaimed, giving Lynn a hug. "I'll be in my toy room if you need me."

Lynn and Mrs. Appleton both laughed.

"Thank you for coming so I can get home to my family," Mrs. Appleton said to Lynn. "You are good for Dr. Peter. No more screaming and yelling. That's much better. Hanna likes you, too."

"It's my pleasure to be here with Hanna. You enjoy your evening with your family," Lynn said.

"Hanna, you ready for your pizza?" Lynn asked after Mrs. Appleton left.

"Sure. Can we eat it and watch television? Dad and I do that sometimes if there's a show I want to watch," Hanna asked.

"If that's OK with your dad to do sometimes, we can do it, too. What show do you like?" Lynn asked.

"I like princess stories. Dad has them set to record," Hanna said as she took over the remote. "Here's a good one."

Lynn set the pizza and salad plates on the placemats on the coffee table, with a glass of milk for Hanna and water for her. Both enjoyed the story of Hanna's princess as she learns life lessons. She hoped she would be there for Hanna as she faced her life lessons.

CHAPTER 56

"Hanna, how about getting ready for bed?" Lynn suggested.

"OK, I'm a little tired. I have school tomorrow, too. You don't have to read me a story. I can read my books now all by myself," Hanna said proudly.

"How about I come upstairs when you are ready for bed to give you a hug and tuck you in?" Lynn asked.

"OK. I would like that," Hanna said.

Lynn finished cleaning the kitchen and was thinking about Hanna, who did not know her mother was in jail for the night.

"I'm ready," Hanna shouted from upstairs.

"I'm coming," Lynn said. "Let's do the hug first and then the tuck-in," Lynn said.

"I'm happy when you come over, Ms. Lynn. You are fun," Hanna said.

"You know I'm always happy to spend time with you," Lynn replied. "Have wonderful dreams."

Once the kitchen was cleared, Lynn lay down on the couch to watch television. She ended up checking out reruns of Blue Bloods. The next thing she knew, Peter was home and covering her with a blanket.

"Sorry to wake you," Peter said. "I just wanted to make sure you were warm enough."

"I tried to wait up for you, but that just didn't happen," Lynn said. "I'm awake now. Tell me about your day."

"First, tell me about you getting attacked again. I've been worried about you all evening," Peter said. "Would you like a glass of wine or Champagne?"

"Let's do champagne. I think celebrations are in order," Lynn responded.

"To us," Peter said as he and Lynn raised their glasses to each other while snuggling under the blanket.

"Here's my story. I was double locking my office this afternoon when a guy came by and slammed into me. I was off balance and grabbed for his arm to steady myself, but I scratched him as he pulled away," Lynn started.

"Were you hurt?" Peter asked.

"No. Stan and Jim showed up right away. Stan was thrilled that I had DNA evidence underneath my fingernails," Lynn said. "Besides all that, the fellow had put the missing diazepam from the crash cart into my jacket pocket."

"He finally succeeded in doing that. Maybe those attempts now are over," Peter said.

"That is the consensus. The other thought we had was that even though this guy accomplished his mission of trying to frame me, it was a dumb move. It would have been easy for me to find the medication in my pocket before the police or security found it. I could have quickly disposed of it in the bathroom," Lynn said.

"That's very true. Are you thinking this guy is not the brains behind these attacks?" Peter asked.

"Yes, definitely. We also eliminated Virginia as being involved. Whoever pulls the strings is smart and has something to gain from discrediting me and probably making sure I was seen as unfit to run the new emergency/outpatient clinic configuration. The question is, who could that be?" Lynn said.

"Let's push that a little further. Suppose you don't get that job; who would get it? I can't see Jim Walker doing it," Peter said. "He doesn't know enough about big emergencies to manage them. Chances are the hospital would have to do a national search for a director."

"They would eventually find someone, but it would take time, maybe even a year," Lynn said. "I've been on some of these search committees for the big jobs, and it's time-consuming."

"Who would gain from delaying this entire project?" Peter asked. "It could give someone time to derail it, but why would someone want that?"

"How about this question? Who would lose out if this hospital became a Level I trauma center?" Lynn asked.

"Certainly not the people who live in this area. The last I looked at requirements, to be a level I trauma center, you need to have 240 admissions a year with an injury severity score of more than 15 (CD 2-4). We see at least 200 of that type of patient in the hospital every year. A good percentage of them get stabilized here and then flown to a type I facility. Others from the area are flown directly to the Type I facility, but nothing is close. I know Dr. Brown has the statistics on those that don't survive the transfer," Peter said.

"If this hospital takes in those trauma patients, then maybe some other hospital nearby with marginal numbers will lose their Trauma I designation," Lynn said. "Maybe that's already on the state trauma plan. Maybe some hospital already knows their hospital will lose status and money if Deer Park Hospital gets their Trauma I designation."

"Just maybe, if that hospital at risk had an extra year, they could do something to keep their designation," Peter said. "Should we or someone talk to Dr. Brown?

"Someone should. If I meet with him, I know he will ask if I plan to take the job. I'm not sure I want it, to be honest," Lynn said.

"Have you clarified any more what you would like to do? I know you said you want to stay away from more administrative paperwork. You also still want to have some contact with patients," Peter said. "Can you bargain that with Dr. Brown?

"Good thought! Maybe I can configure a way to do that, like having an administrative assistant. Let's let that issue simmer for a while. Tell me about your day in court," Lynn said. "It sounds exciting."

CHAPTER 57

"As you know, I was with my lawyer, and Virginia was with hers to process the restraining order. We were in front of Judge Audrey Metcalf. My lawyer spoke up first, listing all the harassment I've experienced from Virginia. The black negligee with Virginia's fingerprints on it raised the judge's eyebrows. The fact that she paid her cousin's husband to pretend to be someone you were dating seemed to get to the judge.

I was happy with my lawyer. I thought he did a great job describing details about true events.

Virginia's lawyer basically admitted that Virginia did all that my lawyer talked about but made the case that it was because of a severe emotional reaction to the divorce, which she did not want to happen. He said she was over the emotional trauma and that none of this would happen again," Peter explained. "It was a good presentation. However, my lawyer then described that the events had been continuous over two years and were recent."

"The judge granted the restraining order, which basically said Virginia could not be within 500 feet of me or anyone I was dating, plus she must permanently restrain from harassing and stalking me and lying about my life in any way. If she continues and ignores the restraining order, she could go to jail," Peter said.

"Holy smokes! I didn't know that part. Talk about being at risk of ruining your life," Lynn said.

"That's when everything disintegrated. Virginia went ballistic. She stood up and started screaming at the judge about how unfair she was and that she would not abide by the restraining order. She pointed her finger at the judge and then told her she was an incompetent ignoramus and a few other choice names. The judge warned her three times to be quiet, or she would be charged with contempt of court. I didn't know contempt of court could be an act of disrespect or defiance even by the defendants."

"That must have been some scene," Lynn said.

"Virginia's lawyer tried to get her to sit down, but she literally swatted him, calling him incompetent, too. The judge said she was in contempt of court and gave Virginia a $5,000 fine and the night in jail to cool off," Peter explained. "The court deputies handcuffed Virginia and led her out of the courtroom. She was still screaming."

"Wow! That must have been some scene. Were there reporters in the room?" Lynn asked. "Do they allow people with cell phones in the court? Someone may have recorded that."

"I don't know, but we will know tomorrow," Peter said. "If the judge ever doubted that the restraining order was a good idea, Virginia showed her she did the right thing."

"How are you after all that?" Lynn asked.

"I'm relieved but a little sad. I put up with all that screaming and name-calling during a lot of my marriage. It felt good to have a judge say, no more," Peter said. "However, Virginia and I both thought our lives would end differently."

"In what ways did you think it would have been different?" Lynn asked.

"We met while I was doing my orthopedic residency, and she was just starting out her design business. We struggled together and supported each other. She thought marrying a doctor would put her in contact with other doctors who had money to hire a home designer. While that did happen, she didn't get that being a doctor often met unpredictable calls to take care of patients," Peter explained.

"When you didn't show up at events that could help her business, she was angry, right?" Lynn asked.

"We were young when we got married, with neither of us anticipating what life would be like when we were going strong in our chosen professions. Virginia looks like the heavy in the relationship, but being married to a doctor wasn't easy for her. I look better because I don't scream as loud," Peter said. "I must admit, I didn't like going to her events, either. Sometimes I could have attended her events but made excuses not to go. It was easy for me to stay later than I had to at the hospital to avoid one of those dinners or talks. Virginia found out a few times that I had done that. I wasn't an angel, either."

"I had a similar issue with Allen," Lynn said. "He was into looking and being successful. He had no use for me handing out $20 to people who could use a boost. He would put me down for not drinking the appropriate wine or wearing white gold jewelry instead of gold-colored gold jewelry, which to him was more sophisticated. I wasn't interested in his parties that were meant to impress people who could afford expensive houses, and he wasn't interested in helping others. We were a poor match and not good for each other," Lynn explained.

"I'm sorry that was a bad experience for you," Peter said.

"Relationships can be tough," Lynn said. "When Virginia and I were together that one time, and she started complaining about you, I cut her off. I said you and I were bound to have some issues, but chances are they would be different from the ones the two of you had. It's like me saying I can't take all the attacks and insisting you deal with those Virginia was creating before we can be together," Lynn said.

"I understood that, and it was OK, although hard not to be seeing you. It was my responsibility to deal with Virginia. The difference is that you didn't scream, and you didn't call me names. You just said what needed to be said," Peter responded. "I could also tell you were going to miss me."

"I'm glad you feel that way. Thank you for that. I must confess I was much more comfortable being here in your house knowing the restraining order was in place and even that Virginia was in jail," Lynn said. "I also missed you a lot."

"It was awful!" Peter said emphatically. "Together is definitely better," Peter said, reaching over to take Lynn into his arms.

CHAPTER 58

The next morning at work, Lynn was having trouble concentrating. Ideas about her relationship with Peter, letting go of worrying about being in court for a trial of Reginald Smith, and now meeting with Dr. Brown kept alternately running through her head. She had called Dr. Brown's office to discuss the new job.

She focused on writing down what she would say to Dr. Brown to make the job work for her. She had decided she would take the job for the first year while the hospital was getting all the personnel and systems organized.

But how can this job be organized to work for me? What do I need? She said to herself.

A familiar knock on her door and a welcome silhouette behind the glass brought a smile to her face.

"Come in," Lynn said. "I desperately need coffee."

Peter laughed as he entered.

"I have always suspected it was the coffee that gets me welcome in your office," Peter said, smiling.

Lynn smiled back. "In your heart, though, you know I love seeing you," Lynn said. Looking at Peter, she thought about spending the rest of her life with him. Was she ready for that commitment? Is that what she wanted to happen?

"I seem to have lost you there for a moment," Peter said. "What's bothering you?"

"I have an appointment with Dr. Brown at 2:00. I'm trying to figure out how to negotiate a structure that would work for me in this new hospital configuration," Lynn answered.

"Change is tough, sometimes," Peter said. "Do you need to have everything worked out today?"

"No, I guess not. I have decided to take the job for at least a year or whatever it takes to set up the new configuration. I do want an assistant who will do a lot of the paperwork, like standard reports and supplies. Beyond that, I don't know. I don't want this job to be my life. I know the staff can handle the patients if I'm not here. Generally, I leave on time without worries," Lynn said.

"Part of setting up the new configuration might involve visiting other places with Type I trauma designations. You will better understand what types of setups work best by hearing what others say work or don't work," Peter suggested.

"Good ideas. I need more information to set something up that would work for me. See, you are more than a cup of coffee. You also have good insights," Lynn said teasingly.

"You have made my day," Peter said, laughing. "I'm always here for you; whatever you need that I can help with."

"Thanks. I'm happy to be there for you, too," Lynn said.

Peter's smile said it all. They had committed themselves to each other spontaneously and felt good about it.

Peter's beeper went off.

"Wanted in OR," Peter said. "See you later, Sweetie."

After Peter left, Lynn realized the big differences between her and Peter and her and Allen and Peter and Virginia were their values. She and Peter had similar values. While they both were successful in their respective fields, their chosen occupations involved helping people. Neither one cared about social standing nor a particular image. Neither one would ask the other to get involved with prestigious gatherings but would understand and support each other, helping patients and other people.

Suddenly, the anxiety about having a committed relationship with Peter left. A feeling of contentment had taken its place.

As Lynn sat in her office, she thought, *no trial, no more harassment from Virginia, no more major fear of getting more involved with Peter; life is getting better.* She was ready to meet with Dr. Brown and then Stan and Jim.

There was a sudden knock on her door with two figures there. Lynn opened the door.

"We know who he is," Stan said. Jim nodded his head.

"The DNA from your fingernails connected us to Ted Oliver, the pharmacy technician," Stan said. "We don't have a motive yet for why he was doing this harassment, but he's our guy. Besides being a pharmacy technician, he's also part of the computer support system in the pharmacy."

"That's huge. What is happening next?" Lynn asked.

We are looking for him in all the surveillance equipment to see whom he meets with and if we can see him in that shirt. Mike from IT is going to be checking his computer. We just need a little more evidence to get an arrest warrant," Stan said. "The DNA is a great help, but he could just say he accidentally bumped into you, and you overreacted. We want to have a solid case before identifying him as the perpetrator of all these assaults against you."

"We are pretty sure he is taking orders from someone else. Who that is, we don't know yet," Jim said.

"I might be able to give you a lead on that, but I need to talk with Dr. Brown first. I have an appointment with him at 2:00 this afternoon. Are you guys going to be around, say, 4:00 o'clock?' Lynn asked.

"You think Dr. Brown has something to do with this?" Jim asked.

"Not the assaults, of course. But he might know someone with a motive. I can't tell you something I know without clarifying it with him first and getting his input. I'm confident I can do that when I meet with him this afternoon," Lynn said.

"This sure is complicated," Jim said.

"That's true, but you are on the way to solving a major part of this puzzle. You know I am so grateful for all your help," Lynn said.

"We will keep working on our end. Looking forward to talking with you at 4:00. Is here in your office a good place?" Stan asked.

"For sure. See you then," Lynn said.

Lynn's next thought was to let Peter know what Stan and Jim had found out. She looked at the OR schedule. *Nothing like having a boyfriend whose daily schedule she could look up on a report!* Lynn thought and smiled.

CHAPTER 59

Lynn was sitting in the waiting area outside Dr. Brown's office a little before 2:00 pm. She thought she still felt like she was waiting to talk with the principal.

"Come on in, Lynn," Dr. Brown said. "Good to see you."

"I have a lot to discuss – some good and some not so good. I don't know if you have heard that someone had been harassing and even assaulting me lately," Lynn said.

"I did hear some rumors about strange emails and your office getting broken into but figured you and security, and maybe the police, were dealing with it," Dr. Brown said.

"Stan Gregowski and Jim Skinner have a strong lead on the person who has been carrying out the attacks. He works in the hospital. However, they and I do not believe he is the mastermind behind making me look incompetent or like a criminal. We think all these attacks are related to the hospital's pursuit of a Level I trauma center," Lynn explained.

"Really? How is that possible?" Dr. Brown asked.

"I have not told anyone about being offered the job to be the Director of the combined ED and outpatient clinics except Dr. Peter Fry, who I have been dating. I know that the pursuit of the Level I trauma designation is in the hospital's rumor mill," Lynn clarified.

"Our thinking is that if I do not get the job because I've been discredited, chances are you will need to do a national search which will take about a year to complete – leading to a year's delay in pursuing the Type I trauma designation. Someone in some other healthcare organization will lose out if Deer Park Hospital gets that designation. Maybe a year's delay will give them enough time to stop this hospital's pursuit. At this point, we are thinking out loud about that. You would have a better idea about the validity of that thought process," Lynn said.

"Wow! I didn't see that coming," Dr. Brown said. "A hospital administrator or board member who believes their hospital will lose money and maybe their Level I trauma designation may have hired this fellow to torment you. Leading to you not wanting to take the job or us not wanting you to be the director. Is that what you are thinking?"

"Exactly. Just as an aside, it may be that someone is extorting this fellow who works here, into doing the dirty work." Lynn said.

"Stan and Jim don't know, or at least I haven't told them, that you offered me the Director position. If they know that, they could then pursue, with your OK, someone who might be the main force behind these attacks with some accuracy," Lynn explained.

"Before I give the OK to say something to Stan and Jim, what are your thoughts about taking this job?" Dr. Brown asked.

"I've thought long and hard about this. I will agree to take this position to establish all the policies and procedures that need to be done in the first year or more. That way, you can move ahead with whatever you need to do to make this Level I designation happen without worrying about immediate management of the units.

I have some reservations and would need further negotiations of my responsibilities to stay in the position," Lynn said. After she said that, she felt good. It was off her mind.

"Great! That's good to know. You are correct, too. You are more than qualified to supervise this new designation, but you are the only one in this hospital. We would need to do a search if you don't take the job," Dr. Brown said.

"I can tell you the closest Level I trauma center is Charity Hospital in Dunkirk, North Carolina. The CEO and one of the board members have been protesting our getting that designation. However, the review committee is on our side. Charity Hospital is close to some of the other hospitals in the Raleigh/Durham area. They have been struggling to meet the minimal number of trauma cases. Without the cases we sent them, they would be unable to sustain that Level I status. The review committee thinks a hospital located where we are could maintain that status level and prevent a delay in trauma care for the population within a 50-mile radius of us. The bottom line is we are looking good, but Charity Hospital is not," Dr. Brown said.

"If you agree to stay in this position during the setup, I'll agree to let you tell Stan and Jim that's what will happen but tell them to keep it between them. They can then pursue the CEO of Charity Hospital, and I'll send you the name and contact information of the board member who is helping him. I'll also announce all this, and you being chosen as the Director. That might take a little bit of time. How does that sound?" Dr. Brown asked.

"That sounds perfect. It's a pleasure doing business with you, Dr. Brown. I'm sure you can contact Stan and Jim about their progress. I know they will welcome any suggestions you might have," Lynn said.

"Thank you for bringing this information to me. Hospital administration is getting tougher all the time," Dr. Brown said. "I'm sorry you have been going through all these attacks. You deserve to be rewarded for all your good work, not assaulted."

"Thanks for that. Stan, the IT department, Security people, and my colleagues have all been terrific and supportive. I couldn't have asked for a better group of people," Lynn said.

"Now, add me to that list of your supporters. My door is always open to you," Dr. Brown said.

"Thanks again! That means a lot," Lynn replied.

At 4:00 pm, Stan and Jim entered Lynn's office. She explained that she had been offered the Director's job in this new configuration, and maybe that's why someone had hired Ted Oliver to sabotage her, to delay the project. She also let them know what Dr. Brown had said about Charity hospital and their CEO and board member.

"It's like a big puzzle finally coming together," Stan said.

"Dr. Brown is in 100%. Feel free to contact him if you have questions. You may get calls from him, too," Lynn said.

"Good job, Lynn," Jim said.

"I'm looking forward to hearing what you guys find out. As for me, I'm taking Thursday and Friday off and going away for a mini vacation," Lynn said.

"By the time you return, we hope to have this all tied up with a particularly nice bow! You deserve to have all this stress over with. Have a fun vacation," Stan said.

"I definitely will," Lynn said.

CHAPTER 60

Lynn and Peter chatted about their days that night. Lynn detailed her meeting with Dr. Brown. Peter agreed it had gone well. Both were excited about their trip to New York City, especially with Lynn taking Thursday and Friday as vacation days.

This morning at work, she was planning to make sure supplies and staffing were good until the following Monday, typically not an easy feat. As she walked from the parking lot to the hospital employee entrance, she noticed a man, just a little ahead of her, with a plaid shirt like the one she, Stan, and Jim had seen on the surveillance cameras. The man had a jacket covering the shirt, but the collar was very visible. Given his height and overall size, Lynn knew the man was Ted Oliver. She quickly texted Stan and Jim, telling them Ted Oliver was at the hospital entrance wearing his plaid shirt. She put her phone on to record her conversation with Ted.

"Good morning," Lynn said to the man, presumed to be Ted Oliver. "Nice balmy day for a change."

The man was shocked to see her. Lynn knew he recognized her.

"Don't you work in the pharmacy department? Isn't your name Ted Oliver?" Lynn asked.

"Yes, it is. I'm sorry, but I can't talk right now. I don't want to be late for my shift," Ted said, picking up his pace and moving away from Lynn.

"I would encourage you to slow down. I have a gun in my coat pocket to protect me from someone who is harassing me. I think that someone is you, and that gun is pointed at you. I want you and me to go through the hospital entrance door and wait for the police to come to get you," Lynn said.

"I'm so sorry. He made me do it. I didn't want to harass you. Everyone says you are a good person. Please let me go," Ted said.

By this time, Lynn saw Stan running toward her.

"How could he make you do all that? Sounds like an excuse to me," Lynn said.

"No, no, you don't understand. My wife works in his hospital. He said he would fire her if I didn't do what he said. We need two incomes to support our family, and my wife loves her job. He promised I would not have to do anything that hurt you physically, which is the only reason I agreed," Ted said.

"So, you agreed to make my life a living hell to maybe save your wife's job? Do you realize you are facing jail time now?" Lynn asked.

"Put your hands behind your back," Stan said to Ted as he approached him. He cuffed him. "You are under arrest for harassment, assault, defamation of character, and theft."

"She has a gun in her pocket. She threatened to shoot me. Arrest her," Ted said to Stan.

"You mean this? It's just the whistle attached to my key chain," Lynn said. "I don't like guns."

"But I do have a gun. You need to come with me," Stan said to Ted. "The plaid shirt is the same one that's on the videos. Great job, Lynn," Stan said.

"Thanks! My very first perpetrator detainment," Lynn said, smiling.

"Let's go, Ted. Maybe we can talk more about who was blackmailing you," Stan said.

Back in her office, Lynn almost collapsed into her chair, and tears started running down her face. *The worst was over*," she thought with relief.

The knock on her door and the silhouette let her know Peter was at her door.

"Come in, Peter," Lynn said.

"How come your door wasn't locked?" Peter asked. "You need to be protected at all times."

"It's because I apprehended the perpetrator of my attacks this morning," Lynn said, wiping her eyes.

"You did what?" Peter asked.

"As I approached the hospital door from the parking lot this morning, I noticed this man with a shirt with a plaid collar in front of me. I started talking to him and asked if he was Ted Oliver. He recognized me and started to take off, but I told him I had a gun in the pocket of my jacket to stay put. I had texted Stan and Jim," Lynn explained.

"Ted admitted to sabotaging me. He also said someone had threatened his wife's job at her hospital if he didn't do the things that made me look incompetent. Stan needed more proof that he was the perpetrator. Since he was wearing the plaid shirt in full view, that gave Stan enough evidence to tie him to the attempted break-ins seen on the videos and his presence at the crash cart," Lynn said. "Of course, they also found a match to his DNA from the blood under my fingernails. His shirt does not have a red line through it as yours does. So, you are in the clear."

"I'm glad I won't be brought to jail as a suspect. All this means they only need to find out who threatened him about his wife's job to end all these attacks. Excellent job, Lynn. You are one brave lady," Peter said.

"I wasn't really scared of Ted. He's a pawn in all this. I'm betting this fellow also offered to pay him to harass me and save his wife's job," Lynn suggested.

"How are you feeling?" Peter asked. "It looked like you were crying when I came in."

"It's this overwhelming feeling of relief. The last few weeks have been the worse weeks of my life. Every minute of every day, I was anticipating an attack from someplace. Now it appears to be over," Lynn said.

Peter got up and locked Lynn's office door. He reached for Lynn to get up from her chair and join him on her couch. He put his arms around her, and her tears flowed steadily.

"It's all OK now," Peter said. "The worst is over. Not only did you survive, but you also apprehended the perpetrator while he was wearing evidence. I want to be there when you tell Wanda you pulled a Blue Bloods detainment. She'll be very jealous."

Lynn laughed. *Life is good again*, she thought. *No, it is better than ever with Peter in her life.*

CHAPTER 61

Lynn slept in the next morning and then did the necessary cleaning of her house. She was ready for the flight to New York City when Peter picked her up at 4:00 pm. It was a short flight of one hour and 40 minutes from Wilmington to LaGuardia. Their most pressing decision was where to eat dinner after settling in the hotel.

"What type of food do you feel like eating, my dear?" Peter asked.

Lynn noticed Peter seemed more relaxed than usual. His manner was more easygoing and unhurried. He also looked happy. Maybe content better described him, Lynn thought.

"Honestly, I would love to go to some little quiet neighborhood place with good food. I can eat almost anything – except maybe brussels sprouts," Lynn said.

"I don't like them either," Peter said. "Let's check with the desk downstairs. They should know some quiet places without brussels sprouts."

Lynn discussed their restaurant idea with a knowledgeable young man helping other guests with their questions.

"Good evening," he said as they approached him. "What can I help you with this evening?"

"We are looking for a restaurant that's on the quiet side, with good food, that's within walking distance," Lynn said.

The young man looked at Lynn and Peter carefully.

"I would suggest a restaurant called Avena. It's right down 57th street," the young man said, writing the address on one of his post-it notes. "It has excellent food, and this time of night on a Thursday should be cozy and comfortable."

"Thank you, young man. That's much appreciated," Peter said, slipping him a $20.

"Did you just slip that young man a $20?" Lynn asked as they were walking to the restaurant.

"I did," Peter said. "It's expensive living in New York City. I know this woman who advocates for distributing 20-dollar bills to boost people. I think she would have approved."

"For sure," Lynn says. "You get great approval scores from her in general, and that tip just added to everything she loves about you."

As they entered the restaurant, they were immediately taken to a table in a location with dim lighting, low music, and in a corner away from the main traffic pattern.

"This certainly meets our criteria for quiet," Lynn said about the restaurant.

"Perfect for a late-night dinner for two exhausted escapees," Peter said.

Lynn laughed.

"I guess we really did escape from work, and for me, the memories of being constantly harassed. There are no words to describe how relieved I am not to be constantly worried about being attacked," Lynn said.

Their waiter approached.

"Good evening. I'll be your waiter this evening. My name is Bruce. Are you interested in cocktails before dinner?"

To the amazement of the waiter, both Lynn and Peter broke out into exuberant laughter.

In between broad smiles and barely controlled laughter, Peter ordered a bottle of champagne for the table.

"I don't believe that just happened," Lynn laughed. "What are the chances our waiter's name would be Bruce?"

"At least we know Virginia didn't hire this Bruce. Or did she?" Peter said.

"We should take his picture, just in case," Lynn laughed. "I am so happy to be laughing at this coincidence."

"I'm just so happy to be here with you," Peter said. "I have always liked coming to New York City for a getaway, but this trip is the way I have always imagined it would be with the right person."

"Me, too. I've been to the city a few times for conferences. I dreamed of coming here with someone special to enjoy the sights and some romantic places. However, I never imagined a Bruce as our waiter," Lynn said.

"What kind of sights and romantic places did you imagine?" Peter asked.

Bruce was back at the table with their champagne. Again, both Lynn and Peter had to stifle their laughter.

"May I take your orders?" Bruce asked.

"First of all, Bruce, we would like to apologize for our smiles and laughter. We have a history with someone named Bruce, and it's just ironic that that is your name, too. Trust me, though; we appreciate that you are a totally different person, and I'm sure our experience will show you to be an excellent waiter," Peter said.

"Thank you, Sir. I must admit, I was a little taken aback by your reaction to my name. You have clarified that superbly," Bruce said.

"Do you have any recommendations for our dinners?" Peter asked.

"Our special for this evening is a pan-seared Chilean Sea Bass with a coconut cream sauce and capers with a creamy garlic cauliflower mash on the side and angel hair pasta. So far, we have gotten excellent customer feedback," Bruce said.

Lynn shook her head yes.

"Do you have cornbread?" Lynn asked.

"Yes, we do," Bruce said. "It's also quite delicious."

Bruce poured champagne into each of their glasses and left to place their order.

"To a wonderful time escaping to New York City. You were about to talk about what kind of sights and romantic places you imagined experiencing here," Peter said. "Do continue."

"I know one place I wanted to see is the Tavern on the Green. It had closed, and I don't know if it ever was reopened. I'll think about other places and make a list," Lynn said.

CHAPTER 62

After an excellent dinner, Lynn told Peter she would think more about what sights and romantic places she had always wanted to see in the city. They kissed good night, promising to get together when Peter finished his workshop tomorrow, which was to stop at 4:30. Peter's workshop included a breakfast talk at 7:30. Lynn was on her own to sleep in, have breakfast, and go shopping at Bloomies.

The next morning, Lynn was up around 9:30, a late morning for her.

"Good morning, Sweetie," the text from Peter at 7:00 am said. "Have a fun day."

"Just getting up, but coffee is in my hand. Hope the workshop is a good one. See you around 4:30."

I wonder if I have some PTSD, Lynn thought. All night she was dreaming about being followed by a man named Bruce. She didn't want to mention anything to Peter and spoil his day.

She had a text waiting for her from Stan.

Ted Oliver told us the man who hired him was Alexander Isdell, who is on the board of Charity hospital. He runs a private investment firm in Dunkirk, NC. We are scanning the videos for pictures of *Ted and Alexander together near the hospital or other locations Ted said they met. If we find that, we will secure a warrant.*

Close to the end of this investigation, Lynn thought.

Excellent work! Keep me posted.

Lynn grabbed a quick breakfast downstairs, showered, and dressed. She was then off to Bloomies. She first went looking for facsimiles of the snow globe with three small snowmen, dish towels with gnomes on them, and elves on wine glasses. The snow globe with the three snowmen that looked like children was easy to find. She had to settle for a reverse of the gnomes and elves, with the gnomes now on the wine glasses and the elves on the dish towels.

Then Lynn looked for a dress for their last evening in New York.

"I'm looking for a dress to wear for a romantic dinner out. Do you have time to help me?" Lynn asked the woman working in the dress department.

"Of course. My name is Betty. You look like you would wear a size small, somewhere between a four and a six, depending on the cut of the dress. Is that correct?" Betty asked.

"Yes. I tend to wear blues and colors with a blue base but more on the brighter end versus the muted colors," Lynn said.

"I can see where that would work for you," Betty replied.

"Let's go over to this women's clothing section which has dresses that are a little more on the dressy side but not over the top. Does that sound good to you?" Betty asked.

"Sounds right on the money to me," Lynn said.

Lynn tried on a maroon short sequined dress which she thought was too much glitter. Then came a fitted black dress cut out near the bust line.

"This one is not quite my style," Lynn said to Betty.

Betty handed Lynn a knee-length, blue sheath dress with small ruffling near and below the waist and slightly cut in at the shoulders. It can fit perfectly.

Lynn went out of her dressing room to look at her image in a full-length mirror. The blue reminded Lynn of a beautiful butterfly she had seen in her mother's garden. A man walked by where Lynn was standing. She could see his thumbs up for this dress.

"I'll take it," Lynn said to Betty.

"Good choice," Betty said.

Happy with her buying experiences, Lynn went back to the hotel.

There was a text from Peter on her phone that he had missed.

The organizer of this workshop has set up a cocktail party for all of us, including spouses, girlfriends, or just friends. What do you think?

Lynn answered.

I'm good with going if that's what you want.

Peter replied.

Ok. I'll tell him we'll be there for a little while before dinner. He gave me some dinner suggestions. I made reservations that I think you'll like. We should leave for the cocktail party around 6:00.

Lynn answered.

I'll be ready. I'll meet you in the lobby.

Lynn was down in the lobby shortly before 6:00. Peter was already there. As she approached him, he looked stunned.

"You OK? Is there something wrong with the way I'm dressed?" Lynn asked in a worried tone.

"I feel a case of Deja vu all over again," Peter said. "Do you remember the last time we went to a gathering of my friends, and you looked ravishing? I warned you that the wolves in my pack of friends would pay you immediate attention. In that dress, in addition to surrounding you, they will throw me out the door to never be seen again. Wow!"

"They may give me attention, but you just know I only have eyes for you," Lynn said. "I'm glad you like the dress. I told you Bloomies was a great department store."

Even though Peter had exaggerated the attention Lynn would receive, it was obvious he was pleased to bring Lynn to meet everyone from the workshop. Conversations went easily, and a congenial time was had, drinking champagne and talking about the workshop. One of the doctors did ask to go to dinner with them, but Peter pulled him aside.

Lynn didn't hear what was being said, but only Lynn and Peter went out to dinner. Peter told the cab driver to go to 67th Street and Central Park West.

"Yes, Sir," the cab driver said.

"Where are we going?" Lynn asked.

"It's a little surprise," Peter said. "You will know the place when we get there."

The cab had stopped at the entrance to the Tavern on the Green, with its iconic red canopy.

"It's so lovely. How did you even get a reservation?" Lynn asked as they walked into the restaurant.

"I must confess to making them as soon as I heard about this workshop, hoping you would agree to come with me," Peter said. "Plus, I had asked George what some of your favorite places might be in New York. I checked, and this restaurant had reopened in 2014."

"Thank you, Peter, for making another one of my dreams come true," Lynn said.

CHAPTER 63

"Good evening, Dr. Fry. Welcome to the Tavern on the Green," the receptionist said after Peter told her about his reservation. "Someone will be right with you to escort you to your table."

A young woman took them inside the restaurant a few minutes later. "Here we are," the woman said, sitting them at a comfortable, private table just slightly off the main sitting area.

A waiter soon approached them.

"If his name is Bruce, we might have to leave," Lynn said.

"Good evening, my name is Martin, and I will be your waiter for the evening. May I interest you in a drink before dinner?"

Both Lynn and Peter smiled at the waiter's introduction. "What would you like?" Peter asked Lynn. "I'm happy to order a bottle of champagne, but we tend not to drink that much."

"I would like a Cosmopolitan," Lynn said.

"I'll have a gin and tonic," Peter said. "House gin is fine."

"Let's look over the menu, and then we can talk," Peter said.

"The salmon sounds delicious," Lynn said. "The bread-basket is fine for me for an appetizer."

"Two salmon dinners, it will be," Peter said.

"Look at this beautiful room," Lynn said. "The Christmas decorations look perfect against the wood and lighting here."

Martin delivered their drinks and took their dinner orders.

"A toast to being in New York City in one of the most iconic restaurants. So many movies have been filmed in here," Lynn said, "even Ghostbusters.

"I hope they took all those ghosts with them," Peter said as they clinked glasses.

"Tell me about the workshop," Lynn said.

"It is so hard for me to even think we could implant body parts printed from a giant computer. That looks like the future, particularly with bones," Peter said. "The presentations were good, but after a day of them, I needed a break. I'm not used to sitting all day."

The breadbasket was now on their table. It contained an assortment of warm bread, biscuits, and muffins.

"Ladies first," Peter said.

Lynn reached for a biscuit. "Still warm," she said.

"So, how was your day?" Peter asked.

"I got a text from Stan. Ted Oliver told them that a man on the board of Charity hospital, Alexander Isdell, was the man who hired him. He runs an investment firm. They are looking for pictures of the two men together near the hospital or in town, where Ted said they met," Lynn said.

"That's big news. Looks like the pieces of the attacks are finally known. In fact, that's great news," Peter said.

"Yes, it is," Lynn said. "Thank goodness. Now all I must do is recover from the PTSD this has created in me. It will take a while to not get tense when someone comes to our table or when I go into my office."

"I am so sorry all this happened to you, especially since someone from my life contributed to the attacks. What can I do to make amends?" Peter asked.

"I'm going to have to think about that one. You know I've wanted to spend a month in Paris. That might help," Lynn said, laughing. "You know I don't hold you responsible for what Virginia did. You took care of that problem and have always been so good to me."

Martin delivered the salmon with an elegance Lynn had not seen before. *What a treat this is*, she thought.

In the middle of eating her dinner, Lynn suddenly got up and went over to a man at a nearby table. A man sitting there was clutching his throat with a look of panic on his face. She stood him up and had him bend over, giving him five back blows. He still couldn't breathe. With her arms around him from his back, her right hand in a fist and the left hand covering it placed slightly above his navel, she pushed up into his abdomen. Out popped a piece of steak that had obstructed the man's breathing.

The man's color returned, and he sat down again, bursting with thanks to Lynn, as did the others around the table.

"It's what I do," Lynn said to the group. Everyone laughed. "I manage an emergency department," she added.

Peter was now by her side.

"This young lady saved my life," the man said.

"Doesn't surprise me," Peter said. "She's amazing."

"Tell me your name," the man said to Lynn.

"My name is Lynn Price. I work at Deer Park Hospital. This fellow here is Peter Fry. He's an orthopedic surgeon at Deer Park."

"If you had broken a bone, I would have come over. Emergencies get handled by Lynn," Peter said. "The important thing is that you are OK."

"Although you are breathing OK, now, you should see your doctor as soon as possible to make sure there are no complications," Lynn said.

"Enjoy the rest of your dinner," Peter said right before he and Lynn went back to their table.

"That was amazing," Peter said. "I love the adventure you bring to my life. You know, I have been wanting to ask you something."

"You can ask me anything," Lynn said.

Peter reached into his pocket and knelt before Lynn with an open box holding a diamond ring in it.

"Lynn Price, I love you. Will you marry me?" Peter asked.

"Yes, yes, I will happily marry you," Lynn answered, pulling Peter off the floor.

"You made me the happiest man ever," Peter said, putting the ring on Lynn's finger.

When Peter and Lynn kissed, the nearby diners clapped and cheered.

Martin came fast, footing it over with a bottle of champagne.

"The man whose life you saved, Miss, sent this over. He also wanted to comp your meals, but our manager beat him to it," Martin said. "Congratulations on your engagement. Can I get you anything else? I can get you a new plate of salmon; these two might be cold."

"The salmon is fine," Lynn said. "Tiramisu for dessert?" Lynn asked Peter.

"Perfect," Peter said, "Boy, do we have stories to tell when we get home."

"George will think we are pulling his leg," Lynn said. "By the way, did you tell George you were going to propose?"

"Yes, and I checked with your mother if it was OK if I asked you to marry me. She said yes, and seemed happy about the idea," Peter said.

"Thank you for checking with her. I know she likes you a lot, but I'll bet it meant a lot to her that you spoke to her," Lynn said.

"She and your dad were always super nice to me when I came to visit," Peter said.

"They often told me they were happy when George was with you because you kept him out of trouble," Lynn said.

"We still managed to have fun. However, this trip for me has been the most fun ever. It's been simply wonderful. I am so excited to spend the rest of my life with you," Peter said.

"I know whatever crosses our path, we will manage it well and be there for each other. I love you, Peter," Lynn said.

"Love you more," Peter said.

"By the way, we have yet to talk about your family. Do you have siblings? What about your parents?" Lynn asked.

"I have a brother and a sister who live in North Carolina. My parents now live in Florida. They are retired spies. I can fill you in when we get home," Peter answered.

The End

CPSIA information can be obtained
at www.ICGtesting.com
Printed in the USA
JSHW020738210623
43508JS00002B/8